SWEET BRIAR

BRENDA WILBEE

The Best in Wholesome Reading
DISTRIBUTED BY
CHOICE BOOKS
POST OFFICE BOX 243
VIENNA, VA 22180
WE WELCOME YOUR RESPONSE

HARVEST HOUSE PUBLISHERS
Eugene, Oregon 97402

SWEETBRIAR

Copyright © 1983 by Harvest House Publishers
Eugene, Oregon 97402

Library of Congress Catalog Card Number 83-080122
ISBN 0-89081-336-1

Printed in the United States of America.

With love to my Auntie Vi...
She told me I'd write.

And to my friends,
Bob
Bonny
Cathy
Candy
Kevin
Leslie
Perry
and Scott...
They helped me write.

INTRODUCTION

> "Surely a kind Providence watched over these unpro-
> tected ones that they might in after years fulfill their
> destiny."
>
> —Emily Inez Denny in *Blazing the Way*

The Boren and Denny families migrated west from Cherry Grove, Illinois, in the year 1851, where destiny carved for them a place in history—that of being the founders of one of the world's busiest deepwater seaports: Seattle, Washington.

Louisa Boren carried with her some sweetbriar seeds. They were her promise of spring, of better times. Today Seattle spreads over the carved-out forests, and sweetbriar grows wild along the beaches, tiny bits of pink in spring green, a gentle reminder of days before.

So much of what is Seattle is because of the Denny family. Street names are the most obvious: Denny Way, James Street, Boren Avenue. Other things, not quite so obvious but well recognized, are some of the city parks, Denny Hill, and the University of Washington. But sadly, so much has been lost and forgotten. Arthur Denny, considered to be the Father of Seattle, in a preface to a small book he wrote in 1888, stated:

> It is now thirty-six years since I came to Puget Sound and I am more and more impressed with the fact as each suc-ceeding year rolls by that the early settlers of the country will very shortly all have crossed over the river and soon be forgotten.... I shall therefore give a brief account of my recollections of early settlements of the Sound, in which it will be my earnest endeavor to state nothing but facts....
>
> The most important thing in my estimation is to make no wrong or incorrect statements. Let it be the pride of old settlers to state the truth. It is no time for romancing or painting fancy sketches when we are nearing the end of our voyage. The work is too serious for fiction.*

---

* Arthur Armstrong Denny, *Pioneer Days on Puget Sound* (Seattle: C.B. Bagley, 1888), pp. 3,4.

The old settlers have crossed over. The facts lie buried with the settlers or shelved in dusty order on library stacks. *SWEETBRIAR* is the recreated story of these forgotten settlers. Despite Arthur's admonition to state nothing but facts, I have taken the facts as they are known, romanticized upon them, and painted a fancy sketch.

I hope to bring Arthur's "old settlers" out of their graves and off the shelves, to bring alive again the beginnings of an important American city. Over a hundred years "after the fact" perhaps the sound of wind can be brought back, the call of the gulls, the wetness of the rain, the throb of the heart. Perhaps Louisa Boren's story can live again. Her sweetbriar still grows— the scent still rides the sea breeze in spring.

—**Brenda Wilbee**

Part One

"What a book the story of my life would make!"
—Louisa Boren

Louisa Boren tried to pray, but the words came hard. She was unaccustomed to kneeling at her bed fully clothed, and thoughts of her plans crowded in. It felt even stranger to be lying in bed with her shoes on, the blankets piled high. But she couldn't run the risk of Ma coming in and finding her still dressed. The blankets would have to stay.

Time passed slowly in the dark. This was her last night in Illinois; tomorrow she would leave for Oregon, the Promised Land. She searched the sounds of John Denny's old farmhouse with her ears, memorizing the creaks and the small groans as the house settled. In the distance she heard the neighbor's dog bark, heard Jonah whine to be let out. "There you go, mutt," she heard her Ma say. They were all going—the whole family.

Louisa sighed, rolled over, and stared absently at the armoire along the west wall of her room. Moonlight made the mirror on it bright, and she found that her heart raced as she thought again of what she had to do. She went over the plans carefully, all the while picturing her wall mirror downstairs, hanging still on the wall in the entry at the foot of the steps. Everything else had been packed; her mirror was to go to Pamelia's in the morning.

The mirror was really her father's, her real father's, and Louisa loved it for that reason. It was a lovely one, framed in dark wood, the beveled glass ground and polished to perfection. Its only fault, if it was one, was that it was too heavy to go out West. But it would go—it had to. After all, it was the only piece she had of

9

her own Pa, the only tangible thing of a forgotten memory.

The stairs complained under the weight as the rest of the family came up to bed. Louisa strained to catch the sound of David's footsteps, but they were lost in the shuffle. She did hear his door shut across the hall from her, and then the easy, quiet banter of his voice as he exchanged good nights with his brothers—her stepbrothers.

David. He was the only reason she was going to Oregon at all, the only reason she was giving up her schoolteaching, saying good-bye to Pamelia. For three years she had waited for David Denny to notice her—ever since John Denny, one of Illinois' state legislators, had married her Ma. But David, even after this time, still treated her the same—polite, at times helpful, but always distant. But for Louisa there was no other choice— she would go to Oregon. David was.

A baby cried in the stillness. Probably Loretta, Ma's new baby—her sister. Louisa thought of her Ma. She was nearly 46 and nursing a two-month-old infant, and not once had Louisa heard her complain about having to leave her home to trek across an unknown wilderness to an even-more-unknown land. Ma was happy. Ma had Pa.

Oh, David! Louisa moaned down inside. She rolled to her back to stare up at the ceiling far above her. She thought of his birthday the month before—Saint Patrick's Day—when he had turned 19. And her? She shut her eyes, tired of wishing that reality was kinder, that she wasn't nearly 24.

Suddenly Louisa was aware of the quiet, of the passing of time. This was it. Everyone was in bed, her mirror left alone. She pushed back the heavy covers and once again knelt. This time she slipped her fingers under the feathered mattress and carefully searched the cold sheeting. "Ah, good..." she whispered unintentionally, her nervousnes creating sound out of what was supposed to have been just air. Her tongue edged her lips and she pulled out several seed packets—a surprise for her older sister someday: seeds from Illinois. Then, plunging both arms under the mattress again, she felt all around to be sure none remained.

The next thing to be done was to pull the armoire from the wall. It gave way easier now that it was empty, and she reached behind and groped through the dustballs for the small shell boxes that she had hidden months ago. They were to be presents for her sister's little girls, gifts for their first Christmas in Oregon. Her fingers closed over one box, then two: one for each of her nieces. Standing, she pushed the armoire back to the wall, where it stood silent and untelling.

Once downstairs, Louisa stood breathlessly before her mirror and gazed at the dim image, at the dark hair that framed her face, the hollow spots where her eyes were supposed to be. Moonlight from the leaded glass window at the base of the stairs caught the glimmer of her silver combs.

She always wore them since David had given them to her last Christmas. She frowned, remembering the hurt. She had been so pleased, so elated that he had chosen her such a perfect gift. But he had spoiled it all by telling her that Arthur had picked them out, and for a long time she hadn't worn them. But now she did; they were better than nothing. And David *had* paid for them. That had to count for something.

A soft creak came from upstairs, and Louisa flattened herself to the wall by the mirror, her heart racing wildly beneath her tight corset. David? Ma? One of the Denny brothers?

But nothing more happened, and Louisa reached for the mirror. The wood was cold to the touch, and she thought of Ma's adamant charge that it was to stay. "You're to take that mirror over to Pamelia's first thing in the morning," she heard Ma saying from somewhere inside her head. "It's going to break...it's too heavy...."

Louisa lifted the mirror from its nail. "Well, Ma," she said to the ghostly face in her hands, "it's going. Whether or not you like it, it's going. It's my wedding present to David." She bit her lip, saying no more to herself.

The dog barked when she stepped out into the night. "Shh, Jonah," she hushed him. "It's only me." The air was chilly, the grass stiff, the mud puddles frozen over in the tease of an Illinois spring. Louisa shivered and hugged the mirror tight to her chest as she bent over the weight. "Want to come along?" she asked the old sheep dog impulsively.

Jonah wagged his tail and bounded after her, and together they hurried along the beaten trail to the covered wagons at the foot of the hill. The moon, ahead of them and full, cast their shadows far out behind, and the dark shapes, stretched and distorted, bobbed oddly over the rough terrain.

Ahead and down the hill were the wagons, four humps of white in the moonlight. Louisa looked into the back of each, trying to find Ma and Pa's. When she found it, Jonah stood guard while she struggled to mount the feedbox nailed to the backboard.

"Can I help you?"

Louisa gasped and lost her balance; the ground spun and drew close. But the man who had spoken was quick, and he caught her as she fell.

"David!"

His arms were tight, hot bands of iron about her. Dizziness descended, and she fought it—that and the gel in her knees, in her whole body. Her heart hammered against the mirror, wedged tight between them. Time stood still. She had heard people say that before and had dismissed it as an expression. But now it did as David's eyes bore into hers. She wondered if she would faint.

Still he stared into her face, and unconsciously she swallowed to rid her mouth of the dryness that had come. But David blinked suddenly, and the tiny movement broke the spell and he let her go. Then she saw the corners of his mouth turn up, slowly at first, the way she loved and had admired from afar. "I might have known you'd be up to something," he grinned.

She swallowed again, and with the gulp, starch stiffened her blood, making her legs and back straight, her breathing steady. "You've got your mirror," he said, smiling fully now so that the soft lines came from the corners of his eyes. She gasped and looked down, then spun so that her back was to him.

"You know nothing of the kind," she told him sternly, in a tone not unlike Ma's. Her voice caught with the sudden fear of being stopped, and she felt his hands on her shoulders, the way Pa would do to Ma when she was upset. She took a breath to calm the inner storm and pain that his touch created. "It's all right," he whispered. "I won't tell."

He walked away from her then, back up the hill to the house. She watched him leave, the stride of his long legs carrying him too quickly from her. "David!" she called, the absence of his touch burning her so that she cried out without intention. He stopped short, but turned slowly. "Wait for me?" she asked weakly.

He came back, but they said nothing. He propped himself against the backboard and rested his weight on the feedbox that Pa had rigged up for the horses. She clambered into the wagon, too clumsily, and she felt the rise of color in her cheek.

"Are you sure you don't want any help?" he yelled up after a bit. She said no and hurried to finish. Her dresses, schoolbooks, and sunbonnets, already squashed flat, lay in a disheveled heap on the floor of the wagon. Moonlight spilled into her empty trunk. Breathing a prayer of forgiveness for her disobedience, she wrapped the mirror between layers of an old comforter she had made as a child and set it carefully along the back wall of her chest. The seed packets and shell boxes were pushed to the corners, and she folded the rest of her clothes in and around them.

She could see the back of David's head as she worked, as well as his shoulders, broad and muscular, and his cap—the one she had given him for Christmas. His hair was long, and it curled a bit under the edges of the hat. The last two things to go back in were her white mull dress—she glanced to David again—and her brass candlestick. Finally it was done, and the rounded lid banged shut. The secrets were sealed.

They walked home in silence. Jonah followed them, his tail still wagging, and when they got to the back door he sniffed at the wooden barrier when it was shut in his face. He whined, then clawed. His tail dropped and he crawled beneath the stoop.

It was David who had shut the door. Inside he hung up his coat next to Louisa's in the semidark. She moved to the stairwell, away from the wall where her mirror had hung. "Don't tell anyone about tonight," she whispered. "All right?"

"I won't."

"And David?"

"Yes?"

She hesitated, then realized that she had never intended to say anything. She just wanted to hold onto him a little longer. "Never mind," she said.

"Good night, Louisa."

"Good night." She walked up a few of the steps and paused. "Aren't you coming?"

"In a bit."

But David was a long time coming. He stayed behind to feel along the empty wall, and when he found the bare nail sticking out of the darknes toward him he grinned, closed his fist around it, and yanked it from the wall.

★   ★   ★

The Denny family was a large one, the combination of two: the Borens and the Dennys. The Borens were Ma, Widow Sarah Boren for the years her three children were growing; her daughter Mary Ann; Carson Dobbins, her only son; his wife, Anna Kays; and Louisa, her youngest daughter. The Dennys were Pa (or John Denny, as the voters of Illinois State called him) and the five youngest of his eight sons: Arthur, 29; James, 27; Samuel, 24; David, 19; and Wiley, 17.

What first brought them together was the marriage of Arthur Denny and Mary Ann Boren in 1843. The subsequent marriage of Ma and Pa five years later united them as a family, and the birth of little Loretta on Valentine's Day, 1851, cemented them together, their blood lines mixing and crossing in the child and sister they all shared.

Other children had been born. Arthur and Mary Ann had two: Lenora (called Nora), three, and Catherine (nicknamed Kate), six. And Dobbins and Anna had a baby now, born December 12, 1850, on Dobbins' 26th birthday. And they all lived together in John's big farmhouse on the outskirts of Cherry Grove, Illinois. Pa was an Illinois congressman, a comrade of Abraham Lincoln, and in spite of the good life they had, his restlessness and energies dictated that they move West.

It was really Arthur who had forced the decision, after months and months of reading and rereading letters from friends who had gone West, and after discussions that waned to the wee hours. But once he had made it known that he and Mary Ann were going come spring, Pa took over. And they all followed—the sons enthusiastic, the women hesitant but agreeable. Pa was Pa, and no one argued. No one wanted to.

April 10, 1851, dawned slowly, caressing the sky with fingers of pinks and blues, spreading satin ribbons along the eastern horizon. Louisa was the first of the family to rise, this last morning in Illinois, and after dressing quickly in the chill, she almost flew down the old stairs. Her eye caught the empty wall on her way out and she smiled, glancing quickly up the stairs to David's room. But she missed the hole where the nail had been; she had only the morning to spend with Pamelia.

Outside, the coolness of the air caught into her lungs and a sharp cry came to her lips. The world was so beautiful, so still. The greenness of the new leaves uncurling from bare brown twigs broke the softness of the sky and a great loneliness seemed to reach out, touching her hesitantly. Then it hugged her tightly, and tears sprang up. Louisa turned from the house and ran down the dirt road into town, sidestepping the frozen mud puddles with little hops and leaps. Once she looked back to see that no one followed or watched out a window. No one was to see that she didn't have the mirror with her.

"Louisa!"

She looked up and saw her dearest friend running toward her. The distance between them closed, and then they were together, hugging each other, both of them weeping.

"Now just look at us," Pamelia scolded as she dabbed at her eyes. "A couple of old schoolmarms crying in the street." She tried to smile. "Goodness, I thought we promised ourselves no scenes when it came time. We did say that, didn't we, Louisa?"

Louisa nodded and wiped her own eyes. They said nothing further as they walked into Cherry Grove, passing by Pa Denny's wagons without comment. Birds chattered, hopping about unconcerned and hurrying to gather their worms. Louisa and Pamelia walked quietly along the picketed fences of Main Street until at last the Dunlap's place came into view. The tangled growth of the sweetbriar bushes, wrapped over and around the arched gateway, let bits of the gathering blue peep through, little twinkles of color through the green.

"Do you suppose the sweetbriar has any blossoms yet?" Louisa asked, scanning the growth with her eyes. They were large eyes, soft, a gentle brown against her fair skin. The cold was bringing the rose flush of her cheeks to a peak, and the color in her face brought more color to her eyes.

"Oh, no, not yet," Pamelia said. "Next month...maybe."

"It's no matter," Louisa sighed. "To eat breakfast with you

this morning will be just as good." They stepped into Mr. Dunlap's garden and she looked about, letting her eyes absorb the spring beauty, the memories of happy times playing here as a child. A table, set up in the corner of the garden, stood waiting for them, laid with Mrs. Dunlap's silver. A few early snowdrops bloomed nearby. "Oh, Pam...it's beautiful," Louisa breathed out. "What a lovely last morning!"

A door slammed and the rounded figure of Mrs. Dunlap came down the veranda steps. In her hand she held a plate of steaming hot cinnamon rolls.

"Good morning, Liza dear!" smiled Pamelia's mother. "What a fine morning for you two!" She set the rolls down and poured a stream of coffee into the china teacups. "Sit down now, girls," she fussed. "There's fresh butter there, Louisa my dear. Fresh from Daisy out back. And the cream came off the top this morning." She stood aside, put her hands where her hips were supposed to have been, and beamed broadly. "It's a fine Pa you got there, Louisa my dear, letting you have the morning with Pamelia." She wiped her apron over her face and coughed, blinking quickly. "Now eat up," she chided. "There's plenty more if and when you're ready." She hurried away, and Louisa listened for the bang of the door.

The morning passed quickly. Louisa and Pamelia shared dreams, hopes, confided secrets. They spoke of everything, of nothing. All the while the sun climbed the sky until it reached its highest point. Louisa looked up at it, her hand shielding her eyes from its intensity. Silence descended, and their eyes met.

"I suppose you'll be having to go," Pamelia ventured. "Your house ought to be empty by now. Your Pa'll be wanting to pull out."

Louisa nodded, afraid to speak. "Anna's folks and some of the Denny relatives were going to divvy up the furniture," she whispered, conscious only that words came from her mouth.

"I know...."

"I got my mirror hidden last night. Ma thinks I brought it to you this morning."

Again silence descended, consuming the unspoken words. A rapping on the window made them both look up, and Louisa waved to the little girl who stood behind the glass. The child's braids hung long over her shoulders, but her bangs, usually so neat and straight, were shoved up her forehead in a tangled meshing.

"Dully's still burning up with the whooping cough, isn't she?" Louisa said. Pamelia nodded. Dully was Pamelia's little sister, the playmate of Louisa's nieces. Three, five, and six, Nora, Dully, and Kate were a threesome, a trio of laughter and bright smiles, and three pairs of legs that kicked out too much on the front pew at the Methodist church.

"Your sister tell the girls yet that they can't say good-bye to Dully?" Pam asked.

"Kate and Nora don't even know we're leaving today. Ma thought it best and Mary Ann agreed."

Pamelia shook her head slowly. "It'll be hard on them. They're inseparable. And Dully's so miserable with this whooping cough. When she finds out—" Pamelia's voice dropped and slowed as they watched Mrs. Dunlap remove the child from the window. "When she finds out that Kate and Nora have gone, and that she didn't get to say good-bye...I don't know...She cries so, even now, wanting them to come play."

Louisa reached for Pamelia's hand and their fingers tightened. "It has to be this way. We can't risk the children coming down with the whooping cough. We've got the babies to think of."

"I know...."

"Come, let's stroll through the garden," said Louisa suddenly. "Then I'll go on." Arm in arm they walked through the carefully cultivated flower beds. Tulips nosed green spikes up out of the cold, hard earth and daffodil stems crowded the fence. Louisa reached out to the sweetbriar and rubbed a tiny bud between her fingers. "If only there was just one in bloom," she whispered. She wanted to see the pink rose, the five petals, the threaded veins of darker pink. Tears gave way. "I just wanted one, Pamelia," she cried. "Just one. I need something to take with me, to hold onto."

They both cried then and held to each other, overcome with the sorrow and pain of it all. "I can't say good-bye," Pamelia cried. "It's like being torn asunder!" A robin hopped close and cocked his head. He hopped away unnoticed.

"The seeds!" Louisa shrieked. She pulled away. "Pamelia,

the sweetbriar seeds we gathered last year! You have them in your bureau! Go get me half! As soon as I get my own home in the Promised Land I'll plant them and send word to you, and you can plant yours! It'll be a tryst between us!''

Pam dashed off and Louisa plucked a closed rose. In a moment Pamelia was back, the seeds tucked away in a linen cloth. She was smiling, and the smile, along with the tear-luster of her blue eyes, made her radiant. "It's a promise!" she cried breathlessly. She pushed the seeds into Louisa's hand. "Blossoms cover thorns! Just remember that, Louisa! Look for the beauty, the spring. Always!''

Louisa threw her arms around her friend. "It's a lovely thought...straight from God, I think!''

"We *will* meet again, Liza," Pam whispered. "On the other side.''

Louisa nodded, then impulsively pressed the small rosebud to Pamelia.

"You write when you and David marry?" Pam asked.

"He doesn't—''

"Shh. Look for the spring. Remember that. It always comes.''

Louisa nodded, tears streaming down her face now. "I will." She bit her lip and nodded again, hugged her friend for the last time, then turned and ran. The seeds were fisted tight in her hand, and when she had passed through the gate she stopped and opened out the cloth. The seeds, the promise of spring, of life, lay in a small heap, so tiny and insignificant: quietly she made her decision—she would place the seeds between the pages of her Bible until she reached the Promised Land of the West.

Then she walked slowly toward the wagons.

"The separation from dearly loved friends, left far behind, wrought upon the mind of the pioneer woman to make her sad to melancholy...."
—Emily Inez Denny in *Blazing the Way*

Louisa walked quickly, not looking back. At times she broke into a run. "Look for spring," Pamelia had said. Head down, she watched her feet move along the road as she fled the hollowness that chased, ready to swallow her up in the vacuum. "Look for spring, look for spring," she chanted in time.

When she came to the place where the wagons were supposed to be, they were gone. For a moment she stood stunned, uncomprehending, and then she remembered. Pa had said they would be up at the house, close to the barn. She turned from the spot and headed uphill, remembering still more things: the children in her class at the one-room schoolhouse, the sewing circle, her voice lesson, and old Mrs. Wessel, who liked to insinuate that both she and Pamelia would always be spinsters. "Stop crying!" she commanded herself through clenched teeth. David *did* care—he had to. She remembered the way he had looked at her last night. His eyes, a warm leather-brown, had looked into hers, and they had seen her.

"Hi, there!"

Louisa's head jerked up at the sound. James Denny waved and drew close. "Just coming to meet you!" he called, running the last of the distance. "Pa's ready to head on out!"

At 27 James stood a powerful man, his muscles keenly developed from hard work on the farm. The Nordic blood that cropped up now and then in the Denny line had come to James, for his skin was almost a russet color. His hair and beard and mustache were red too, but more the color of burnt fields in autumn. Everything about him was red—everything but his eyes. "Like baby robin eggs," Louisa always thought. A handsome man, full of strength and warmth, temper and vitality, he was

Louisa's favorite—next to David, that is, and Dobbins, her own blood brother.

Louisa reached for her hair to push it from her face. She felt her fingers tremble against her temple.

"Louisa? You all right?"

"Oh, James…"

In one stride he had her in his arms, and she pushed her face into his shoulder. "Liza, it's all right," he whispered. "It's bad, I know, but it'll pass. I promise."

"I miss her already," she cried into the blue flannel that was his shirt.

"Who, honey?"

"Pamelia…how about Ma, the babies…what if something were to happen, James?" She looked up at him. "I'm afraid…."

He said nothing and she searched his face for assurance. He always had it for her. "It's going to be all right," he told her, and she felt his arms tighten about her back.

"How old was your Ma when she died?" she demanded suddenly, pulling back.

"What?"

"I want to know how old your Ma was when she died."

James whistled through his lips, yanked his cap from his head, and ran a hand through the thick hair. "You know all this… happened maybe ten years ago now…."

"How long was she ill?"

"I don't know…as long as I can remember. What's this got to do with anything?"

"I don't know. Guess I was just wondering about my own Ma."

"Ah!" He laughed—suddenly, spontaneously, as all the Dennys did. "What'd you and Pamelia talk about anyway? Rattlesnakes and Indians?"

"Of course not!"

He grinned and leaned forward, hands on his hips. "We got to get you laughing again, Louisa Boren." He spoke to her as he did to Kate and Nora. "This is a good day and we can't have you spoiling it. What is it that Ma keeps saying? 'This is the day that the Lord has made. Let us rejoice in it and be glad'?" He gave her a prod. "Get going. Can't have Ma seeing that long face of yours, so we're going to have a race to that oak tree over there.'' He laughed low in his throat, and gray darts of light came to his eyes. "It's where I kissed my first girl! Go on, I'll give you a head start!''

She laughed then. James could always make her laugh. It was the way he took charge, the way he smiled and gave in so easily to his own laughter, as if he owned it all and was willing to share it. "Go on!'' he hollered.

She ran swiftly, lifting her skirts high as she leaped over the mud puddles, soft and messy now with the warming sun. The breeze lifted her hair from off her neck and whipped into her cheeks. She could hear him lumbering up behind, closer and closer, until his arms swung out and caught her. She hugged tight, head down, as he twirled her in mad circles.

"Stop!'' she screamed. "Enough, enough!''

"No more pouting?''

"No!''

"Promise?''

"I promise!''

The earth scraped her toes, her feet dug in. The world still spun out of focus; only James held it in place. Then slowly, slowly, the whirling, the reeling, unraveled and she crumpled into his arms. "Oh, thank you!'' she laughed. "That's just what I needed!'' His hand came up and cupped the back of her head; everything was stable, secure. He was her friend, her brother, and she kissed his cheek the way she always did.

He rubbed the spot with the back of his hand. "Come on, we better be going on, or Pa'll be sending someone after us.''

Neither of them saw David on the crest of the hill. He stood looking down on them, his jaw drawn tight like the string of a readied bow. His boot swung out, kicking the air, and then he spun about and disappeared over the ridge.

★   ★   ★

"Yip! Yip!'' a whip cracked the air.

Wagons groaned, then lurched forward. Wheels circled around, gathered momentum, and slipped into an easy roll. Louisa, in the lead wagon, sat with Kate and Nora under each arm, and the three of them swayed as one to the jostling motion. The children were strangely quiet as they passed the house and headed west into town.

The farmhouse, empty now, stood with its door open. The entry, with the coats packed and gone, looked large and desolate, and the garden, neglected for other things, was rioted over with weeds.

"Wait!" Louisa's sister jumped from a wagon and ran to the wide veranda. The porch swing was still hung, and her skirt touched it as she pushed past.

"What are you doing?" Arthur thundered after his wife. "Come back here!" But Mary Ann was gone.

Louisa watched Arthur closely from where she sat in the wagon ahead. She could see the muscles of his face ripple as he forced his mouth into a straight line. She had always thought Arthur to be attractive in a masculine sort of way, with his hair the color of clean sand and his eyes blue like the soft yarn that Ma used to knit baby shoes with.

Arthur was the one who most looked like his father. But he had benefited by the sorting out and handing down of genes, for he had none of the scragginess of John Denny's face; Pa's rough features and prominent nose had settled more calmly on Arthur.

And like the similar-yet-altered physique, Arthur had Pa's temperament. They were both men driven by a restlessness, a discontent to let mediocrity reign. If there was a better way, it was to be sought after. But as Pa was patient in his persistence and carrying out of plans—never one to lose his sense of humor or to take himself or anyone else too seriously—Arthur was brusque and impatient when his plans or ideas were crossed or delayed. Louisa saw the straight line of his mouth give way to a scowl. "What in tarnation is she doing?" he bellowed. "Jumping from a moving wagon in her condition! She'll miscarry for sure!"

"She needs one last look, Son," said Pa from up front. "Don't let your impatience and concern get tangled! Let her have it in peace!" No one said anymore while they waited.

The canvas sides of the wagon were rolled high, and Louisa had little trouble seeing the forlornness of the farm. She could see the barn; the roosting house for the chickens (they had all been shared by neighbors); and the privy, its rusted gate hanging lopsided and open. Mary Ann, she saw, moved from room to room in the house, appearing first at one window, then another.

When Mary came to the door she stood a long time. The horses whinnied in impatience, and Louisa could see that Arthur remained quiet with great difficulty. The knuckles of his hands were white from gripping the reins so tightly; it was what made him so fine—his control, the way he could check his agitation.

"What's Mama doing?" Nora asked suddenly, breaking the strain. The child slipped away from Louisa to hang over the backboard. "Hello, Papa," she called to her father. Arthur nodded at the three-year-old, his eye still on Mary Ann. She had gone to the garden and was pulling weeds. When she finally stood she had one in her hand, its long, tangled roots dangling from her closed fist. It hung limply, dropping bits of soil back to the earth. Mary held it out, her hand open now, palm up, and then her fingers dropped low and the weed fell without sound.

Arthur helped her up without a word, and Mary Ann sat beside him stiffly. Her hands were set over her stomach where it had just begun to swell with her pregnancy and her face looked west. "I forgot to pack flower seeds," she whispered.

Mary Ann rarely cried, and she didn't now. Louisa glanced back to her trunk; it was wedged tight with flour sacks, barrels of salt pork, bags of cornmeal, and other things. For a moment she debated, then settled back. The flower seeds could wait. Mary was strong.

The wheels turned again and the wagons moved on. Pa led the horses into town, turning them to Main Street, where he stopped to let the other three wagons lead out. All along the white picketed fences their friends stood, and Louisa gasped at the roar of the shouted good-byes. Arthur and Mary Ann pulled out first. Dobbins and Anna, with little Gertrude balanced on a lap, went next, and James third. Pa cut in, and slowly they made their way through Cherry Grove. All the friends held handkerchiefs high overhead, and the white fluttered against the blueness of the sky, like little clouds skittering in the wind beyond.

"Look! There's Dully!" shrieked Kate, and before Louisa could stop them, the children had scrambled over the backboard and were racing back to their friend. Too short to see over the fence, they kissed Dully between the narrow picket slats.

David was there instantly, galloping up from the rear. He pulled the girls away gently, prying their arms from the posts, and carried them on the back of his horse to Louisa. For a moment their eyes met. But the softness that had been there the night before was gone. Louisa blinked in hurt dismay. "The good-byes are hard," she mumbled. He nodded, clucked to his horse, and was gone.

Louisa looked back, out to the mass of friends, blurred now by her tears. Someone ran to the middle of the road. It was Pamelia, her arms raised high, waving, disappearing, swallowed up in the distance. A wave of overwhelming sadness burst from the pit of Louisa's stomach, and she rose up on her knees as if to see better was to ease the pain. She waved until her shoulders ached, until her arms dropped without feeling to her side. Too soon the friends were gone, and only the ruts of the wagons marking the mud trailed out behind them, stretching like spoiled ribbons back to a world that had gone forever.

3

"To add to the worry and discomfort of Mary Denny,
who was expecting her third child in a few months, Lenora
and Catherine developed whooping cough as a result of
the kisses stolen through the picket fence."
—Roberta Frye Watt in *Four Wagons West*

"Auntie, I'm so hot..."

"I know you are, Kate," whispered Louisa. She laid a wet
cloth across the six-year-old's forehead. "You try to sleep." The
child sighed and let her cheek fall onto the pillows. A tiny smile,
half-hidden in the coverings, came, then went. She shut her eyes
and slept.

The first two weeks of the journey had been pleasant. The
fresh aroma of spring had scented the air, and flowers of every
color had dotted the miles between towns. Iowa tumbled and
rose up like the waves of the sea; green grass, lush and thick,
passed underfoot as John Denny led them westward. The days
blended together as the travelers adjusted themselves to the
change. But then Kate had sneezed, Nora's nose had begun to
run, and the contentment that had permeated the four wagons
dissipated with the realization that the whooping cough had come
with them.

Now both Lenora and Catherine lay ill in the back of a wagon
as they jounced over the road, too listless to even raise their heads.
Hour by hour Louisa told them stories, bathed them down, and
told them more tales. Only an attack, vicious in its grip, interrupted the routine, jerking their sweated bodies up spasmodically
to cough. It was with great despair that they kept going, one
warm day at a time, and the women said nothing as each morning Pa hitched up the horses, facing them still westward.

"Maybe we'll find a doctor in Kanesville," Pa said one day
at the noon stop. Mary Ann sighed and looked away. "They'd
be just as sick at home, Mary," he told her kindly. "And like
I said, maybe there'll be a doctor in Kanesville."

"Kanesville?" Mary's faced showed the strain. "Isn't that where we cross the Missouri?" Pa nodded.

"How can I take my babies out into the prarie when they're so ill?" He didn't answer.

"We won't." Arthur faced his father. "Not until they're on the mend will we proceed."

"We'll waste time, Son. It's imperative that we keep moving."

"We're not going until the girls are stronger. Look, Pa, you've said more than once not to get my impatience tangled with my concern. So this is the way it's going to be."

John Denny rubbed the back of his bowed head with both hands. They were gnarled, showing the nearly 58 years of wear. One nail had been hammered clean off and another was split like the cloven hoof of an animal. The knuckles were round and red, the veins prominent. "You're right, you're right," he said wearily. "We'll wait. But mind you," he added, looking Arthur in the eye, blue against blue, "I'll not hole up too long."

The afternoon passed slowly, and the children's fever seemed to mount. Louisa rode in Mary Ann and Arthur's wagon, where she could tend them, and she passed the time watching David. She could see him off to the left, pushing the five milch cows that they had brought along. He hollered something to Wiley, the youngest of the Denny brothers, and the seventeen-year-old boy moved east. The cattle bunched together and continued forward.

Lenora stirred and Louisa wrung out the cloth to bathe little Nora's flushed cheeks. Mary Ann was asleep too, sheer exhaustion finally putting her down. She lay with her feet propped up on a pile of bedding, her shoes off. They had begun to swell a bit, just enough to pinch, and her only relief was to set them up barefoot. Her hand, as almost always, rested over her stomach, a small four months swollen. Just yesterday the baby had begun to kick.

Suddenly Kate sat and coughed violently, over and over, while her lips took on a bluish tinge. She clawed at Louisa, her brown eyes wide with fright, windowing the terror within. Mary Ann was awake instantly, and together she and Louisa thumped the girl's back with quick, firm slaps. Mucous drained from Kate's mouth, and before she could catch her breath, she began to retch, spewing more of the mucous, thick and green, down her front. Louisa shoved a basin under her chin to catch what was left, and in a moment it was all over and Catherine began to cry.

"How long can this go on?" Mary asked as she rocked Kate in her arms. Already the little girl slept. "The cough only gets worse."

"I expect it will before it can get better. That's what Ma always says," Louisa added.

"Pa says there'll be a doctor in Kanesville..."

Louisa forced a smile. Mary Ann had heard what she had wanted to hear. "They'll be just fine. You wait and see." Pa hollered "Whoa!" and the wagons came to a standstill. "Looks like we're stopping for supper. I'll go and wash out the basin."

Favorite chores had been established, and everyone went about his own with few words. Worry hung heavy, although hope held on. Prayers were made each night and whispered through each day, and so far the two babies, Ma's and Anna's, showed no sign of the whooping cough; perhaps Gertrude and Loretta would be spared.

Night came on and the sunset, full of vibrant colors, washed the sky with brilliant reds and yellows. While Louisa helped Mary Ann put the girls to bed (sponging them down, helping them into fresh gowns, and forcing a bit of soup into their mouths), she watched David brush down the horses—all 18 of them. He was good with animals and worked slowly. They had three four-horse teams: one single-span and four other horses that they used for riding cavvy (and, once they got out to the prairie, for scouting ahead). But David ignored Louisa as he had been doing, going about his business with a strange silence, as if that last night in Cherry Grove had never happened.

Louisa sang softly to calm herself, to hide her loneliness, to soothe the children. She told them stories of Moses and the Promised Land while the reds of the sky stretched out long and thin, giving into the pinks underneath. And when the pinks gave way to gray she found the girls asleep, their breathing too harsh and too short. She could feel the heat of their fevers from where she sat, and for a long time she stayed between them, staring out to the gray.

★   ★   ★

Night was upon them in earnest when Louisa ventured out. "You sure you don't want me to come along?" James called after her. It was his turn to take the first watch; the others were all in bed.

"No, I want to be alone."

The moon was bright and round, marking clearly the distant horizon, and Louisa set off toward it. She didn't know where she was going, or why—she just had to walk. The wind rippled the tops of the grasses, and iridescent shades of gray shadowed over one another. As far as she could see, Louisa found only these varying grays, gray upon gray. Upon turning back, even the wagons appeared shrouded in gray.

Her thoughts, as gray as the air she breathed, swirled inside of her head. She thought of David, of the children. Would there be a doctor in Kanesville? And if so, would he be of any help? Was there any help to be had?

And the babies—could they survive the whooping cough? On and on the thoughts swirled and spun, spinning around and around in the recesses of her mind. Finally they stopped and centered on her father, the man who had given her life.

His name had been Richard Freeman Boren, and he had been a man dedicated to the spreading of the gospel. He had died before Louisa could walk, and she wondered what he had been like, what kind of a smile he had, whether he liked to laugh.

Suddenly she realized that she missed her father. "I've missed him all my life!" she thought. "I'm a part of him, and a part of him lives on in me. Maybe we've shared the same thoughts, felt the same things! It is too bad the good die young...that's what was said, wasn't it?"

A new thought slammed into Louisa's head. A terrifying one, and it made her turn and run. She had to see the girls! The grass yielded to her, standing back in place as she passed, hiding where she had been.

Suddenly Louisa clutched her throat and backed up, her eyes riveted to the grave. She hadn't seen it on the way out. Now she nearly tumbled over it. Two wagon wheel spokes, tied to form a crude cross, stuck up out of a small mound of bare earth. From the top of it hung a sunbonnet, tiny and ghostly white in the grayness. And two ties dropped to the ground lifelessly.

Her arms fell to her sides like lead, dropping heavily and without feeling. Her fingers clawed her skirt, dug into the material, caught it up in a frozen grasp. Her knees buckled. "I will not faint out here," she thought. Strength surged and she ran.

Her breath came in great gulps as she neared the camp; the pain of it seared her lungs like daggers into flesh. "Dear God!" she cried. "Don't let them die! Not out here!" Tears rolled off her face. "Please don't let them die!"

James saw her coming. He bolted up and stared horrified as she ran toward him. Her hand reached for the nearest wagon, and for a moment she leaned into it, breathing wildly. Her hair tumbled about her shoulders, her face white. Then she was in his arms and he held her close, feeling the tremble of her body as she clung to him.

"A grave..." Her eyes filled with tears. "A baby's grave...a dead baby's grave..." She choked, and he reached up to wipe her cheeks.

"Shh...don't talk..."

David heard and vaulted over the wagon base in his stocking feet. Pebbles bit into his heels at the same time he saw them.

"There was a sunbonnet," Louisa sobbed. James kissed the top of her head, the way he always did.

"Shh," he whispered, holding her tighter. Blood whipped in his veins and he knew, more than ever, that he had to have her. "Liza," he whispered, setting her away from him. But he caught her again, held her face in his hands. He stared into her eyes, shining with tears and moonlight. How anyone could have such black hair and such fair skin was beyond him. In the daytime she was beautiful, and at night.... He bit his lip.

"There were ribbons, James. Little ribbons, still wrinkled. Just dangling in the wind, just hanging there..." Her voice broke again. He held her, let her cry. He talked on and on of nothing while inside his head he cursed himself, chastised himself for the relationship they shared. How could he have let it go on like this when every part of his body ached to really hold her, to really kiss her, to really comfort her?

"I'm all right now," she said, but he didn't hear her. She said it again, but he couldn't let go.

"Stay with me awhile," he whispered.

"No, I'm fine now. I really am," she said. He watched helplessly as she climbed into Arthur's dark wagon. David, perched on the tongue of the supply wagon, watched helplessly too, his face and thoughts masked by the shadows. Louisa undressed and slipped between the children. They were still hot, and when the ties of her gown caught tight around her throat she stifled the scream that wanted to come, and then grabbed the ribbons and tore them free. The gown ripped to her breast, and pulling a blanket up over her, she curled into a ball.

4

"The great Missouri was crossed at Council Bluffs [Kanesville] by ferryboat on the 5th of May.... From thence they followed the beaten track of the many who had preceded them to California and Oregon."
—Emily Inez Denny in *Blazing the Way*

"No, Ma'am, there's nothing can be done for them." The words came from a small man, and he passed a hat from one hand to another. It was a gentleman's hat—black and rounded on top. "A bad case of the whooping cough, that's clear enough," he said. "Maybe lung fever."

"Lung fever?" Mary Ann looked up sharply. She was a small woman, like Louisa, but her face was fuller, her hair lighter and always pulled back into a knot. The past days had etched scratch lines under her eyes and the flesh puffed out, dark from the lack of sleep. "I knew it!" she said to Arthur. "All along I knew it! I was just too afraid to face the truth!"

"Now, Ma'am," said the little man, the doctor, again. "Don't be so alarmed. The fevers aren't as high as they come. I say with time and—you have a good milch cow?—time and plenty of warm milk, that should bring them out of it just fine." He smiled, showing his uneven teeth, yellow and crowded. "Just fine."

"There is nothing at all to be done?" Mary Ann asked again. "We had so hoped...once we got to Kanesville..." Her voice trailed off and a shadow crossed her face. "Surely you've got something!" she cried suddenly. "Surely you do!"

"Well, Ma'am, there is something I've heard tell of. But I don't know where you would get lemons from—not this time of year."

"Lemons?" Arthur spread his feet further apart, set his hands on his lean hips.

"If you can find the lemons, there is." The doctor ran a hand over the dome of his hat again. "Dissolve an egg in the juice

31

of one lemon and it helps the cough. But like I've said, I don't know where you'll find one in these parts."

"Where'd they get this lung fever from anyway?" Arthur demanded.

"Easy enough in a wagon. They get damp at night." The doctor put his hat on, covering the baldness of his head. He nodded and touched the soft brim slightly. "Good day, Sir. I'll be around to pick up my fee."

Louisa, standing with the others, watched the man leave. She stiffened and her eye involuntarily moved toward the tent where the children rested. Pa had just purchased the tents so there would be more room at night to stretch out. For now they served as temporary houses while they camped out at the edge of the Missouri River.

Kanesville was the last of civilization until Fort Laramie, a good 500 miles out into the prarie. Pa worried about the delay, but Arthur was adamant. They would not leave, they would not cross the river until the children were on the mend.

Silently Mary Ann walked to the tent. Louisa followed, and together they began once again to bathe down the girls. They said very little as they worked, talking mostly in hushed tones to Kate and Nora. Sunlight, warm and comforting, shone in and Louisa turned to see who had pulled open the tent's door.

It was Arthur, and even in the semilight she saw that his cheeks were wet. "Have you seen my diary, Mary?" he asked, his voice hoarse.

"Top of the bedding. Why?" Mary Ann reached for the quilts nearby, fumbled through the squares of color, and handed him the hardbound book.

"I want to make an entry."

"What are you putting down?"

"Just that it's April 30th and that we've made it to Kanesville and the Missouri River."

"Nothing about the children?"

Arthur rubbed his nose into his shoulder. "We don't know anything yet, do we?"

The excitement of the morning was past. The Dennys had crossed the Missouri and were on their way again after five days of just sitting. It felt good to be moving again, to walk alongside the wagons, to see new country. Louisa sniffed the clean air. There was a faint smell of dust, of dry things, but the scent of spring was strong. Buffalo grass, bent and curled, grew everywhere, and the terrain spread out all around with soft rolling hills. Off in the distance stood rocky hills, the scanty vegetation blurred by great distance. The best part of the day, though, was not in the scents or scenery. It was in the sound of the children's laughter. It came easy to them, at times bringing on a cough, but that quickly disappeared to more of the laughter.

The children had rallied quickly after that first day in Kanesville—almost overnight. They had all been surprised with the marked improvement, but the doctor that Arthur had found seemed almost angry with the change.

"You're fortunate," he had said when looking in on them earlier that morning. "Lung fever can really settle in."

"Whooping cough," Arthur corrected him.

"With a little lung fever," the small man tenaciously shot back. He took off his hat and passed it nervously from hand to hand. "About my pay…" He coughed uncertainly.

"You've done nothing," said Arthur, "except to give us a good scare when we weren't in need of one."

"Oh, come now, Arthur," Mary interrupted blissfully. "He's made himself available. And the children are better."

Arthur shot her a look that meant silence. "They've mended themselves, as far as I can see," he said, looking back at the doctor. "No thanks to your skills with medicine."

"But there's nothing to be done for whooping cough! Sir!"

"Precisely my point."

The man drew himself up as tall as he could, until he stood on the toes of his carefully polished shoes. "I have made myself available! Like your good wife says!"

Arthur stroked his beard, sandy like his hair. He stroked it so long that it began to shine with the sweat of his palm. "So you have," he said at length. "And I am a man who pays what is due. There you are, Sir." He slapped a few coins into the open hand.

"But, Sir! It's only two cents!"

Louisa looked out to the left of the wagon, out to the Platte River. She smiled, remembering the astonished face, Arthur's look of smugness, Mary Ann's horror. "Good for Arthur!" she thought.

The Platte was a lazy river, looking too tired to flow anywhere in a hurry. Long islands poked up through the water in spots to make it look like a great collection of rivers. Its source, some 500 miles west, spent its life winding through miles and miles of wasted prairie, emptying finally into the Missouri River. There it sacrificed its life with little fanfare to the river that divided the country in two, a cutting line that marked the security of civilization against the uncertainty of the wilderness.

Like the river, the afternoon seemed lazy. It grew hot and oppressive. The travelers were only one week into May and already the sun burned too hot. Louisa squinted up.

She climbed into the wagon, and Arthur, bent over the reins on the wagon seat, turned around to smile at her as she crawled over the flour sacks and a small rocking chair, then squeezed past his old desk—the only large piece of furniture that had been permitted. He smiled absently as the sun bounced off his hair.

A ragged storybook poked from beneath Kate's pillow and she pulled it loose—carefully, lest she disturb the girls while they napped. Idly she thumbed the worn pages, smiling when she saw the portraits of Little Bo Peep, Jack and Jill, and other memories of her own childhood.

"Can get kind of lonely out here," said Arthur suddenly.

"Mm-m," she answered, then began to fan the girls. It was no use looking around for David; Pa had said he could ride scout, and he would be far ahead.

"The weather's got the horses skittish," Arthur went on. "Feels awful still, like a storm brewing. I don't like it. How are the girls?"

"Sleeping." She fanned harder to stir up a bit of breeze. Back and forth she waved the book. Back and forth, matching the rhythm of the circling wheels and the gentle plop, plop of the horses' hooves hitting the soft earth. The grasses passed by, never ending, never changing, and the book waved slower and slower until the small stirring of air died away.

The book fell, jerking Louisa awake. Her eyes flew open. Was that a bit of breeze that brushed her cheek? It didn't matter because she slept, dreaming of a coolness that used to sweep her hair as she returned to the old swing that had hung from Ma's apple tree of so long ago.

Everything stopped. The swing sat still, close to the ground, and refused to climb again to the sky. Louisa sat slowly, blinked, then rubbed her eyes. The soothing jolt of the wagon had ceased and the stillness suddenly penetrated. She jumped up, surprised to feel the strength of the wind. Where were the children? Arthur?

Long shadows pulled out from beneath the wagon and stretched back toward home. A wave of homesickness flooded Louisa and she lifted her face to the sky, to where God lived. The wind was strong and cold, and she thought of the spring days in Mr. Dunlap's garden, of Pamelia.

"David! Secure the picket lines! No! Get the horses tied!"

Shouts, the whinnying of horses, babies crying—the sounds exploded into Louisa's dulled senses. Her weariness, her thoughts of home, vanished. Camp had been set up, the tents stood in a trio near the fire, and Mary Ann's iron cooking pot hung from its tripod over the flames, swinging madly in the wind.

"Samuel! Wiley! Where are you two?" Pa's voice thundered. "Help me drive these tent pegs further into the ground! It'll be a good one! Don't want us blowing away! Sarah! Ma! Get some of the extra bedding! We'll be needing everything tonight just to keep dry!"

Loose clumps of dirt skipped across the fields, blowing nowhere, and pieces of shrubberies rolled over the grasses, dancing high, then scooting close to the ground. The sky was dark, a deep blue edged in black. "Louisa! You're awake!" someone shouted. Ma waved from one of the tents; she waved back. "Help us with these blankets! Pa says a dandy is blowing in!" Mary Ann followed Ma into the tent with a basket of biscuits. Dobbins grabbed the handle of the pot, howled, then took the rag Anna offered and lifted the heavy pot from its hook.

Louisa turned to see what bedding she could find. Lightning jumped down out of the sky and startled her. She tripped. The dagger of light pierced through the blackened clouds and bit into the ground with a crack. Thunder followed, rolling across the expanse, drowning out the frantic shouts and orders as everyone rushed to complete the preparations. "I'll have to hurry," she thought. How had she slept through it all? She thought of her blue cape folded away in her trunk. That would keep her warm.

Another clap of thunder rang out, and darkness blew in. Beginning to frighten now, she turned back to the end of the wagon and jumped. "Oh darn it all!" she muttered angrily. "I didn't get the blankets!" She scrambled back in, feeling along the bottom, for the sudden darkness made it almost impossible to see anything. She found a blanket, folded it hastily, then grabbed for another. The wind pushed in and tugged viciously at the blanket under her arm.

The sides of the wagons were still rolled up! For a moment Louisa stared out to the thunderclouds between the naked bows of the wagon. No one had untied the canvas. If the rain got in.... The blankets dropped and she vaulted over the wagon base. She had to get the canvas untied, the sides pulled down! Her skirt caught and tore, and she fell. The wind hurled her into a wheel.

A sharp cry escaped—she heard the sound of it in her ears. Hand to her side, another anchored to the spoke of the wheel, she stood and braced herself to the wind. Leaning in, she tore at the knots of the canvas ties.

The sunlight, what was left of it, bowed to the storm. Louisa, teeth clenched tight, felt for the bindings. Her skirt bunched around her knees, then billowed out, and a chill stabbed through, running down her back.

Oh David! Where are you? More lightning daggered overhead. Thunder followed almost immediately, and Louisa stood up on her toes and bit, clawing at the ties in desperation. She couldn't let Arthur's desk get ruined. And the flour sacks? What good would they be if they got wet? "This is no use!" she screamed. A raindrop fell into her face, then two. Blinking against the glare of repeated flashes of lightning, she gave a final tug. The ribbon tore. Once section dropped at an angle.

Another crack of the lightning ripped through the air, a terrifying crack, sudden and sharp! More of it shattered the dome of the prairie, splitting it in sections clear to the ground. The thunder rolled, and a fear, a lonesome fright, pounced upon her. Where was everybody? David?

"David!" she screamed, but the strength of the wind shoved her cry back down into her throat. Then it was raining, coming down in torrents, biting into her head and bouncing off the ground. "David!" she screamed again as she threw her arms up over herself in futile protection against the onslaught. "David! Ma!" The lightning quivered, pierced the darkness, over and over, and flashed glimpses of the foggy outline of the three tents.

Louisa pushed toward them but the wind jerked her back. Her foot slipped, the dust of the prairie instantly slick, and she slammed into the ground, belly first. She spit the filth from her mouth and groaned—a long, slow, agonized groan as air found its way back into her lungs. Standing, she pushed on, only to slip again.

Her teeth chattered uncontrollably and she shoved her tongue between them to soften the jar. Panic surged and she screamed. Her hair, matted with knots, whipped about her face in sudden, harsh lashings. Her sunbonnet flapped behind her head so that the ties dug into her wet throat. The lightning played, livid and glaring, and she screamed again.

Suddenly she stopped. Biting back the tears, she forced herself forward again, this time dragging along the ground on her knees. The lightning came often, crackling, scarring the heavens. The thunder boomed, rolling around the perimeter of the prarie, fencing everything in, letting nothing escape its fury. And the rain hit hard, needles upon her head, wetting her to the skin.

Then finally she was there. Her fingers groped for the flap that was the tent door, found it, then lost it to the wind. Again she found it, and this time her hand held tight. She fell inside.

The blackness of the interior startled her, and she stumbled over something. "Catherine? Lenora?"

No one answered.

"Katy! Nora!" she screamed the names again. "Ma?" Only the fierce wind and the crash of the continual thunder responded. She knelt, felt around the floor and found the blanket she had tripped on. "Isn't there anybody in here?" she shouted.

The tent snapped and pulled at its pegs. Louisa turned, went back to the door, and looked out. The wind caught her hair and whipped it into her eyes so that it took both hands to pull it away.

Lightning forks laced the sky, outlining the four wagons, the horses nosed up to them, almost hidden in the downpour. Their feet raised and set in rapid succession and their necks jerked frantically on the lines that held them.

Where were the other tents? Where was everyone else? She

stepped out, then fell, stifling a scream. Both arms went around her knees. Crying, giving in at last to the tears, she crawled back to the empty tent. Why didn't they miss her? Probably each tent figured she was in the other. But why wasn't anyone in this one? She shivered, convulsively, her chin bouncing into her knees.

The blanket. She felt around again for it, pressed it to her face. So warm, so dry.

"Louisa?"

She knew his voice anywhere. "David!"

Louisa sprang up. Her foot caught the hem of her dress and she felt it tear as she spun. "David!" she gasped again. For a moment she stood stunned, stunned to see anyone in a world gone beserk.

"Louisa." He crossed the tent floor and reached for her. His touch was wet and cold, and it tightened about her wrist, bringing a strange warmth and comfort. It was as if he felt it too for he let go just briefly before grasping her hand more firmly.

"Louisa." He took her head in his hands and held her, and she felt a calm, dizzy quiet as he pulled her close. Could this be happening?

"We've got to get to another tent. One where the others are— you'll get lung fever." He spoke directly into her face.

"No... the storm." She started to sob again. The thunder boomed, loud and defiant. The lightening flickered. David brushed a wet strand of hair off her face, his fingers lingering, then running down to her chin. She bent her face into his touch.

She could only look at him. Her shivering passed and she was still, waiting. "Come on," he said.

He led her toward the other tents in the blinding rainfall, holding her fast, pulling her over the slippery earth. She could see the other two tents, the lightning blinking them into vision in bright darts. And then they were there.

"Ma? Oh, Ma!" Louisa felt the dry warmth of her cape being pushed into her hands, and she pushed her nose into thick, warm pile. Louisa pulled her face away in a start. Ma had been in her trunk! Had she seen the mirror? She felt David's hands grip her shoulders from behind, and then he was gone. The wind tore at the tents. The lightning flashed again, brilliantly, and Louisa saw Ma's face. Ma knew.... Well, it didn't matter anymore. She thought instead of David. And the storm raged on.

5

"One of the hunters, D.T. Denny, said it might have
been a very serious matter for them to have been charged
by a wounded buffalo out on the treeless prairie, where
a man had nothing to dodge behind but his own shadow."
—Emily Inez Denny in *Blazing the Way*

It took two days to dry everything out. David worked with
unabated energy, a fresh vivacity—and a little more daring in
his surveillance of Louisa. He was still hesitant to draw close
and was puzzled how he could have been so audacious during
the storm, but she made no show that she had minded, and he
took heart. He smiled more and whistled, and even James
couldn't annoy him.

Louisa was a puzzlement to David. He knew from watching
her that it had been a long time since anyone else other than
James had merited her attention—maybe even as long as the
three years that Ma and Pa had been married. And it wasn't
that suitors hadn't been around—plenty of them had. But Louisa
had seemed to see only James.

David grinned, feeling again the way she had clung to him,
hearing again the way she had cried out his name. The familiar
stirring deep inside whipped about—as if Ma had taken an egg-
beater to his intestines, and he heard himself whistle.

"Buffalo, Pa!" David pulled in his horse, swung around, and
lined up his stallion next to the head wagon. They were three
weeks into the plains, and he and Dobbins were supposed to
be out scouting. "A whole herd of them, Pa! A few miles to the
northwest!"David's words came in surges as he gulped for air.
Beneath him his horse panted, flanks heaving. The muscles
quivered from the run. Dobbins rode in close behind.

"Get your gun, Pa! You said we were needing meat!"

Louisa sat with Pa, her face protected by the brim of her sunbonnet. She wore her blue calico (his favorite, David noted).
He grinned and waved up to her; she smiled, waved back, and

pushed at her hat to see better. "Buffalo? Is it safe?" she asked.

"You take the reins, Sugar Lump." John pushed them into her hands. "Dobbins? Can I ride with you? Liza! Here!" He picked up the reins he had dropped. "You take the wagon! Tell Wiley, should he catch up with you, that we've gone hunting! Doubt those cows will mosey on any faster than they're going, though…. Must be miles back by now." He grabbed the rifle that rode behind them.

"Good-bye, Mother! No time for a kiss!" he hollered into the interior. He checked his ammunition and was gone. Arthur and Samuel, the middle Denny brother, the one who found his place between David and James, were just as fast. Louisa, Anna, and Mary Ann shrugged, then cracked their whips over the waiting horses.

James drove the fourth wagon. "Where's Ma?" he demanded, steering in close to Louisa. Sweat beaded his forehead and he swiped at it with the back of his bare arm. His brows were knit together in a wet, red ridge over his nose.

"Tending the babies in back!"

"Well, can't she take my wagon awhile?"

"What horse you going to ride? Pa and Dobbins already had to ride double!"

"Oh, criminy!" James lifted his quirt and let it fall over the backs of his team. They bolted forward, snorting their pain and surprise, and jounced past the others in a fog of dust. The women watched him go, knowing that his frustration would drive him far. Ma poked her head out of the canvas to shake her head and mutter, "The fool will ride himself into nothin' but trouble. And don't tell me it's his red hair. It's his temper, sure as God made little cricks in a back."

James drove straight west. The other men veered north a few degrees, beyond the swelling horizon, with David in the lead. Here he was in command. He had grown up with a gun in his hand, a veritable Nimrod, and the others followed him confidently.

David liked to be out. He liked the vastness of the prairies, the odd sense of isolation it gave him. Pa had given him the regular assignment of riding scout, and he gloried in it, feeling akin to David of long ago, shepherding his sheep outside Bethlehem. The only drawback to the task was that he didn't get to see much of Louisa. "It's just as well," he thought as they galloped toward the spot where he had first seen the buffalo. Trying to interest Louisa wasn't a thing he could rush. He puckered his lips and bit on the inside bulge of his cheek.

"There they are!" shouted Samuel. Sam resembled James in appearance—rusty, with congeniality sketched in his face except for when things didn't go his way. He pointed down from a hill they had just crested. The valley was long and lush, with unusually green vegetation. The whole of the low-lying region was the color of Ma's green peas back home on the pantry shelf.

There were no large bushes, though, and David knew that before another month passed this grass too would be gone, having yielded to the sun. He thought of the passage in the Bible that spoke of the withering grass, of the flower that falleth. He knew it wasn't speaking of the great plains at the end of May. He would have to look that up later—maybe tonight.

"There's hundreds of them!" Samuel whistled. He stood in his stirrups to get a better view, his eyes shielded from the sun's brightness.

"More like a thousand of 'em," mumbled John. "Maybe two..."

"Suppose we can get one?" Dobbins laughed halfheartedly.

"I don't know," said Arthur. "Just look at the size of them! I've never seen such beasts!" The herd moved toward them casually. Their heads, massive and mangy, nosed to the ground, their tails twitching spasmodically.

"How do you go about shooting one of those brutes?" Samuel asked. "Anybody know what we're doing here?" David saw one of James's grins on Sam's face.

He held a finger out ahead of him, brought it to his lips, wet it, then stuck it back out. "Wind's comin' from the south. We'll circle to the north and close in behind them, a little to their left. Don't want them to get a whiff of us."

"Who says you know what you're doing, Dave?" Sam asked.

"I read, don't I?"

"He knows what he's doing." Arthur clucked to his horse. He and David were close. "What do we do, Dave?"

"Well, you can either ride right into them like the Indians do and get yourself killed, or you can do it the easy way..." He paused to stare down into the low basin.

"Which is?" John urged.

"You can take a pop at 'em downwind. Hit 'em right and they'll fall over dead. Hit 'em wrong and you got one mad buffalo on your hands!" He whistled and shook his head slowly. "Sure could be a serious matter to be charged by one of those fellows. No trees, nothing to hide behind but our own shadows." He tapped his horse slightly with the reins, then pulled up sharply. His body bounced comfortably as Jonathan broke into an easy trot.

He was happy—a horse beneath him, rifle clean and ready, game just ahead. The best part of it was that there wasn't a cloud in the sky and James was stuck back at the wagons. He grinned and bent to slap the muscles along Jonathan's neck. David and Jonathan. They were a team. "I'm going to get one, Dobbins! Feel it in my bones the way Ma does the weather!"

"Pretty cocky, aren't you?" Dobbins ran a hand through his hair, and it reminded David of Louisa. She did the same thing at night, when the fire was still burning, the cold beginning to come on. "Know where to shoot?" Dobbins hollered.

"Yup!"

"Shh!" ordered John. "I hear their hearing is good. Eyesight bad, but they got ears."

"Pa, they're too dumb to know that we're even after them," said Samuel. "Dumbest animal next to the sheep."

"Just the same, be quiet!"

They circled in silence, their eye on the herd. Great bare patches of skin showed through the black wool, the wool ragged and loosening for the summer.

"Would you just look at those eyes!" whispered Samuel. "About the size of one of Ma's teacups..."

"Shh-h!" John waved his arm, silencing them.

Dobbins was the first to fire. John leaned way back to give him room, then straightened at the sound. Dobbins hit one of the larger animals, a bull who paid little attention to the infliction in his side. He merely flipped his tail, then chewed on as before. A few of the buffalo lifted their heads, as if to acknowledge the gunfire, but returned their noses to the grass unconcerned, slobbering saliva from their leathery mouths.

"So much for keen ears, Pa!" said Dobbins. He scratched his head and looked to David. "Don't exactly spook, do they?"

"Don't exactly mind a bullet in the gut, either. Here, I'll show you how it's done." David looked down the barrel of his gun, the familiar sight lining up the clear patch right behind the shoulder point of a cow's foreleg. His finger curled around the trigger and he clamped his teeth together, squeezing hard.

"You hit 'er! By gum, you hit 'er!" Samuel hollered. A tiny spot of red bubbled up. "What's wrong with these critters?" The cow, like the other, stood unaffected.

Suddenly she lunged, bellowing out in rage. The herd charged, en masse, to the southeasterly horizon, all of them snorting and trumpeting in confusion.

David's prey fell behind, her legs buckling beneath the weight. She stood again and braced, a spurt of purple bursting from her mouth and draining from her nostrils. She staggered, turned, came back toward the men, then fell, kneeling as if in prayer. Her head dropped to the ground.

The men watched in awe as the animal fought her death. Like a lion claiming his kill, the cow tossed her head, the mane rolling with motion. But her mouth was empty, save the tongue that hung from it—thick, pulpy, and red with blood.

In a final surge of power, the buffalo plunged forward. But she slumped only yards from where they sat atop their horses. Her side hit the earth, her legs shot out. Without a sound she raised her head to stare out of the massive, unseeing eyes. Then her head fell with a thud against the ground, stilled upon the prairie. The men stood unmoving, hardly daring to advance.

"Pa! The buffalo! They've stampeded straight for the wagons!" Arthur thundered.

David slapped the rump of his horse and they were off, all of them, spurring their animals into a hard gallop, the dead buffalo forgotten as they raced over the flattened grass.

The rest of the herd had spread over the plains, their hooves hitting the sod in a thundering roll, tearing up the grass with the force. They reached the rim of the basin and disappeared, sending up a cloud of dust. David blinked from the grit that hovered.

"Louisa!" he screamed, then buried his face into the crook of his arm. He gave Jonathan the lead, trusting him to make it through the dust that blew up. "Come on, boy," he coaxed. Nothing mattered anymore. Only Louisa, the others. What a fool! Shooting into a bunch of wild animals that were facing east! He felt his horse slow, snorting on the pulverized earth.

"Louisa!" he screamed again. But the din of the stampeding buffalo erased his call, and he dug his heels into the flanks of his faltering horse with desperation.

★   ★   ★

"Auntie! What's that noise?" Kate sat with Louisa, her arms bared to the sun, her sunbonnet pulled back. Louisa listened. There *was* a noise, a soft rumble.

"I don't see any clouds," she said. "Surely we're not in for another thunderstorm..."

Nora rode in the wagon ahead, bouncing along with her arms dangling over the backboard. They were passing through a particularly barren section, devoid of the lush grass that marked the lower-lying terrain, and Louisa steered her wagon a little to the side of Mary Ann's to avoid some of the dust.

"Look!" shrieked Kate.

Anna screamed. "It's the buffalo! They're headed straight for us!" A dark line marked them along the edge of the plains, miles off but advancing. A long, low cloud of dust haloed the approaching herd, staining the blueness of the sky.

Louisa stared in horror. She could see James several miles ahead, safely out of the buffalo's path. Wiley, she knew, was too far back to be of any help. And she didn't want to think of him alone back there, with only the cattle, his horse, and Jonah.

"Nora!" she hollered to the child in the wagon ahead. "Climb up to your mother and tell her to move to the south side of Aunt Anna!" But Lenora clung to her spot, rooted with fear. Only her curls bounced alongside her rounded cheeks and widened eyes. "Quick!" Louisa screamed. The little girl's skirts twitched and then she was gone, climbing and stumbling her way to the front. The wagon veered to the left and Louisa lashed at her horses, steering them to the northwest. She pulled up between Mary Ann and Anna, making a line of the three wagons, facing the marching line that grew bigger. Then it hit her! The horses! What if they spooked?

"No!" she screamed. "It's all wrong! The horses! Turn around! We've got to turn around!"

"What?" shouted Mary Ann. The distant rumble was loud now, a rolling thunder, ominous and chilling in its sound.

"Turn back! Around!" Louisa motioned, circling her arm, then pointed behind. Mary nodded, then turned her wagon. Anna sat numb and the earth trembled. The horses reared, afraid to keep their feet on the ground.

"Turn you idiot!" Louisa shouted. Anna turned, circling wide, fighting her team, then lining them up next to Louisa's and Mary's.

"They're going to trample us!" she cried.

"Hold your horses tight!" Louisa shouted. "If we stand still I think we'll be wide enough to make the buffalo go around us! But you've got to hold the horses in!"

"I can't hear you!"

"Hold the reins! Tight!"

The buffeting of the hooves reverberated across the earth, vibrating everything that touched it, swallowing up all other sounds of the great plains.

"I can't do it, Liza. I can't!" Anna sobbed.

"You can! And you will!" shouted Mary Ann. "You get a hold of yourself!"

"I can't hear you!" Anna screamed, again and again. "We're all going to die!"

"Shut up!" Louisa raised her hand but grabbed the reins as the horses pulled.

"Louisa!" Ma spoke up sharply, and suddenly Louisa was aware of Kate beside her. "Katy!" she shrieked. "Get yourself into the wagon!" The girl didn't argue; she dropped backward into her grandmother's arms.

The horses yanked at their harnesses in terror, whinnying, rearing up. The leather reins bit into Louisa's hands. The horses threw their heads from side to side, their eyes rolling and blinking from the dust that was upon them.

The horses bucked, pulling the wagon up off the ground, then dropped it again. Louisa's neck snapped. "Whoa!" she screamed. "Whoa!" But it was no use—the horses were off, fleeing the dread behind them. "Whoa!" she screamed again as she wrapped the straps around her wrists to keep her grip. "Whoa!"

Anna's team bolted past, and she nearly pitched head-over

into the wagon tongue with the jerk. "Dear God," thought Louisa, "what a way to die!" But God was good; Anna hung on.

All three wagons careened forward, bouncing wildly. Then the beasts were upon them. They charged by, skirting them neatly as they passed. The horses snorted, spewing mucous and dust from their noses. They plunged on, heedless of the bits that brought blood to their mouths.

Louisa grabbed hard at the reins, pulling in tight, only to have them snapped back out, yanking her arms out straight. A searing pain shot through her shoulders, and she felt warm tears spring up from her eyes. Her vision blurred. The dust closed in, a golden color of choking filth.

On and on the monstrous buffalo came, brushing close, with the horses driven in the midst of them, wild with fright. Louisa forgot everything—the torment of her shoulders, the ache in her chest, everything but keeping the horses from running in front of the buffalo. Rounded humps rushed headlong beside her, mound after mound, making her so dizzy that she feared she might pitch over the side.

Then they were gone. But the horses continued to run, and Louisa screamed until her voice quit. At last they slowed, then stopped. Their coats glistened with sweat; saliva, thick with dirt, and blood dripped from their mouths.

Louisa jumped from the wagon, collapsed, picked herself back up, and staggered to the horses. "Shh," she crooned, rubbing her hands along their necks and down their shoulders, both hands moving swiftly, calming their terror. Ma joined her, handing her the canteen.

The water ran from Louisa's chin and splashed onto her skirt. She drank, savoring the wetness as it softened her throat and filled her stomach until it ached. Splashing some onto her palms, she rinsed her face, sensing too late her own blood. It smeared, and she rubbed it into her dress along her thighs.

"The buffalo! They're crossing the Platte!" Louisa looked out, then took Mary's hand in hers. Ma and Anna stood beside them and they all watched woodenly as the herd waded through the water. The ground felt strangely still, the air strangely quiet. Slowly the dust settled, and Anna flopped herself against a horse, her arms thrown up over its back. She pressed her forehead into its flank and sobbed.

Louisa walked over to her, touching her hand on her trembling back. "You did just fine, Anna. I'm sorry for what I said. I spoke hastily. I do that, you know…it's a bad habit of mine. Ma's been…"

"I want to go home… I just want to go home!"

"It's all over, Anna. We're safe. God took care of us."

"Here comes James," continued Louisa. Ma stood with her hands on her hips, a small woman with flashing black eyes. James had the horses trotting, creating more dust, coloring the air again. He jumped from the wagon with a "whoa" and a toss of the reins, then ran the remaining few feet, his eyes searching theirs.

"We could all be dead!" Anna screamed. Tears muddied her cheeks, and the green of her eyes looked like glass.

"If you're all right I'll go see about Wiley." He looked to Louisa, but she kept her eyes cast downward. "I'll be off then." He yanked off his hat, then donned it again with a plop. He walked to one of Louisa's horses and unleashed him from the harness. "I'll go see what I can find, Ma'am," he said to Ma, swinging up on Pete and onto the path. It was a new path, beaten wide by the buffalo, and stretched along the river. Beyond it was Wiley. Somewhere.

Louisa stood motionless, feeling the pain now. Wiley? Where was Wiley? And David? She limped to her wagon, startled to see the chaos inside but too weary to care. Numbly she thought about her mirror and figured it was probably in a million pieces now.

She cleared a small place, lowered herself down carefully, and set her back against her trunk. Her head dropped backward until it rested on the hump. Her arms ached, and she curled her fingers into her lap, afraid to open them for the pain. She wondered if her shoulders had been dislocated, but decided they had not.

"Dear God," Louisa said silently, "thank you for sparing us again. Please, please let Wiley be all right…and David and the others."

David? Where was he? She took a deep breath, forcing herself to calm down. She saw Anna pitching forward, heard her own sharp words, felt the yank in her arms. Tears fell as she jerked forward, reacting to the imaginary pull of the reins. "Breathe deeply," she told herself. "Just keep breathing deeply."

"Louisa! Sarah!" Pa's voice drifted through her fatigue, the swirling space, but she made no move. The sound of the horses, galloping in closer and closer brought back her fright, and she fought the terror, clenching her teeth, willing herself not to scream. There were more shouts. Anna was crying, and the children...

"Louisa?"

She opened her eyes slowly and saw him. He was perched beside her, staring into her face. "The buffalo, David..." she whispered. "They—"

"I know... It was all my fault..." He broke off, unable to say any more.

"Oh, David! No!" She tried to sit straight, opening her fingers to the tears that streamed down his face, falling unchecked from his jaw. He grabbed her hand and she winced.

"Yes, it was! Louisa, listen to me! I shot one! I shot a buffalo! None of us knew what we were doing, but I shot one!" He dropped her hand and leaned forward over his buried face. His shoulders heaved as he cried out, "I nearly killed you, Liza!"

"No—"

"I started the stampede!" Their eyes locked. "I could have killed everyone! You!"

"No, David, no..." Her pain was gone now—only David's was there. She reached for his hand, and at her touch he took it, then softly ran a finger across her palm, across the lacerations and blood. He turned it over and touched the rawness of her wrist. Their eyes met again, and he calmed. He reached for her cheek to smooth the hair from her blood-smeared face. "I think you better go," she whispered, not taking her eyes from his. "Your buffalo...it'll need butchering."

He sniffed. "All right." Backing out, eyes unable to let go, he dropped to the ground. For a moment they held each other, and then he was gone.

6

"So the prairie schooners ploughed their way, day after day.... The monotonous days lengthened into weeks. The sun beat down upon them with its relentless heat; the flowers and grass withered; the earth became hard and parched; the horses jogged along with heads hanging."
—Roberta Frye Watt in *Four Wagons West*

"This place isn't fit for anybody but Indians and buffalo," said David. He scanned the miles ahead, taking in the numerous prairie-dog holes of the Laramie Plain and the scattered buffalo bones—huge and bleached white by the sun. They lay everywhere, humps of death in the desolation.

Behind towered Scott's Bluff, along with other rocky buttes. They rose out of the prairie stark and grotesque, almost torturous in their appearance among the withered grass—burnt red against burnt amber.

Louisa sat with David. She had invited herself along, unable to stand his quietude anymore. Two and a half weeks had passed since the buffalo stampede. Her mirror hadn't broken, but David was spoiling it all by his old aloofness. She didn't know what had happened. Was his quiet due to the fight he and James had after the stampede? The two of them had accused each other of being totally irresponsible and Pa had had to break it up.

Well, today, for a reason she couldn't explain, she had just climbed up on the wagon seat beside him and said hello. She sat close so that her thigh touched his, and the kindling of warmth of it pulsated through her. Something deep down had pushed its way up after years of being carefully buried by proper training. Maybe it was that she had just had her birthday; June the 1st she had turned 24.

In her hands she held one of Pa's shirts. He had ripped out one of the buttonholes, and she was trying to salvage the wreckage. It was hard to do, bouncing along, and once in awhile she would wince and suck at the blood on her finger. She thought of Fort Laramie somewhere ahead, and her fingers pulled at the threads quickly; the excitement of seeing new faces, maybe even having a bath, quickened her movements.

The days were going slowly now—always the same. Each morning before the sun was up Ma would have a fire going, the biscuits rolled, the bacon sizzling. She had become an expert at preparing the cornmeal, rolling out the cakes, and then tying up the sack again. Once in awhile she would come across an egg insulated in the flour and they would have a treat.

Breakfast over, they would hitch the horses and start the long walk all over again. The children still coughed from time to time, but the worry of the whooping cough was gone. Even the memory of the buffalo stampede had subsided, and nothing but a few wandering Indians created a stir. It would be wonderful to get to the fort. Pa had said maybe tomorrow.

"Makes you wonder how they survive out here," said David. "The Indians, I mean."

"I suppose they wander, follow the buffalo or something." She didn't look at him. He was talking now, and she didn't want him to stop.

"Remember the day I shot the buffalo?" She nodded. "A verse—well, part of a verse—came to my head that day. Something about withering grass. I looked it up last night." He laughed suddenly and she glanced up sharply. "It's in James! Imagine me finding anything useful in James!"

She pushed the needle into the small pin book that Ma had made for her once. "Want to hear how the whole thing goes?" he asked. "No, wait, I'll tell you anyway. 'Let the brother of low degree rejoice in that he is exalted, but the rich in that he is made low, because as the flower of the grass he shall pass away. For the sun is no sooner risen with a burning heat but it withereth the grass.... So also shall the rich man fade away in his ways.' " He paused. "James 1:9-11. Interesting, isn't it?"

"You think you're going to be rich someday?"

"That's not the point. James is the rich brother. I'm the one of low degree."

"I'm not sure I understand."

He smiled slowly and she watched his mouth turn up. "Well, I do, Liza. I do..." His voice trailed off and he smiled again. "I'm going to memorize the whole thing, you know."

"The whole Book of James!"

"It's not that long. Five chapters, 108 verses, whichever you prefer. Counted them last night. Thought the idea of memorizing James somewhat funny." He turned on the seat to face her. "You don't see the humor in that, do you?"

"No, can't say that I do."

"Well, I do. Yup, I'm going to memorize that whole book. Might help me out when it comes to that brother of mine. Like the bit about controlling your tongue... Oh, forget it." He tugged on the reins, urged the horses faster. He laughed again.

"You're jealous of James."

"What?"

"You're jealous of James, David. I see it all now. You are, aren't you?"

He propped his elbows on the worn threads of his pants and stared out over the backs of the horses to the prairie. He fidgeted with the leather straps in his hands, rubbing his palms together so that the reins rolled from the base of his palms out to his fingertips and back again. He turned to look at her, his eyes dark from the squint. Then deliberately he wrapped the reins to the post alongside him and took her face between his hands to kiss her.

She gasped from the suddenness of it and pulled away. But he grabbed tight. The sun burned hot on her face and he kissed her again. His lips were hard and unyielding, then harsh and painful.

"David!"

"I don't see you getting in such a huff with James!"

She pushed her fallen sunbonnet back into place and tied the ribbons tight under her chin. She did it slowly, aware of the wrinkled satin between fingertips, of the chasm that seemed to only widen between her and David. "That's different," she whispered softly. "This is you and me, David. We're different. Aren't we?" She looked up and saw that he had withdrawn completely, and she blinked and wiped her eyes. "Don't do this to me, David," she pleaded. "Please don't shut me away. Please! James—"

"Don't mention James to me again!"

"But he's my brother, David... Your brother."

"He *is* mine." David's voice was cold and he stared straight ahead. "He is *not* yours."

"David." She paused. "James and I have been friends ever since Ma and Pa got married. We have fun together..." She stopped abruptly.

"So I've noticed," David mumbled. He slapped the reins in his hands.

"He is my brother, David. What—"

"He's no more your brother than I am!" He snapped the whip and the horses bolted. Louisa had to hold fast to keep from being bounced off. "There's nothing in the law, Louisa Boren, that says James can't up and marry you! And let me tell you something, that is just what *my* brother intends on doing!"

The wagon lurched forward, the desert passed by. James? He wanted to marry her? Louisa sat stunned. She could hear David talking to the horses, felt the wagon slow.

"You're wrong." She was afraid to look at him now. "James doesn't want to marry me or he would have asked a long time ago."

"Don't mention James to me, Louisa. I told you that."

"James—"

"I'm sick of hearing his name! I'm sick of the whole business!"

"You're not trying to understand!"

"I understand plenty!"

"Hey, there! Whoa!" Dobbins rode up on David's horse. He came out of nowhere, startling them both. Louisa felt her face warm. "Pa says for you to ride scout with Samuel, David! I'm to take over here!" He dismounted when they stopped.

David handed the reins down and fell into Jonathan's saddle in almost one motion, and Louisa watched as he galloped away from her.

"David can only see James just now, Sis," said Dobbins. "And it's churning his gut." He hopped up and got the wagon rolling again.

"I don't know what you're talking about," said Louisa. She tossed her head.

"James casts a pretty big shadow. A bit of advice, Sister. Stay away from him. You'll lose David."

Louisa saw no reason to answer her brother. She licked the salty tears from her cheeks and sniffed. Dobbins dug through his pockets, pulled loose a dusty handkerchief, and without a word handed it to her.

"Thanks," she whispered, then blew her nose.

7

"On June the 6th, thirty-two days after crossing the
Missouri River, the Denny party reached Fort Laramie,
five hundred thirty miles distant."
　　　　　　—Roberta Frye Watt in *Four Wagons West*

The women were keenly disappointed and the children cried.
And Sarah noticed that Anna said nothing.

It had been hard to cross the Laramie River. The water,
churning and sucking in swirls of soapy foam, had nearly pulled
one of the wagons under. It had been a battle to save it. But
another battle, a silent and deadly one, had been declared
unknowingly. Pa insisted on passing Fort Laramie without stopping, without even going into it. The battle was started, and
the hidden foe of resentment and anger gained swift advantage
because no one knew it was being waged against them, or waged
at all.

They had planned well, Pa said. No need to waste precious
time for foolishness. They needed nothing. They only needed
to get to Oregon.

"Oh, please?" asked Mary Ann. "Can't we just stop a few
hours?" She looked around at the gardens that grew, the corn
that reached up out of the earth, coming almost to her knees.
"Please, Pa? I want to see if they have any flower seeds. I forgot
to bring any."

"No, Mary, we've got to keep going. If we stopped every time
there was an excuse, we'd never get to Oregon. And you don't
want that baby of yours to come while on the trail, do you?"
She gathered her skirts and walked away, and the wind pressed
her clothes to her stomach, outlining the growing child beneath.

"What about Arthur's ague?" James asked.

"What about it?"

"It's bad this time. If it keeps up he'll be needing more
quinine. And the fort's bound to carry some."

Mary Ann turned around, her eyes wide and hopeful.

Louisa smiled with the sweetening of the tension.

"All right. But wait!" Pa held out his hand, stilling the excitment. "Only James goes in. The rest of us go on. You can catch up with us best you can, James. Buy some flower seeds while you're there."

"Flower seeds?" James shifted his feet, pulled the hat off his head, and smashed it back on. "Flower seeds?"

"Please, James?" Mary pleaded. "Any kind will do. I don't care. Just so they're pretty ones. Please?"

"But, Mary—a grown man asking after flower seeds?"

"Never mind." Mary walked away, and Louisa watched her sister limp to the wagon, where Arthur lay huddled beneath a pile of blankets, shivering despite the heat of the day.

"You could have asked, James," Louisa muttered as she pushed past him and Pa. He stuck out his hand to catch her by the arm, but she yanked away. David hadn't spoken to her at all since their scrap yesterday, and now James annoyed her.

"What's the matter with you?" He caught up with her and blocked her way, then grinnned and crossed his arms over in front of his chest. "I'm not letting you go until you spit it out, Liza. You look mad enough to kill a dog."

"Oh, stop it."

"Hey, I tried! I tried to get Pa to rethink! How was I supposed to know he'd just send me?"

"I'm not angry about that. Well, I am...but I'm angry with Pa. A few hours wouldn't have hurt."

"Then what are you angry with me about?"

"The seeds, James. Can't you see how important they are to Mary Ann? Her feet ache—it's not any fun to be pregnant and have to walk all day, you know—and Arthur's ill, and all she wants are a few flower seeds!"

"But, Louisa! I can't go in there and announce that I'm needing some flower seeds!"

"Yip!" Pa cracked his whip. The wheels turned, pushing through the soft soil. The other wagons inched forward, and Louisa left James to go find Ma.

The women walked together behind the wagons. Tepees were pitched in clusters, spread about the valley, and old squaws with tangled hair and worn teeth watched the travelers as they made their way past Fort Laramie. They walked stiffly, their eyes focused on the distant blue rim of the Rocky Mountain foothills. Louisa was resolved not to look behind at the adobe walls of the fort; but then, she didn't need to—she had memorized what the structure looked like.

It had two blockhouses on opposite corners, a bastion over the open gate, two shiny brass cannons pointed out to the desert, and hundreds of tents.

Louisa kicked clumps of earth and tried not to think about the fort, of Mary Ann, of the solemn Indians, of David. If she thought too long she might be tempted to scream, and she might give in and show Mary Ann the seeds in her trunk. And she couldn't do that—not yet.

"Say, look at this!" Ma pointed just off the trail. A tiny cradle, baby clothes folded neatly inside, had been discarded. They stared down at the soft colors of the handmade things and blinked. It hadn't been dumped because it weighed too much. Louisa started to walk again, afraid if she looked far she would see something else she didn't want to find.

A lot of discards sat forlornly along the trail. All along the way they had seen them, but not like this. Hundreds of belongings lay everywhere, cracked and warped, dead and forgotten. There were pieces of old wagons, splintered and too decrepit to carry on. There were rocking chairs, broken dishes, rotting bedsteads, and chests with lids that hung open. There was even a sign with faded, lopsided lettering that read HELP YOURSELF. They passed a sideboard, the mahogany still waxed.

"Hey, look, Ma!" Louisa exclaimed suddenly. She bent over a glitter of sunlight in the grass. "It's an old mirror!" The beveled glass was cracked and one corner was shattered in the twisted frame.

"Now that's exactly what would have happened to your lovely mirror, Louisa, had you insisted on bringing it along," said Ma. Louisa squinted between the jagged pieces and patted her hair, wiping the perspiration from her cheeks. "Aren't you glad to know that it's still in one piece, quite usable, decorating Pamelia's fine house?" Ma went on. Louisa glanced over and saw her mother watching her as if amused with something.

She dropped the mirror, her fingers numbing. "Yes, Ma," she said slowly. "You were quite right. You always are."

Ma laughed. Louisa flushed and hurried after her, sidestepping an old tea kettle. Ma continued to laugh, and thoughts of the fort were temporarily forgotten as Louisa listened to the sound. Ma had been in her trunk. Ma knew, and Louisa wasn't so sure she liked the way anything was turning out.

★   ★   ★

"Where's Anna?" asked Pa at supper that night. They sat in a circle, tin plates in hand. They had given up the fancy ordeal of spreading the checkered tablecloth and setting out the plates for dinner, but they still, without fail, remembered to bow their heads in thankful prayer before begining to eat what had become monotonous to them.

It was always lentils, saltport, and sometimes biscuits or corn cakes. The dried fruit had run out long before—no cobbler anymore. Sometimes David or Dobbins was able to bring in fresh meat, and that was always a treat, and they did have some of the dried buffalo meat ground into pemmican.

Louisa missed the milk most. Three of the cows still gave a little of it, but only enough for the children. The buckets that Pa had hung beneath the supply wagon bounced empty, for butter was the thing they had given up first.

The cows couldn't be blamed. The lush spring grasses were gone and they were tired from the long miles of walking. The oats and grain that Pa had brought along served only to keep them alive, not to make them fat and full of milk. Perhaps when they got to the Rockies, where it was cooler—where the grass would be green and full of nourishment—perhaps then they would give more milk, enough for everyone—and butter.

"We can't eat without Anna," said Pa again. "Where is she?"

"She won't eat." Dobbins sat cross-legged, his plate balanced carefully.

"Not eating? She's not ill, is she?"

"I don't know what's wrong with her, Pa. She won't talk to me. Just lays there and stares at nothing. Ever since we passed Fort Laramie this afternoon she's been like that. Can't make any sense of it. Can you?"

"I'll go talk with her," said Wiley. He was fond of Anna.

"No, not you," said Ma. "Dobbins needs to go to her."

"She doesn't want me, Ma!"

"She needs you, Son."

"No, I don't think so."

"Go on—we'll wait for you."

Dobbins unfolded his legs, long and thin. There was a red patch on the knee of his right leg, and when he stood it wrinkled. "I found some baby booties in an old cradle outside of Laramie," he said. "Maybe she'd like them for Gerty."

"Anna?" he called, setting his elbows on the feedbox. "Everyone's waiting for you." There was no answer and he climbed inside. "Can I bring you something?" he tried again.

She refused to look at him, and when he reached to wipe the perspiration from her temple she rolled her face away from his touch.

"Please, Anna. They're all waiting."

"I want to go home."

"Look. See what I found for you? For Gertrude?" He lifted her hand flat. The booties fluffed up.

"Baby booties? You brought me a dead baby's booties?" They dropped from her hand. "My baby is not dead, Dobbins! Not yet, anyway!" she screamed.

He dropped back, stunned. Anna clung to Gertrude and wept. She rocked the baby back and forth, moaning to herself. She smoothed the infant's hair from her cheek. "I'm sorry," she wailed. "I just want to go home!"

Dobbins rubbed his head with both hands, holding the hair between his fingers. "We can't Anna. We just can't."

"Just can't? Or just won't? Which is it, Dobbins?"

"We can't."

She laughed a small sound. "You mean you won't." And then she cried.

"Is there any hope of happiness for you, Annie? For us?" he asked. She cried softly and sobbed into the baby's blanket. It bunched in her fist and Gertrude peered out—quiet, her eyes unblinking, two little round, dark buttons. The baby shoes fell to the wagon floor.

A disquietude, a heavy despondency, settled in after that. The battle was on, claiming each of them to some degree. The Sweetwater guided the wagons now. Unlike the Platte, its waters were cool and clear, and green grass edged its banks as if to add a bit of tatting to a ribbon. But the fields on either side were awash with alkali, and each day put them further and further into the worst of it. For nearly a week they pushed forward and each day dragged longer, until it seemed that this was all they had known.

John Denny sat alone on the wagon seat. With eyes stinging, he watched his horses step cautiously forward. They set their hooves down gently, deliberately careful, into the powdered dust, so alkaline and caustic. He rubbed his eyes, but the sting remained. He blinked and wished for tears to soothe the burn.

Turning, he tried to see inside the wagon, but the opening was pulled tight and only a dark, empty hole met his gaze. All the wagons had the canvas coverings pulled in—an attempt to keep the alkali from penetrating. But it seeped in anyway and dusted everything, burning whenever it grated between sweated skin and clothes.

John cursed himself silently. It wasn't the desolation around them that was to blame for the oppressiveness. It was him. The desert merely intensified what he had started. The women rarely spoke, Anna not at all. She hadn't eaten much. The only thing she communicated was that she wanted to go home. And even Louisa was quiet.

John looked to the river, where Louisa and Mary Ann walked. Mary's limp was worse. He could see that their lips moved, but there was no laughter, no smiles. "Flower seeds," he said aloud. "All she wanted was flower seeds." He watched Mary limp on, her shoulders stooped over the burden she carried in front. He moaned and rubbed his eyes again.

Even Sarah hadn't been able to hide her disappointment. She had withdrawn from him, serving his needs perfunctorily, leaving the warm caresses, the tenderness for little Loretta. He missed her, missed her touch. He felt old without it.

Ahead the foothills of the Rockies still shaped the horizon, tantalizing his torment by appearing to draw no nearer. But they did bring a softness, a shade of color to the harshness, and he focused his attention on them. He stared out, then squinted. Was that a rise, a swelling? Had they come to Independence Rock?

He called a halt for the noon meal. The women routinely went about in the preparation, the serving, the cleaning up. Anna remained where she was, a shadow in the wagon box, her face too thin, far too white.

John sighed and cracked the whip. Time to move on.

The sun scorched everything. It sweltered those who sought refuge beneath the canvases, baked those who walked, and burned skin, making bare arms brown. Like the Rockies, Independence Rock seemed to grow no bigger. It stayed shrouded in the dim distance and to John it seemed to remain aloof—like Sarah, too displeased to draw close.

He leaned into his elbows, the boniness of them piercing his knees. What had he done? Had a few saved hours been worth the gloom that pervaded? His eyes stung and he bowed to welcome the relief of his tears, the utter desolation that consumed him. More tears came, but only God knew his anguish, for he sat alone.

★　　★　　★

Like a turtle hibernating, its head and legs tucked out of sight, Independence Rock lifted up out of the burnt grasses, a dark mound of chalky amber. It humped up, scarred and secure in its assigned spot, ageless in its existence.

As the travelers neared, its sharp and smooth surfaces separated to reveal a long fissure that cut through the granite. Its ancient face, clearing with each step closer, began to show the newest of its scars: the etching of hundreds of names, some carved deep into its skin and others painted with tar on its cheek.

The wagons creaked to a stop and the horses dropped their heads wearily, uninterested. Everyone silently gathered—everyone but Anna, who sat in her wagon—and solemnly stared at the giant monolith. No one moved, the oppression robbing them of the pleasure at having reached another landmark.

"May we write our names, Grandpa?" Kate tugged at John's gnarled hands, her voice plaintive and pleading. He squatted beside her, his eyes brought to the same level as hers. He saw Mary Ann's eyes pleading to stay on at Fort Laramie, and he blinked away the memory.

"I don't know," he drawled slowly, watching her carefully. "Seems like a horrendous waste of time." He winked, and she laughed. The sound was sudden and clear, like music on a cold morning, and it caught everyone off guard.

"Come on, Nora!" she sang. "We're going to have some fun!" She caught her grandfather's arm and pulled him forward, then stopped to dance, filling the air with her happiness.

"I'll take them, Pa." Louisa stepped forward. He looked at her, and she saw the miniscule red veins webbed in his eyes, the sense of isolation and self-disparagement caught in the broken look. "You've had a hard day, Pa," she whispered. "And I don't mind. I'd really like to."

David jumped from the supply wagon and set a bucket of tar down with a thud. Dust poofed up. "I'll get you something to slap it on with!" he hollered. The children clambered around Louisa and pulled on her arms. "Come on, Auntie!" they sang out, jumping again. Their bubbling excitement was infectious, and a new sense of gaiety percolated.

"I'll carry the tar!" said James. He swung the bucket up easily, a smile on his face. David returned with a flat trowel.

"Thought I was doing the tar," he said.

"No problem for me, little brother!" James took the tool and jerked his head to Louisa. "Come on!"

"You coming, David?" she asked. He had that expression again—one she had grown used to, but couldn't understand.

"No, thanks, I've got other things to do."

The momentary bubble of happiness popped. "Come on, Liza!" James shouted. The girls, anxious to be off, tugged her along, dragging her away, and she looked back at him helplessly.

"Give me your hand and I'll give you a boost!" James stood about four feet off the ground, his boots planted in the gouged fissure of the rock. She let him pull her, then of necessity help her with her skirts. They stood in the crevice, the carved letterings surrounding them: hundreds of names and messages, recordings of death, birth, words of love—all carved or painted on the granite.

The fissure ran along the rock at an incline and gave them an ideal way to mount the rock. Almost crawling, they scooted up, using their arms like a monkey. Once James slipped and nearly lost the tar. But when they reached a place that was smooth and unblemished, Louisa straightened and gasped with surprise. They were up much higher than she had thought, and she could see for miles.

An excitement came as she breathed in the clean air, free of the dust that plagued the lower levels. The Sweetwater River flowed casually eastward and the Rockies looked blue. Sweat ran down her back and ran in itchy rivulets between her legs, but it felt good because there was a breeze. She saw David standing just as she had left him—feet spread, hands in his pockets—and the excitement was fed. She wanted to laugh, to be happy again.

"Look!" James backed into a jagged etching. "I'm sitting on Mrs. Van Kloegen!" It was silly, but the excitement exploded and she laughed. She felt no shame, for she wanted to laugh so badly. They all laughed and read aloud the names that were around them.

David watched awhile and then turned away. "Couple of fools, aren't they?" he said when he passed Anna in the wagon. He stopped and leaned against the wooden base, his elbows resting on it behind him, holding him up. The minutes passed and Anna leaned forward, propping her arms beside David. Both of them watched as Louisa and James slapped the tar on the rock.

"I miss your singing," he said, not looking at her.

"Why don't you tell James to leave her alone?"

"What?" The question startled him.

"Louisa loves you. Why don't you tell James to mind his own business?"

He turned to look at her. Anna was gazing up. "It's like a monument," she whispered. "Marking our existence."

"We do exist."

He didn't know what else to say to her.

"There's a song, David, something about a rock in a weary land."

"Jesus Is the Rock in the Weary Land?"

She nodded and the tears fell.

"Sing it for me. I like that hymn."

Her voice was clear and high, like a nightingale's. The melodic strains lifted over the heat waves, quietly at first, then more sure. The silly laughter on the rock stopped. Down below everyone hushed. They all listened.

"Wiley! Help me with the tents!" shouted Pa. "Well? Don't just everybody stand there! We've got work to do! You know what needs to be done! We're making camp!"

The girls scattered to collect their buffalo chips for the fire. Everyone jumped to his tasks, afraid that Anna would stop. But she didn't, and when supper was served, she helped Ma pour the molasses over the hasty pudding.

★   ★   ★

"What did you say to her?" whispered Louisa. Her hands were buried in the sudsing water as the sun painted its pastels across the sky behind her.

"I don't know as I said anything," David answered. "She seemed to take comfort in seeing her name on the rock."

David and Louisa stood on either side of the washtub, scrubbing the supper plates before setting them out to dry. Each time their fingers touched beneath the foamy water, their eyes met and a burning tingle intensified. "It's as if our names bring on immortality, a hope of life forever," Louisa said. She smiled. "At least an assurance that we'll make it to Oregon despite it all."

"We'll make it. We'll make it forever, too." David's eyes were soft in the dusk.

"David?" she said quietly. "You're so jealous of James, aren't you?"

"Let's just forget it, all right? I'm immature. Anna, in her own way, pointed that out."

"You're not immature." Louisa ran her hand along the bottom of the old tub to feel for any lost dishes. Only the lukewarm water slithered around her fingers, then something grabbed and held tight. She looked up, startled, then suddenly was very shy. David separated her fingers with his own and she felt her wrist bend upwards as his palm met hers. A butterfly flew down and rested on a dusty stalk of grass nearby. David lifted the heavy tub, splashed its water in an arc over the thirsty earth, and the butterfly flew from the splash. It spread its colorful wings, then darted up out of sight.

8

"...while they were making camp for the night a lone Indian made his appearance...."
—Roberta Frye Watt in *Four Wagons West*

Being together was new for David and Louisa, and they guarded the relationship carefully, forcing a casualness between them, as if afraid that somehow the closeness might drive them apart. The days were spent separately—David riding scout, Louisa helping Mary with Kate and Nora, Ma and Anna with Loretta and Gertrude. But in the evenings they came together through stolen glances and inobtrusive brushes, continually testing, yet not pushing.

The days passed quickly this way. The trail leading out from Independence Rock to the South Pass of the Rockies was a relatively easy one, a gradual ascent up a grassy incline, making the days pass pleasantly as well as swiftly. The wagons followed the Sweetwater, and at times the travelers walked the riverbed to save the horses' hooves from the searing heat of the sand. On the 21st of June they reached the summit.

At first Louisa was disappointed. While trekking over the endless miles of prairie she had somehow come to think of the South Pass as being monumental, jagged and harsh, perhaps even having streams foaming and spilling their way down either side of the great Continental Divide. Yet it had been only another hill of blowing grasses and sand, the summit hardly recognizable. But they had celebrated the entrance into the Territory of Oregon by shouting, "Here's Oregon! Hurrah for Oregon!" and by stopping just long enough to throw their hats and sunbonnets high.

From there they descended into the desolate Green River Desert, a 53-mile stretch of orange barrenness. To save the animals (and Arthur, who had succumbed to yet another attack of the fever and ague), they crossed the worst of it at night. Starting out at four o'clock in the afternoon, they traveled over the arid waste, a strange journey in the dimness of the summer night, with only starlight overhead.

In the morning, when they finally reached the Green River, the horses bolted and made a rush for the water. They didn't stop until they stood in it up to their bellies, with the wagons dragged in after them. And so once again the travelers were forced to stop and dry everything out. But it gave Arthur time to rest, to rally, and when it was time to go on Louisa watched him struggle to help Pa hitch his team. For most of his adult life he had had frequent attacks of the ague, and she secretly wondered if that had been his main reason for leaving Illinois; Oregon was rumored to be a cure for the illness. After all this trouble she hoped it was true.

The approach into Fort Hall on the Snake River was rough. The terrain was alternately rocky then too sandy. The grass was poor, so the cattle and some of the horses deteriorated drastically.

One of the horses, Pete, the stallion with the yellow star, slumped while dragging Pa's wagon out of the Portneuf River, and Pa had to cut him out of the harness to free the other horses of the dead weight. He didn't even bother to bury the horse; he figured the wolves would get him anyway.

They came into Fort Hall on the Fourth of July, and were surprised at its dilapidated appearance. Surrounded by high walls and acres and acres of discards, it sat like a dethroned king in a refuse heap. As at Fort Laramie, there were hundreds of tepees dotting the valley, and there were patches of gardens, but the produce was poor. The Indian squaws stared at the travelers without expression as they pulled in beside the decaying structure.

Inside the fort, however, there was an air of primitive festivity. Mountain men from hidden crevices of the distant Rockies had come out of the rocky folds to celebrate Independence Day, and they laughed raucously at one another, slapping each other on the back and betting whiskey over arm-wrestling. Tobacco juice stained their whiskers and missing teeth made their weathered faces take on a beaten yet very-much-alive look. Their eyes glistened from both the excitement and the bottle, and when the Dennys arrived there was much eye-winking, and pushed-back belches, and "Yes, Ma'am"'s with exaggerated bows.

Louisa, Mary Ann, Ma, and Anna looked quickly through the mud-covered trading post. Once an efficient Hudson Bay outlet for goods of all kinds, it now offered little to sell. Mary Ann asked after flower seeds and the coarse laughter of the men congregated about a table in a far corner almost made her cry. Pa paid for a new horse harness, and after talking with the superintendent awhile, he said, "This place is devoid of decency and human feeling. We're moving on." The remark was greeted by more of the laughter, and someone spit at Louisa's feet. When she looked up the man grinned through his overgrown beard. His lips puckered with a kiss and she pushed past.

They camped along the Snake River about a mile west of the fort. Occasional gunfire sounded across the distance as the evening wore on. It grew more intense as the celebration came to a climax. No one said much, too disappointed to find much to talk of, too aware of Pa to complain. He had let them go in, and it had been a change. Suddenly David laughed.

"Hey, come on! It's the Fourth of July!" He pulled the trigger on his gun and they jumped at the blast. He grinned, then pulled two candy sticks out of his pocket—one for Kate and the other for Nora. "And I have something for you, Mary," he said. "I've got it hidden in the supply wagon. Got it at the fort this afternoon," he mumbled as he shuffled off to get it.

When he came back he had a small parcel in his hands, wrapped carefully in brown paper. He set it in her lap and she looked up at him, a puzzled look in her eyes as she searched his in the soft light of the low sun. "Go on! Open it!" he urged.

"What is it?"

"Might find out if you open it, Mary, " said Arthur. He tossed a twig into the flames. Mary Ann slid a finger under the edge of the paper and ran it along the length. The rest of the wrapping fell as she caught up a pair of soft moccasins to her cheek. "Oh, David..." she breathed out heavily. A flush of pink washed her face. "You shouldn't have...."

"Louisa told me your feet were hurting you some." David jabbed a finger down under the collar of his shirt nervously and scratched his neck. "Figured maybe it was your shoes."

Suddenly Mary was crying.

"Hey! Don't fret! Just wanted to do something nice for you. All right?" Mary Ann bit the tremor of her bottom lip, the way Louisa at times did, and nodded quickly. Louisa watched her sister try on her new shoes and wondered how long it had been since she had seen her so happy. Mary held out a foot so they could all admire the beading along the toes and the soft fur that spilled out of the ankle. When David saw that Louisa watched him he smiled, then shrugged, and she smiled back. It made him laugh.

But then a movement by one of the wagons caught her eye. An Indian stepped out of the shadows. He was alone. His hair was caught and tied behind his neck, and his chest was bare. His copper-colored frame showed strength; his face was strong but old. His eyes were black like the approaching night, and they focused on Louisa. She gasped; her fingers came to her lips to stop the sound, and she jumped quickly to her feet. Mary, she saw, edged closer to Arthur. David stood.

The Indian didn't blink. Drawn in by the unflinching gaze, Louisa stood motionless, mesmerized by the stare. Cold sweat broke out on her brow, in her palms; it mingled with the dried sweat on her back and dripped uncomfortably down until it caught at her waist. She tried to swallow. The Indian moved. He moved in a slow circle about the camp, poking his nose into the frying pan, a flour sack, the end of a wagon, but always returning his gaze back to Louisa. She turned with him, afraid to look away, yet afraid to watch. And when he returned to the spot they had first seen him, he stopped.

A smile, slow and deliberate, wrinkled a jagged scar that ran from his eye to his left ear, revealing white and even teeth. His eyes darted down, then up, and Louisa shuddered and shut her own eyes to block out the shameless stare. Someone touched her from behind and she spun in terror. It was only James.

"Oh, James!" she sobbed, falling weakly into him, under his protective arms. "Oh, James..."

"Shh...he's gone now. It was nothing. Just curious is all. And he's gone."

"But he was staring at me! He was—" She couldn't say it, and instead clung helplessly to the soft flannel that was his shirt.

"Let me take her," she heard someone say. David? Was it David? Her cheek pressed into James's chest as his hand held her close and firm.

"Don't you think I'm quite capable of this, little brother?" The vibrations of James's voice came through the flannel and she felt him walk her away from everyone. She went numbly, unable to think, to understand. They walked a long ways, until they came to an old wagon wheel, rotten, warped, and half-buried in the shifting sand. Half the spokes were missing.

Cold came off the ground, and she shivered. A more violent shudder passed through her but James held her still as she shook, then gently eased her down, where they sat side by side in the dark. She could dimly see his face, but she could see the Indian's clearly: his eyes, the way he had stared at her, the lurid smile. Again the shudder swept through.

"Hey, nothing will happen," she heard James saying. The volley of gunfire from Fort Hall ripped through the air, staccatoing the night with harshness. Time passed. The moon slid out from behind a cloud, a round hole in the gray-black of the night. Strange shadows lay out over the bleakness, catching the points of the tepees, staking out dark shapes along the ground. David? Where was David? Why didn't he come? The Indian! Where was he? She jerked forward, searched the shadows for the black, cold eyes.

"Liza! It's all right! He's gone! I'm here!"

David? No, it was still James. She stared at him curiously. He was so agitated, almost hurting her arms where he held her. And where was David? She had to find him. He wouldn't like her to be out here with James. She started to rise, to run. She ran in time to the gunfire.

But James grabbed her from behind, spinning her about so fast that it hurt her head. "No!" he whispered fiercely. "Don't go!"

"I have to, James. I have to find—"

"I love you!"

She stopped short. He stood before her, his face masked. His hands pinched tight about her upper arms as he bent into her face. "If that Indian so much as stepped near you I would have killed him! Do you understand me?" he whispered savagely, his face two inches from her own.

"You're hurting me. My arms..."

"Do you understand me?"

She shook her head and dropped low, away from his powerful grasp, but he yanked her back up. "He was..." The words stopped as he kissed her.

"No, James, no..." she whimpered.

"Don't, Louisa! Don't pull away from me! I need you!" His breath was hot on her face, his lips hot. As she tried to turn away, he caught her dress, tearing the bodice.

"James!" she screamed.

She stood in front of him, sobbing, her arms crossed over her face. Great sobs shook her body as her fists clenched and unclenched. He took her gently, absorbing her smallness in his power. "Oh, Liza, don't..." he cried. "I'm sorry. I'm sorry..."

He was just her brother again, and Louisa sobbed in his arms. "Can you forgive me?" he asked. He stroked her hair and kissed the top of her head. "Can you?" he asked again. She nodded, and he held her while she wept.

When she pulled away, moonlight caught the tear along the front of her dress, and vaguely she wondered how she would explain it to Ma. Sniffling, she tried to tie herself up. A gentle pressure behind made her turn. Then, crying again, she found James's arms, the warm curve of his shoulder.

"Do you love me?" he asked hesitantly.

"I can't..."

"I told you I was sorry. I was just afraid... I lost control..."

She lifted her head. "I can't love you, James. I love David." Even the fireworks in the distance seemed quiet. "I love David," she said again.

"David!" James exploded and stalked off toward the fort, the tepees. He turned. "David!"

"I can't help it...I just do. I always have."

"But David? Liza! He's just a kid! He's only 19!"

"I love him!"

James strode back to Louisa. "I'm not going to give you up, you know."

"It's no use, James."

He took her by the shoulders, his hands large and heavy. "I told you I'd kill that Indian. How do you think that makes me feel about my own brother, Louisa?"

"You can't kill anybody."

"Cain did."

"Let me go, James."

"Louisa! Liza!"

She left him standing there, his arms held stiffly at his sides, and headed for the glow of the fire and the rounded humps of the four wagons. As she neared she thought she saw David's face shadowed by the flames, but when she got to camp it was only Dobbins. "Where's David?" she asked.

"Stormed out of here like a—well, never mind." Then he saw her dress. "I told you to stay away from James, didn't I?"

"Oh, Dobbins, what am I going to do?" She dropped wearily to the ground and set her face in her hands. Dobbins rubbed his hands over his cheeks and lowered himself slowly down beside her. "I don't know, Sis, I just don't know. He didn't—"

"No, Dobbins. James didn't hurt me. He was just upset." She sniffed back the tears. "The Indian? Will he come back?"

"We'll keep a watch. Why don't you crawl into bed with Anna tonight?"

"What about you?"

"I'll be up all night."

She nodded and went to Anna's tent. Anna was asleep already, and beneath the cool sheets, Louisa stared up alone at the dark ceiling. Her nightgown was cold, and she shivered. Her chin chattered into her chest, and unconsciously she felt where James had touched her. Black eyes seemed to stare out from the shadows, and she shoved the back of her hand over her mouth. "Oh, David," she moaned. Tears dripped noiselessly onto the pillow.

★   ★   ★

David kicked an old anvil that had been discarded. Verses from the Book of James rattled in his head, verses that he wished he hadn't memorized. They bombarded his brain, pounding the words over and over. "Ye lust, and have not: ye kill, and desire to have. Ye lust, and have not: ye kill..." Over and over they came.

The Indian had been bad enough—but James! He had seen his brother's face when he took Louisa away. David's hands fisted tight and let go, then fisted again. Fear of what he was capable of doing gripped painfully.

A fresh assault of gunfire rattled the sky, and he slammed his foot into the side of an old bureau. The wood, dry and brittle, sprinkled the ground in tiny bits.

The Fourth of July died eventually. Mary Ann slept close to Arthur, her hand over his, her new moccasins on her feet.

Dobbins stood guard. He waved to James when he came to crawl into bed, and he waited long into the night for David to return.

Louisa and Anna were both quiet the next morning. Anna nursed Gertrude while she watched Sarah mix up the cornmeal, shaping it quickly in her hands. With a sense of urgency, the men pulled the tent pegs and folded the canvases into tidy piles. While they worked Anna watched and thought of the Indian. She shuddered, remembering the lurid eyes and the slow, deliberate stare.

Dobbins came up from the river, shouldering the washtub. The water splashed over the rim carelessly and he set it down beside Sarah. She said something to him and he shrugged. Dobbins liked it out here. Anna bit the swell of her bottom lip.

"Anna?" She jumped, but it was only Louisa. "Want a corn cake?"

"Thanks," she whispered, feeling the heat of it burn her fingers.

David walked past, looking like he hadn't slept. Dark stubble shadowed his cheek, and both Anna and Louisa watched him cross camp to the tub. He rolled his sleeves, then dipped his bare arms up to his elbows in the icy water. Sarah handed him a towel, and when he saw Louisa he dropped it and hurried in the opposite direction.

"David?" Louisa called. He broke into a run and disappeared into the back of the supply wagon. Louisa hesitated.

"Go on," Anna urged. But Louisa had gone only a few steps when an Indian galloped up. He came from the east in a cloud of dust, and as he drew near everyone stopped what he was doing, not sure of what to do or what to expect.

He was a younger man. A handsome mare pranced beneath his lithe body; his bare thighs held the horse tight, restraining the energy, and behind him trailed a long string of ponies. A whinny broke the stunned silence.

"I come to make trade!" the young brave announced. He thumped his chest. "Good trade—my ponies, your woman!" His brown finger stabbed the air toward Louisa. Anna leaned into the wagon base in dizzy numbness.

"Break camp!" Pa hollered. He tipped a bucket of water over with his boot to kill the fire. It died with spits. "Break camp!" he shouted again.

"No!" The Indian jumped from his horse noiselessly and pulled a chocolate pony in closer. He went to Pa and held out the rope. "Yours!" he beamed. "And mine!" Again he pointed to Louisa.

"David!" The scream made Anna's skin crawl. "David!" Louisa screamed again. Again and again. "David! David!"

Anna stood slowly, inching her way up the side of the wagon. David vaulted the backboard of the wagon and raced over the piles of tents and beddings.

"No trade!" Pa said. He pushed the rope away. "She belongs to us. No trade!"

"My father! He say pretty woman! I bring you his ponies to make *good* trade!" He took a step forward and the muscles along the inside of his thigh rippled. Louisa cowered in David's arms.

"Get her out of sight, Dave!" James jumped in front to block the advance. David began to back off, pulling Louisa with him. "Get her out of here!" James thundered. "Get her out!"

He stood an impressive blockage, hands on his hips, legs spread. The Indian stood before him, motionless except for his eyes. They darted quickly from side to side, calculating. "Move on," said James.

The brave was fast. His bare foot flew up and clipped James beneath the chin, and he went down with a thud. The Indian delivered a second blow, spinning James's body out ahead of him, and before anyone could stop him, he had James's fallen rifle and had rammed the butt of it into his stomach. He snarled, then raised the gun again to bring it down hard.

Anna turned and ran.

9

"The leader, attired in a plug hat and long, black over-coat (and nothing else), flapping about his sinewy limbs, gun in hand, advanced toward the [wagon] train calling out, 'How-do-do! How-de-do! Stop! Stop!' "
—Emily Inez Denny in *Blazing the Way*

Inside the wagon where David and Louisa hid, David yanked on the rope that brought the canvas opening tight. It narrowed and left only a small circle of sunlight. Then he stomped over the disorder inside the schooner, tripped over Louisa, and pulled the front tight. Darkness closed in on them, and dust danced in the two streams of light that penetrated.

He stood, slightly stooped, his eye to the front hole, his gun in hand. "Samuel and Wiley have the Indian," he muttered. "Pa and Arthur are carrying James into a wagon."

"Is he hurt?" Louisa whispered.

"Yeah, I think so. Ma's tending him... No, Mary is. Can't see much. Dobbins is getting the rest of camp picked up." He smiled weakly and Louisa nodded, her eyes fastened to the bit of sun that shone around David's profile.

"Everything's loaded... Here comes Ma and Pa!" The wagon sank, then sank again. "We're ready. Sam's letting the brave go!"

Pa's whip snapped the air and they were off. David tumbled his way to the back, and Louisa pulled in her feet to make room for him to pass. Again he stooped, his eye to the hole.

"He's following us!"

Louisa watched David's face, his arms—the way his muscles knotted as he unconsciously gripped his gun. His sleeves were still rolled, and she could see that his biceps were strong. She took comfort in his strength. The wagon bounced and she bounced with it. David's body swayed, held in place by hands that locked about the arched bows overhead. His rifle lay at his feet now, but he still guarded, his eye not leaving the small peephole.

"Still there?" Louisa asked after a time. Her throat was so dry she could hardly speak. "Still there?" she squeaked out, louder this time. David nodded. "How long? How long has it been?"

"Hasn't been that long, not really. But he's still coming. Creating quite a bit of dust, that's for sure. Oh, wait!"

"What, David? What?" Louisa scrambled to her feet, but a sudden turn sent her sprawling and she crashed her head into the corner of something sharp. It dazed her for a moment, but then she was up again. "What is it?" she demanded, trying to see. One of David's arms dropped from the bow, and he held her to his side so she could see.

"He's leaving!" she shrieked. "He's turning back!"

David dropped his other arm. The wagon bounced and they fell to the floor. Blankets had been tossed in earlier over the backboard, and David and Louisa tumbled into their bulk, their arms locked. David laughed and let himself fall back. He pulled Louisa on top.

"He's gone!" she laughed with relief. She set her chin on his chest and smiled down, then laughed again when she felt the push of his stomach beneath hers. The wagon rolled, their bodies rolled with it, and David's cheek, rough with stubble, bit into hers. A fleeting memory flickered, was lost, then came again. It was her Pa, her own Pa, his cheek rough at the end of the day, rubbing hers, as he tucked her into bed.

David reached up and pulled the silver combs from her hair. It fell down around them. "Arthur didn't buy you these," he whispered, touching his lips to hers. "*I* picked them out." He kissed her again and she yielded to his warmth. "I picked them out because I loved you, always have...."

"Shh..." She kissed his cheek, the ridge over his nose, his mouth. His lips opened. Sunlight broke in, shattering the dimness. Louisa looked up with a start. "Ma!"

Sarah sat on the wagon seat peering into the dark interior. "And just how long has this been going on?" she demanded sternly.

★   ★   ★

"Yes, Ma'am," said Louisa. She wasn't really listening to her mother. She was really watching David. It was the morning after Fort Hall, July the sixth, and they were breaking camp, getting ready for yet another day. Nerves were short and the tension was still there. Although the Indian had given up his chase, the scare still hung. Only David seemed to be free of it, and he whistled while he strapped the last of the teams to the wagons. Louisa watched him slap a mare on the rump, then run his hands along her flank to double-check the buckles of the harness.

"You're not listening to me," said Sarah crossly. Her voice was strained, the words harsh.

"What was it you said, Ma?" Louisa asked. She stuffed some of the bedding over a feedbox, then felt it slide and settle into a heap inside the wagon.

"He's five years younger than you."

"Who, Ma?" She glanced again toward David, then walked to the edge of the trail to look at the tumultous falls that cascaded over a brink above them. The American Falls, that was what Pa had called them, and they were beautiful. Louisa breathed in the fresh scent, the moist air.

The falls were formed by the Snake River dropping from a high cliff. Water foamed and bubbled as it hurtled over the edge, showered up, splintering into thousands of droplets, then fell back again to a large pool down below. From there the Snake River continued west, winding its way through the dusty gullies and rocky folds of earth.

Louisa knew that James watched her. After sleeping out the bulk of yesterday he was up and around this morning, although when he walked he still held a hand to his stomach and took small, careful steps. She had thanked him for his protection and he had nodded painfully. Now they had little else to say and judiciously avoided each other, although he watched her carefully, always following her about with his eyes. Even when she would excuse herself to attend to private matters, he would watch her go. She glanced now to the brooding eyes, but Ma stepped close and she looked away. She still hadn't decided what to do about the dress James had torn.

"David is five years younger than you, Louisa," Ma said again. Louisa sighed wearily. The discussion was getting nowhere, and she was tired of it. It didn't even matter what Ma thought.

"Five years is a lot of difference. David is just a boy."

"Mother!" Louisa put her hands on her hips and turned to look into her Ma's face. Sarah Latimer Boren Denny had a stern face, thin at the chin, broad at the brow, and she wore her hair, graying down the center, in a severe knot in the back, tied low on her neck. Age had taken the softness from her hair and it lay flat to her head. Small growths popped up on her face, one just inside her right eye, another alongside her right ear and a third between the fold line of her cheek and nose. But she had taken care of her skin and few lines marked her face. "David is not a boy," said Louisa irritably to her mother. "And if you'd look you would see that I'm right. He rides scout all day every day for Pa. He takes his turn with guard duty, sometimes double duty. Ma! That's half a night every night! And he and Dobbins keep us alive with the fresh meat they bring in. He is the best man with the horses! Do I need to go on? And do you ever see David getting upset? Angry? Impatient? Do you, Ma? Or does he conduct himself like Pa? Like a grown man?"

She stopped to take a breath. "I am right, Ma. And I *am* right about some other things, aren't I, Ma?" She looked at Ma directly, questioning her with her eyes, and then deliberately turning her gaze to the wagons, to where her trunk was.

"Not always, Liza. We have yet to see about your mirror. The trip isn't over yet. I worry that you forget your place."

"And what is my place?"

"A daughter should always obey her Ma." Louisa said nothing and Sarah continued. "And a grown woman of your age does not go about kissing a boy of only 19 in the back of a wagon!" She paused. "It's downright shameful and immoral."

"Oh, for heaven's sake, Ma! Since when is love shameful? And we've done nothing immoral." Louisa looked out to the roar of the falls. They stood on a ridge about halfway down the falls. "Look," she said more calmly. "It's the Sabbath today, Ma. Let's not spoil it. See?" She waved her hand over the scenery, the usual sandy terrain, the scrubby sagebrush, the occasional wildflowers that brought specks of color to the landscape. "Isn't it all so wonderful, Ma?"

Sarah's face lost its sternness, and the lines that framed her mouth melted as she smiled. She patted Louisa's arm, then shaded her eyes to peer over the edge. "He makes you happy?" she asked.

"Yes, Ma. Very."

"How long, Liza. How long have you loved him?"

"I don't know. Maybe always. Does that sound strange?"

"Yes."

They were silent awhile, letting the others finish with the chores that needed to be done. The din of the falls—music, really, after the monotony of endless grasshoppers and crickets—reminded Louisa of Pamelia on Sunday mornings at the Methodist church in Cherry Grove. She played the small pump organ for morning services. Did Pamelia pray, even now, for her as she did for Pamelia?

"Promise me something," said Ma.

"Depends on what it is."

"Promise."

"How can I if I don't even know what it is?"

"Just promise me because I'm your Ma and I love you."

"You know I can't do that, Ma. You'll have to tell me first."

"I want you to marry James."

"James!" She squealed his name too loud and slapped a hand over her lips. "James?" she asked again. "You want me to marry James?"

"He's closer to your age. A good man. And he loves you a great deal."

"I can't."

"Why not?"

"I love David."

"But you love James, too. I know you do."

"I love James, Ma, because he is good to me." She swallowed quickly and darted her eyes to the side, where she could see him sitting, still watching her. "But I love David more, Ma. And it's the marrying kind of love, Ma. I shouldn't have to explain that to you. It's not like you're too old to remember. You got Pa."

"Louisa!"

"I'm going to marry David, Ma. Nothing you can say will change that. I love him."

"David is only a boy."

"He is not!"

"You're getting impertinent, Louisa Boren."

Louisa clenched her fists beneath the covering of her skirt, where Ma couldn't see. "Well, you needn't worry about us getting married today. He hasn't asked me."

"Impertinent," Sarah muttered.

Louisa's fingers unfolded; the fight went out of her. "I'm sorry, Ma. I really am. I won't marry him until you see that we really do love each other." She clutched her skirt again. "But be warned, Ma, I won't put it off forever. Only for a time."

Sarah frowned and Louisa leaned over the ridge to peer below, as her mother was doing. "What is it, Ma?" she asked.

"Look, Liza...something's odd about those ducks in the pool way below. Have you seen so many in single file before?"

"They're headed for the ravine." She looked down the rutted trail to the ravine below. The road widened considerably as it descended to the wide gully. From there it came together again, up and away from the river. "Ma..." Louisa whispered, staring down. "You don't suppose they're Indians, do you?" A cold wave of horror passed slowly down her throat, through the trunk of her body and into her legs.

"It is..." whispered Ma hoarsely. Louisa nearly pitched forward from the sudden weakness that zipped through her veins. Ma grabbed her sleeve and they fell backward to the rough road.

"Indians!" they screamed in warning together. Louisa clambered to her feet clumsily, unable to find her footing, dragging Ma along with her. David appeared out of nowhere and pushed them both into the closest wagon. "I got to drive the head wagon!" he hollered. He didn't wave, but turned and ran along the trail, his steps long and hard as he raced forward.

"Hold on there!" Pa shouted. "We can fight them!" But Arthur, Wiley, Samuel, David, James, and Dobbins all leaped for the wagons. "I say! We can hold 'em off!" Pa thundered.

"Forget it! We're running!" For a moment confusion prevailed as they accounted for everyone. Orders were shouted, but no one listened. The cattle were forgotten.

"We can fight them!" Pa bellowed again, waving his gun.

Ma screamed. "Get in here, you fool! Get in!"

Louisa stared.

"You heard me!" Ma shrieked, her fist raised. "Get in!"

"How-de-do! How-de-do!"

An Indian popped out from behind a large boulder, waving a top hat in his hand. Louisa gasped with the suddenness of his appearance, then gasped again at the man's nakedness. He wore only a black swallowtail coat, and it flapped open in front, exposing his body. "Stop!" he shouted again. "Stop!" Pa took one look and leaped up to the wagon seat.

"Yip! Yip!" The whip cracked and the wagon hurtled forward after the other three. "Yip!" he shouted again. "Yip! Yip!" The canvas was rolled up and Louisa looked out as they bumped madly down the trail to the open ravine, gaping in astonishment.

"Stop!" the Indian hollered after them. A pistol gleamed in the sunlight and Louisa ducked. A shot rang out.

"Get along there!" Another crack of the whip, a second. A third. Again and Again.

"Liza, look!" Ma pointed out to the river, her face drained of color. Her chin jammed down into Retta's bonnet as they bumped downhill. The "ducks" rose up out of the water, really black topknots of tens of Indians, all howling, arms whipping overhead.

"They're going to cut us off at the ravine!" Louisa screamed.

"Get me my rifle!" Pa shouted. "Take the reins, Sarah! I got to get a shot in at these varmints!"

"Pardon?"

"Take the reins!" Pa bounced on the seat, sliding back and forth. His cap blew off. Ma inched forward.

An arrow pierced the dome of the wagon and sailed straight through, leaving a jagged tear. Louisa threw herself to the floor on top of Kate. She felt the girl cry beneath her. Ma crouched, then half-knelt, half-crawled her way to the front, slamming back and forth into the crates and sacks. From inside the wagon she reached for the reins and held on, kneeling, her head bent low.

Kate pulled free and peered over the backboard. Louisa hauled her back down just as another arrow whizzed by. It stuck into a sack, the end quivering, the head held fast. She watched it in terror as they careened on. She could only thank God she'd pulled the child down in time.

But what if a linchpin were to break? An axle? Rifle shots echoed overhead as more arrows penetrated, zinging and quivering. Pictures of the horses slumped over, arrows tunneled through their bellies, flashed through her head. She envisioned wagons overturned, dishes scattered, bedding strewn, and babies with their skulls draining. Louisa moaned, sickened by the terror. She grabbed for Kate and held on.

"Dear sweet Jesus, don't let this happen to us! Give us the strength to keep going!"

The wagon strained and the horses panted. They were climbing now. "Why don't we hurry?" she wondered. "Why doesn't Pa lay on the lash?" They were high up, the ravine below. The Indians were behind, running up, arrows drawn. She ducked. One flew and she felt the warmth of the air as it whizzed close. The horses snorted and she rose up again, just sure that one had been hit.

"Stay down!" Ma screamed. Pa was gone, and the wagon had stopped. "Stay down! Stay down!" Ma cried. Then, "Loretta! Where's my Retta?"

Louisa reached along the rough floorboards to the baby and pulled her close. "I got her, Ma! She's all right!" The rise and fall of her small abdomen told Louisa the child was wailing. But she couldn't hear it—only the gunfire, the shouts, and more gunfire. Kate clutched her neck and Louisa fought the spasm of her own lungs, commanding them to be still, to be calm.

★ ★ ★

The horses were tired, weary from the fast pace they had been forced to go all day, fleeing the Indians. But still the whips cracked, urging them on. On and on.

Louisa sat next to David, feeling his strength and the peace he brought her. He held the reins, his right arm free to snap the quirt, and she could feel the tautness of his body. They had to press on; the Indians could still be trailing. They hadn't been killed, but had only been scared off. The sun hung heavy as the evening chill crept in. Louisa shivered and moved closer to David.

"Don't know as I want to experience such a shave again. Ever." David turned to look at her. She nodded, not wanting to think about it.

"You don't suppose it was on account of me?" she whispered finally.

"You?"

"I mean on account of that business with the Indian outside of Fort Hall. You don't suppose he was angry enough to come after us, do you?"

"Of course not!" David said it too quickly, and she knew that he wondered about it the same as she did. They lapsed into silence again, listening to the creak of the wheels, the sounds of the trailing wagons, all of them hurrying forward away from the horror.

Louisa thought of the buffalo stampede, the brave at Fort Hall, the children's whooping cough, Arthur's ague. She thought of the river crossings, the narrow escapes, the horrible screams of the Indians coming up out of the water. "Do you think we'll ever get to the Willamette Valley?" she asked quietly. She set her hand on David's leg; the pants were rough, stiff, and crusted with dirt. He took her fingers and set her hand into his pocket.

"Don't let it frighten you." He paused. "God will take care of us. I really believe that. I don't mean to sound just like a pulpit preacher." She smiled and he set the whip between his legs, took the reins in his other hand, and put his arm around her waist. His kiss was tender and assuring, and when she let her head fall to his shoulder he gave her a squeeze. Spring always came. Hadn't Pamelia said that? Her eyes closed and she saw a small, flickering fire in the dark. So warm.

"Louisa?" David jostled her. "Wake up. We've run into company."

She bolted up, stiffening instantly. But David laughed softly, kissing her again. "Good company, Liza. Sunday company." He pointed ahead. A distant fire crackled, shedding a cozy light. Someone sat by the flames, and happy laughter sifted out on the night air.

10

"The two parties joined forces at this time...."
—Roberta Frye Watt in *Four Wagons West*

"A sight for sore eyes, that's sure," said Pa, shaking the extended hand.

"John Low." The man that spoke was of medium build, with a strong face and a long, thin beard that grew from just his chin; his cheeks were shaved clean. He seemed to smile easily, and casually waved to the other man by the fire—a shorter man, full-bearded, with eyes set so deep that they were lost in the dark. "William Bell, my partner," John Low said.

"Pleased to meet you. Both of you!" Pa pumped the hands again and grinned. "Name's John Denny," he said, then beckoned to the rest of them to come forward. "My family's tired. Had a close call with a renegade band of Indians early this morning and we haven't stopped since."

"Oh?" John Low frowned and tugged on his beard. "You kill any of them?" Pa shook his head and John sighed. "We'll put a double watch on anyway. You never know. Lose anyone yourself?"

"Lost our cattle. We'll have to send back to see if we can't locate them. Came all this way and can't be letting them wander now, can we?"

"We got a herd. Beef cattle."

"Ours were milch cows—for the children."

"Well, come, come." Mr. Low lifted an enamel pot from the hot rocks set around the fire, and Louisa wondered how old a man he was. "The wives and children are put to bed," Mr. Low said. "But there's coffee here and I can rustle up some grub as good as Lydia's. That's my wife."

Louisa let David help her from the wagon, welcoming the strength of his hands, warm and firm under her arms. She wasn't too tired to enjoy the closeness, the cover of night that hid them from the others—from James. She ran her hands up his arms

81

and clasped them behind his neck. He kissed her, and she marveled that she was actually with him. Had it been only yesterday morning that he had taken the silver combs from her hair, that he had told her he loved her?

"Come on," he whispered.

The fire was hot and crackling, and Mr. Bell motioned for them to sit. Louisa could see that he wasn't a man to talk much; he merely nodded as they introduced themselves. The children curled into tiny balls and fell asleep at once.

"No kidding!" she heard Mr. Low say. "We crossed the Missouri the third of May! You crossed the fifth?"

"We waited five days in Kanesville for our girls to gain strength." Mary Ann pushed a biscuit in the gravy on her plate. "They had the whooping cough."

"And now?" The man's voice was kindly, and a wounded look came to his eyes.

"Oh, they're fine now." Mary Ann nodded to Kate and Nora and smiled. Mr. Low looked down at them too, his eyes thoughtful, as if remembering something painful. "Two of ours are gone," he said quietly.

"Tell me," said Mary Ann, putting a hand out to him.

"Susan Frances died on her first birthday. She choked. There was nothing we could do."

"I'm sorry."

"That was in '45. Then in '48, our Martha Ann passed on. She was almost eight. A happy child." He stopped.

"You said you had other children?"

Mr. Low nodded. "Four. Two girls and two boys."

"Well, we can thank the Lord for them," said Mary Ann. "Are you a God-fearing man, Mr. Low?"

"Please, Ma'am. It's John. Mr. Low makes me sound old. I'm only 34." He smiled, and Louisa decided that she liked the man, God-fearing or not.

"It's a wonder we didn't run into you along the way," said Pa. "Did you take the north side of the Platte?" He took a swig of the coffee and spun it around in his mouth. Firelight caught the blue of his eyes and he winked at Louisa when he saw that she watched him.

"Nope. South side," said William Bell for the first time.

Louisa listened to the men talk. The deep resonance of their voices was soothing, their sudden bursts of laughter assuring. Once she tilted her head to smile up at David. He returned the smile. The fire made his face gentle, and a feeling of possession quickened within, a feeling of being possessed, and she rested her head into the soft hollow of his shoulder. It was made for her.

The flames danced high in yellows and whites, spitting at times. She felt David relax, was conscious of his arms circling her, caging her in, his hands clasped loosely in front of them. James watched them, but it didn't matter anymore. She slept while David held her. She was his. They all knew that now.

Morning came early and Louisa hurried alone to find Anna and Dobbins' tent. Camp was quiet, the sky still hazy gray, the air clear and chilly. "Anna?" she called softly. "Can you go with me to the river?"

"Mm? Louisa? That you?" Anna rose up on an elbow and pushed her long hair off her face. Dobbins groaned and rolled over.

"Yes! Will you come hold the blanket for me? Please?"

"All right... Just a minute!"

Louisa let the canvas door fall. She shivered and wished that she had gotten dressed first. At least she should have put on her shoes. The earth was cold and already her toes were numb.

When Anna came out she had a heavy shawl over her gown, and she wore shoes. "Got the blanket?" she asked.

Louisa held it up. "Drank too much coffee last night," she whispered. "Couldn't even wait to get dressed. Sorry I had to drag you out of bed."

They slipped past the wagons. Mr. Bell and Wiley, standing guard, politely turned the other way, away from the trail and the small stream it led to.

"Think this'll be all right?" Louisa asked when they came to the bubbling tributary of the Snake.

"I don't care!" Anna chattered through her teeth. "Just hurry up. I'm about to freeze!"

Louisa looked around quickly. The wagons were well-hidden by a knoll, and the country across the river was empty, almost lonely. And the sun, shedding its mantle, brought a bluing to the horizon. Birds chirped. She would have to hurry.

"Say, Anna?" she asked when the blanket was refolded. "Are those tracks across the water?"

"I don't see anything. Come on."

"No, wait! They *are* tracks! I'm sure of it!"

"Then let's get out of here! It's probably the Indians!" Anna drew back in alarm, but Louisa stepped closer to the water's edge. The fear of yesterday was gone in the peaceful setting of the quiet day.

"And go alarming everyone needlessly?" Louisa demanded. "We better make sure, Anna!" She stepped into the icy cold and pulled up on her nightgown, baring her legs.

"Louisa! Come back here!"

"For heaven's sake! We have to check first! What if it turns out to be nothing?"

"I'll scream, Louisa! I swear, I will!" But Louisa kept on, inching her way further into the icy water, wading in deeper until her feet could no longer feel the sharp pebbles, until her gown could be raised no further. In the dusty gray of morning she could clearly see the shoeless tracks. Indian ponies...

"DOBBINS!"

Louisa froze and Anna screamed again. She spun and saw that Anna was alone, that no Indian had scalped her.

"What in the world are you doing?" Louisa shrieked, flying out of the water. Somehow her gown got drenched, and she stood on the shore shivering violently. Her teeth banged together as she struggled to speak. "You nearly scared me to death, Anna Boren! And for no reason! And now everyone will be up and just look at us!"

The men crashed through the brush as she spoke, leaping the sagebrush and small boulders. Wiley and Mr. Bell came first, then James, David, Pa—everyone. Louisa hurried past, leaving them to stare, and nearly collided with Dobbins.

"Anna? Is it Anna?" He grabbed her elbow but she jerked loose. Her nightie stuck fast to her in wet, cold folds and she tried to pull it loose as she stumbled back to camp. Cold tears came.

"What's going on?" David ran up from behind and caught her. She refused to look at him and he pulled up on her chin, forcing her to look. "Was it Anna that screamed? Or you? Answer me!"

"It was Anna!" Louisa wailed. "She just panicked is all!"

"About what!"

"There's tracks on the other side of the stream."

"Tracks?"

"I went over to look, to make sure, but the water..."

"You went over to check? You what?" David stepped back and she cringed under his stare. She shivered and hugged herself, hiding from his eyes. "Of all the stupid things to be doing!" he shouted. "A bunch of Indians gone mad nearly swipe our scalps one day and you think nothing of swimming..." He waved at her wet nightie and continued, "...swimming across an unknown stream the next?"

"I didn't swim! Anna screamed and it scared me! I don't know how I got wet!"

"And suppose one of those Indians was still around, Louisa! Then what? Good-bye, Louisa? Is that it? Or maybe just..."

"That's enough!"

James stepped up suddenly. Louisa ran. "Can't you see that she's wet and cold?" she heard James holler. "Embarrassed, to say the least?"

The humiliation was too much. She stumbled on until she found her bed. Stripping down, she shivered beneath the warm covers. How could she have gone out in only her gown? And David *was* right. She never should have gone into the stream. As soon as she saw the tracks she and Anna should have run right back to camp. She should have...

"Louisa?" Ma poked her head into the tent. "Are you all right?"

"Go away, Ma. Just go away," she sobbed.

★   ★   ★

Both the Low and Bell families had four children. Lydia Low was a large woman with a square chin, and she managed her four children with a strong hand and a gentle voice. Mary, her eldest, was nine, a quiet girl with a somber face. Alonzo, seven, was just the opposite of his older sister—handsome and full of mischief. Little John was four and Minerva was two. She was a tiny child for her age, and she looked out at the world from large gray-green eyes that were out of place in her peaked face. Her hair was straight and thick, and Lydia always brushed it back from her forehead, where it was tied securely behind with a wrinkled ribbon.

The four Bell children were nine, five, four, and just a few months old. All four were girls, and all were delicate in build, with soft, fair skin like their mother. Sarah Bell, or Sally, as they had begun to call her, was fragile and worked slowly, as if strength were something unknown to her. Her husband did the harder work, and his deepset eyes followed her always. Whenever there was something Sally could not do, he was right there to do it for her.

And if William Bell rarely spoke or smiled, his wife did both. She talked often, smiled often. Her laughter was fresh and clear, bubbling up from deep inside, where happiness and contentment are rooted.

Their first day together passed quickly. The horses rested; the women shared stories and laughed and made fresh bread from the dwindling flour supply; the children ran and played; some of the men scouted about for further signs of the Indians (who had obviously come as far as the stream). But the Indians had disappeared and the Denny cattle had been found. Following a rutted trail was all they had known for so long that they did it automatically. The wonder was not that the cows had found their way, but that the Indians hadn't taken them.

★   ★   ★

"Well? That settles it then?" John Denny dumped the old tobacco from his pipe and David watched his father polish the bowl on his pant leg. "We join up?" Supper was finished. Tomorrow they would head out.

"No doubt about it... it was our united forces that kept the riled Injuns 'a yours from doing anything last night," mused John Low. He tugged on his beard. His hand clamped tight at the end of it so that the whiskers were hidden in his fist.

David lost track of the discussion. It was evident enough to him that they would all ride into the Willamette Valley together. The roughest part of the journey was yet to come: the Blue Mountains and numerous rivers, many of them treacherous. The extra help would be beneficial for both parties, especially so since Arthur was always coming down with bouts of the ague.

David watched Louisa. He could see that she was tired by the way she slumped wearily against one of the wagon wheels and watched the activities listlessly. She had been crying—he could see that too—and he shoved his hands into his pockets, feeling the fuzz that had collected along the bottom seam. How could he have hollered like that at her? He felt like crying himself.

"Can we talk?" David lowered himself beside Louisa and ignored the flush that floated to her cheeks. "I'm sorry for earlier," he said quickly. "I was worried out of my head, Liza, that's all. Do you know what I would have done had any of those Indians been out there? If they had hurt you? Or rode off with you? I can't forget that fellow back at the fort—his eyes, the way he stared at you..."

"Shh, don't talk about it."

"James was right, you know," he went on. "You were embarrassed. I should have let you go." He ground his teeth together. "James is always right, isn't he?"

She cut him short. "I think I'm beginning to understand what it is between you two." She looked at him. "You don't love me just because he does, do you?"

He didn't know what to say.

"It's been that way between you two for a long time, hasn't it?"

"What way? What are you talking about?"

"The competition between you two. All your lives. You and James. And now I'm the booty."

David stood abruptly. His pant legs fell smooth and unwrinkled, and he flicked a bit of dirt from one of the knees. "Tell Ma you're riding with me."

They talked a long time. No, David had never really thought much about himself and James. They had always been at each other in small ways. It was something he was used to.

"You see, Liza," he said. "When we were boys our Ma was always ill. Arthur had to drop out of school half-days to care for her, but James always got to go on. He liked school, and had no interest as far as I could see in making Ma happy. At the time I was too small to be of much help, but it bothered me that James didn't seem to care, and made no effort. Guess I've always resented him for it."

"What about your other brothers? Samuel? Wiley?"

"They were around. Wiley was too little to do much of anything, but Samuel, I remember, used to bring Ma flowers after school. James did nothing but cart his books back and forth." He paused, then went on. "It's probably pretty silly, but I think I've been trying to make up for James all my life.

I loved Ma. Arthur did, too. Maybe that's why I respect Arthur.''

He was silent after that, and Louisa tried to think of what it would be like with no Ma. David had been nine when his Ma had finally died, and she had been ill for years before that, an invalid. He and Wiley had pretty much been on their own from the time they could walk.

"James isn't such a bad sort," she said after awhile. "I think he's quite sensitive, a little too happy-go-lucky perhaps. But that's part of his charm. I like James."

"So you've told me."

"We're not going to start that again, are we?"

He tucked her hand into his jacket pocket and smiled. "No, Liza Boren. Of course not."

But it was time to stop. Another river, swift and white, blocked the trail. David jumped down to get the tar and tallow, but Louisa sat on the seat a long time while the men plugged the holes. There was a lot to think about.

11

"The Blue Mountains were decidedly more difficult to cross than the Rockies. Beautiful in distance, they soon became stern realities. Soft contours vanished; huge crags and steep walls—rough, rugged, and cruel—exacted every ounce of the travelers' strength and endurance. Even today the trees along the old trail bear mute scars made by the chains that were passed around the trunks to act as brakes for the heavy wagons of the pioneers."

—Roberta Frye Watt in *Four Wagons West*

The Dalles was a collection of traders' tents, a small cluster of civilization along the Columbia River. It was the last outpost before the Willamette Valley, Fort Vancouver, and Portland. Because of its relatively close proximity to the Willamette, there was an optimistic air, a kind of oasis to the desperate struggles of the trail. The end was in sight, the destination could be tasted. The Dalles was a reminder that there *was* an end, that trial would soon be rewarded.

For the Dennys, and the Bells and Lows, when they arrived on August 11, they were in need of that assurance. The Blue Mountains had demanded every ounce of their strength. Stunning from a distance, the trail had been harsh and demanding. One miscalculated step could easily have sent any one of them to his death, his body lost forever (as some previous travelers had been) to the bottomless ravines.

At times they had had to use chains for brakes, strapping them around the stoutest of the trees and letting them out a bit at a time so that the wagons could be inched slowly forward down the incline. The embankments had been too steep, the inclines too sharp, for them to have descended on their own safely. The sheer weight of the wagons would have pushed the horses to their extinction.

And then the dread mountain fever had taken them, a high burning fever peculiar to the area. Mary Ann, almost to the end of her pregnancy, came down with it the worst. No one complained of his discomfort, for it was nothing compared to what Mary endured.

The morning after they arrived, John Denny and John Low talked with the traders and the women rested. Mary Ann slept on a mat in one of the tents. Whenever she awoke it was for short periods of time, and Louisa was always there.

About noon, when the day was at its hottest, Mary Ann awoke enough to talk. "Liza?" she whispered. Her eyes focused on Louisa's face above her. "He's talking about going up to the Puget Sound." She reached out for Louisa but her hand fell short and dropped weakly to the sweaty mat.

"Shh," Louisa whispered. "Arthur's just talking, that's all." She wiped her sister's cheek with a cold cloth and Mary sighed.

"No, Liza, he's not. And you know Arthur—once he gets an idea, there's no shaking it out of him."

Arthur *had* been talking of the Puget Sound. In fact, it was all he talked about lately, and it bothered Louisa as much as it was now bothering Mary Ann. "Now why would anyone want to go up there?" Louisa asked. "It's not even officially part of the States yet. There's no one up there but the Hudson Bay and Indians."

"Some fellow we met on the Burnt River... Remember, Liza?"

"Brock?"

Mary nodded and licked at her lips. Louisa slid an arm under her head and raised it so that she could take a small sip of water. "He says the Willamette is all filled up, that all the good land's been taken, Liza."

"Well, we haven't seen that for ourselves, have we? Oregon's a mighty big place. I'm sure there's plenty of land."

Mary groaned and curled into a ball. Her arms reached around her unborn child, her fingers dug into the pain. A sharp cry escaped her throat, and she rocked back and forth until the spasm passed. Exhausted, she fell back to the mat while perspiration poured from her temples. Louisa said nothing but wiped the wet skin with a clean towel.

"Think I'll lose the baby, Liza?" The question came quietly, more air than sound.

"Of course not!" Louisa spoke sharply. "You are a strong

woman, Mary Denny! I won't have you talking like that, you hear?'' Mary Ann didn't answer, and Louisa took her shoulders roughly. ''You got only three more weeks to go!'' she cried. ''And you're not going to give up now! We're nearly there! Only a little way more!'' Suddenly she felt her sister's frailty and let go. She stared into the deep color of Mary's eyes, as brown as the bottom of the well back home on a hot summer day. ''No, Mary, '' she said. ''You're not going to lose the baby.''

''Where are we?''

''I've told you a dozen times—''

''I'm sorry, Liza! I'm sorry! I can't remember!''

Louisa sniffed back the tears. ''No, Mary, I'm sorry...''

''Where are we?''

''The Dalles. The Columbia River.''

''We're finished with the Blue Mountains?''

''They're behind us. Yes.''

Mary Ann again tried to reach out to Louisa. Seeing the effort, Louisa caught up the warm hand between her palms and blinked rapidly to dam the hot tears. ''We're at the Dalles, Mary,'' she said again. ''The Columbia River. At the bottom is Portland. The Willamette. There's only the Cascades to get through.''

''How far until the Puget Sound? How far north is it?''

Louisa sighed. ''You just forget the Puget Sound. Arthur's just talking. I told you that. Here, let me read to you. Where's your Bible?''

Mary turned her eyes to the far corner of the tent, and Louisa saw the black, leatherbound book. She settled comfortably and began to flip through the worn pages for something appropriate. A new sound came to her ears. Startled, she looked up sharply. Mary was laughing gently, and she turned her head to smile at Louisa. ''Now don't you be reading Psalm 23 to me,'' she whispered.

Louisa chuckled. ''I wouldn't think of it. You are going to get Revelation and the dragons that come up out of the sea!''

''Is it what I deserve?''

''It's what you deserve, Mary Denny.'' And so Louisa read until Mary slept, and there was a new heaven and a new earth, and the sea was no more.

★   ★   ★

When Louisa left the tent she almost collided with David. "Just coming to find you," he said. "I've got something to tell you."

"Something wrong?"

"Pa's splitting up the group." He took her by the elbow and led her out past the tents, on out past the wagons. "Mary's too ill to get over another mountain pass. The Cascades are about as bad as the Blue Mountains—maybe worse, according to some of the men around here."

The full afternoon sun brought out the gold in David's eyes, small flecks of light in the soft brown. "I'm not going to be forced to stay behind while you go on, am I?" she asked.

"It's not that bad, Liza. We'll all get to Portland about the same time. Pa's found a man, a Mr. Tudor, who rents boats down the Columbia as far as the great Cascade Falls. He supplies the oarsmen and they bring the boats back up here."

"And what about us?"

David grinned. "This is your chance to make history, Louisa Boren. There's a man by the name of Chenowith who's starting a tram road down and around the falls. He's got about three miles cleared, with a track laid, and once you get to the bottom he's got an old brig—uses it to haul salmon in—that gets you and the salmon down to Portland."

"How many people have used this tram road?"

David grinned again. "You'd be the first, Liza. Up until now the only way was Barlow's Pass and the overland trail. But this Chenowith fellow and this Mr. Tudor, they've been putting their heads together 'cause this other way looks a whole lot easier. And quicker. You can be into Portland in a week."

She looked out to the wide river. Placid, tranquil, soft waves lapping the shore. "In a week, David?"

He nodded. "Pa's idea is to ship all of you down the river along with Dobbins and Arthur, John Low maybe. And the rest of us will go over Barlow's Pass as planned."

"But David! That means we'll be—"

He tried to smile, but seeing her stricken face, he reached for her in a gulp of a choked-backed cry and buried her head into his shoulder. She pushed her nose into the warm curve.

"You're concerned that I don't really love you," he whispered in her hair. It was clean and smelled of sweet things. "That I'm just in the game because of James. Be honest."

She didn't answer. She couldn't. But it didn't matter anymore! Not really! It was enough that he held her, kissed her, told her he loved her!

"It's for the best. Really," he said. "You'll see that I love you after this separation. That I will always love you. Maybe Ma and Pa will see it too," he added slowly.

"Who'll cook for you?"

He laughed softly and took her face in his hands. "I will." He kissed her. "And William Bell…" he kissed her again, "…says he's not too bad. We'll get along, don't worry."

"Just keep holding me? Please?"

He set his chin over her head and stared out at the water. At the Dalles the Columbia River was wide, with gravel shores. But further on, he knew, the river changed. Running west, it had to cut through mountain gorges; the trip would not be without its dangers. But it had to be done. Mary Ann simply could not go any other way. And the separation *was* needed, not so much for them but for Ma and Pa.

He felt her arms tighten, her fists grab his shirt. He remembered Fort Hall and the lone Indian. Louisa had been in James's arms then. But now she was in *his* arms and she didn't cry.

★　　★　　★

A full moon reflected off the peaceful water of the Columbia when they started from the Dalles that night. The two boats were large, one six feet wide at its broadest and ten feet from bow to stern, the other eight feet wide and fifteen feet in length. Both had planks stretched across their widths to serve as rough seats, and both were white wherever the paint still clung. Their sacks of provisions for the few days' journey sat in cluttered heaps at the bottom of the splintered floorings. In the larger boat the women and children and a Mrs. MacCarthy, who had joined their party for the duration of the boat trip, settled in the best they could. Arthur, Dobbins, and John Low rode in the smaller boat.

The oarsmen, ten in all (six with the women and four with the men), set their paddles neatly into the water with a soft wisp and pushed the two open boats forward in quiet jerks. Anna listened to the dip, push, lift of the paddles.

The sound bothered her; it reminded her of the sound the wagon wheels had made turning over the sand away from Fort Laramie—the soft continuance, the empty noise. She put her hands to her ears. Gertrude slept across her lap.

"Mel! Pass the jug!"

Anna sat straight, startled. One of the oarsmen caught a blue jug with both hands; it had been tossed to him from a man in the bow, and he popped the cork out of the neck with his teeth and spit it to his lap. Sharp stubbles bristled around his mouth as he guzzled the brew. He gulped loudly, then belched and sighed. The moon caught the glint in his eyes and he winked when he saw that Anna watched him.

"Keep 'er goin'!"

The jug was pitched carelessly to the oarsman closest to Anna, and she pulled back as the bottle knocked into a sack at her knee.

All the boatmen were coarse; they had scraggly hair and were dirty and unkempt. Knit toques matted with dust were jammed down and around their ears. Anna cowered low in the boat, as if she could escape their crudeness by her position. And Dobbins? What did he care? He didn't. It was all adventure to him.

Dip, push, lift. Dip, push, lift. The sound took over again, getting sloppier as the night wore on. The small jug went from whiskered mouth to whiskered mouth, was replaced by another, and the oars started to slap the water instead of slice it.

And the river lost its placid nature. It began to foam up in sections, spitting white to the moonlight. Anna could see the dim outline of the men in the smaller boat ahead and wondered which was Dobbins. And she wondered why she bothered.

"Anna?"

Mary Ann, resting against Louisa's lap, looked up at Anna. Kate and Nora slept at her feet, sprawled uncomfortably between the piles of bags and sacks. In the shadows her face looked oddly pale, her eyes oddly dark.

"Will you sing for us, Anna?" Mary Ann asked. She didn't lift her head, and Louisa adjusted the quilts to cover her better.

"You want me to sing now?"

"Yes, a Christmas song. Doesn't it seem like Christmas to you?" Her voice was weak, almost ghostly, and it scared Anna. She thought of the Virgin Mary, traveling a road, her stomach swollen with the Christ child.

"Anna?"

"Yes, Mary."

"Are you all right?"

"I'm fine," Anna lied.

"Will you sing then?"

"BART!"

They all jumped. The oarsman closest to Anna shoved a hand to his ear, and the loud voice from the boat ahead came again. "Bart! We got a leak!"

Bart grabbed his oar and pushed it to the water. The jug he had held rolled to the floorboards and settled against a sack and two other blue jugs. Anna watched the man's face as he hollered out the instructions—the way the left corner of his mouth dropped as he shouted, the way the moonlight washed over his cheeks, showing the thick stubble and the dark recesses of his eyes. She didn't like the eyes, and a shudder shot down her back. Her shoulders went back in reaction to the jolt.

The boat veered to the left, closer to the sharp rocks that pushed up along the river's edge.

"This ain't no place to push ashore!" shouted a man from the boat that pulled in beside them. Anna saw Dobbins.

"Well, there's a place not too far back!"

"We're leakin' fast, Bart! I told you that!"

"Then you'd best follow fast and shut your ugly face!" roared Bart as he paddled into the small inlet. A steep bank rose up sharply from behind a narrow beach. Water bounced against large boulders, then washed over and onto smaller rocks beyond. Spray splashed.

"This place ain't fit for a grandmother!"

"Thought you said you was drownin'!"

"So I did!"

"Then stop your yellin'!"

"We can't pull these boats up onto two feet of beach!"

"You keep on blabberin' and you'll choke on yer tongue 'fore the river gets to ya!"

Gertrude wailed and Anna bent over the baby. Bart swung around and shoved a finger into her face. "And you!" he thundered. "You shut that brat up, you hear?"

Arthur's fist caught Bart under the chin, and he spun sideways and out. When he came up out of the water, sputtering, Arthur lunged for the back of his neck and hauled him out. "I've had just about all I'm going to take!" he growled, then shoved the surprised man's face back into the foam.

"Stop it!" Mary Ann tried to stand in the boat, to reach out to the struggle, but Louisa pulled her back. "You're going to kill him!" Mary screamed. "Stop! Arthur! Stop it!" Again she reached. The boat tipped and Anna screamed.

Arthur's arm shot out to steady the craft, and Bart stumbled to his feet. Water dripped from his ears and the end of his dark chin. The pale blue of his eyes penetrated the gray of the night and he stood shivering from the cold. His toque floated on the water by his knee. He mumbled an obscenity, then wiped the back of his hand over his mouth.

Arthur reached for the man's throat again and lifted him against one of the boulders. The other oarsmen protested but did nothing. "Now look here," Arthur spit out. "I paid a fair price for a safe passage to the Cascade Falls, and by gum that's what you're going to deliver. And you'll do it with some degree of civility! Seventeen dollars a person entitles the women and children to some degree of decency! Do I make myself clear?" Bart nodded and Arthur set him down. "Now," Arthur went on. "I'm taking my family up to the top of this bank where we'll try to get some sleep before sunup. You and your boys will make sure our provisions are taken out of the leaking boat and secured someplace dry. Then you're going to climb that bank and get some sleep, and you're going to say good-bye to your jug! Do you understand that?"

Bart swung away, saying nothing. Arthur grabbed an elbow and pulled him around. "I asked you a question!"

"Just going to do it is all." Arthur let him go, and Bart walked over to the leaking boat and began to pull wet sacks out and toss them up to the beach. The other men joined in, pushing the bags to the back, as far from the water as possible. Not that it mattered. It was all wet anyway.

At the top of the bank was a small clearing. Woods edged close, and the travelers did their best to make up beds in the cramped quarters with what they had. Ma, Louisa, Lydia Low and Sally Bell spread out quilts, some of them wet, and tucked the children and Mary Ann under the driest of them. John Low got a fire going. The first of the flames licked the night tentatively, then caught and pushed to the sky, darker now without the river's full reflection. Strange shadows, long and dancing, played the earth, and Anna listened to the whispered prayers of the children, the hushed good nights, the grumblings and cursings of the boatmen below the bank. She kissed her own child, and, after tucking Gertrude into a dry flannel blanket, she left the sleeping infant alone so that she could sit awhile by the fire. She was cold and needed the warmth.

Dobbins sat on the other side of Anna and didn't notice that she had come or that she shivered. He sat with his hands held out to the fire.

Arthur sat across from them, and Anna could see the worry etched in his lean face. He was a handsome man. Mary Ann slept at his feet, and the light from the fire showed that her face was flushed again. Arthur put a hand to her cheek.

"John? Will you get me my Bible?" he asked suddenly.

Anna watched while he leaned into the fire, getting the light to go over the pages. He squinted at the small print.

"What 'ave we 'ere?" The oarsmen, laughing raucously and singing their own song, clambered up the bank. "Why! A bunch of Bible people! Might have known!" One of them laughed.

The Bible dropped. Louisa retrieved the book and straightened the pages while Arthur sprang to his feet. The man chortled. "We're goin' to 'ave our own part-y!" He held up the forbidden jug and grinned, touching the side of it to his rough cheek. "Any joiners? A swig of the Blue Ruin beats all!" He and the others laughed again. Bart pushed forward and took a well-aimed spit.

Arthur wiped his face clean and slowly rubbed the spittle over his thigh. Slowly he turned his back.

When he hit Bart it was sudden and forceful. Bart buckled and folded at the waist, dropping over as he clutched his belly. He moaned and staggered painfully sideways. Suddenly his foot came up and he swung out.

"GERTRUDE!"

Only Anna saw Bart's boot catch her baby's blanket. "GERTRUDE!" she screamed again. Her feet slipped as she pushed sideways to catch the rolling bundle. Her fingers caught an edge of the flannel but the baby hurtled past. She lunged again and threw herself over the bank, and the sound of the rushing river below couldn't drown out her scream.

12

"The solitary watcher stirred uneasily, looked at the long lines of foam out in midstream and saw how fiercely the white waves contended, and far swifter flew the waters than at any hour before."
—Emily Inez Denny in *Blazing the Way*

They found Anna crying over her baby. She stood in the river, moaning and rocking the limp body to her breast. Arthur reached for the infant, but Anna screamed and pulled away. But Dobbins wrenched the child from her arms and scrambled back up the bank with Gertrude under one arm. Pebbles and clumps of dirt slithered back down to the beach.

"Ma!" Dobbins yelled. "Get me something warm! Quick!" He tore at the baby's wet nightgown and diaper, then pushed gently on the small stomach with his open palm. He rolled Gertrude facedown on his lap and water spilled onto his pant leg. He did it again, and again, until no more came, then blew gently into his baby's lips with his own. Ma wrapped the baby while he worked. John Low stoked up the fire.

"Plug her nose, Ma!" Dobbins commanded, then went back to work, breathing in tiny, quick, soft breaths of air. Anna crawled up beside him and watched without emotion. One braid had come loose and hung dripping over her shoulder. She shivered.

Suddenly Gertrude sputtered, then coughed and wailed. Her feet thrashed and kicked the blanket off. Dobbins snatched it back on. Anna lunged for the baby but Arthur pulled her away.

"You got to get something dry on," Dobbins told her. "We got to get Gerty warm." Anna nodded numbly and went to change. She said nothing as Louisa worked the buttons from their wet confines and dropped a dry gown over her shoulders. She said nothing as Ma and Dobbins and Sally Bell worked the baby over, rubbing the tiny arms and legs briskly. She said nothing as slowly the blueness faded and the pallor gave way to pink. But when they put the baby to her breast, and when Gertrude began to suck noisily, Anna looked up at Bart with her piercing eyes.

★   ★   ★

The next morning nothing was said. There was nothing that could be said. Coffee was boiled strong and black. The oarsmen were given all they needed in silence. Hostile glances were exchanged.

Five more days passed. They went slowly, and tension mounted. Wind and more leaks caused delay after delay. Frequent stops, often whole days, would pass without going further than a few miles. Food ran out and clothes were never dry. Salmon snatched from the river kept off hunger pains, and it was eaten morning, noon, and evening. The night of the 15th Dobbins went out and hunted down a quail, but it had been feasting on salmon too, so it tasted more fish than foul. Arthur flung it out to the river. "Plague take it," he said.

The evening of the 16th the wind was at a low, and Bart decided to push on. "If the weather holds," he said, "we might make it to the Cascades before morning. Them falls ought to be near here, near as I can figure."

"You mean you *don't know*?" Arthur demanded. "You *don't know* where you're at? You *don't know* where Mr. Chenowith's landing is?" He whipped off his cap and wiped his brow impatiently. "You!" he shouted, sticking a finger into Bart's broad chest. "You *don't know what* you're doing!"

"I know what I'm doing, *Mr.* Denny," said Bart through clenched teeth.

"You know to stop before you get to the falls, Bart?" Arthur cut in.

"Get off my back, man!"

The moon was no longer full, as it had been when they had first started off. Now it was just a sliver of gold on the low sky. Only starlight illuminated the dark river, catching the white foam that sudsed. The two boats bobbed and bounced on the growing rapids, but in time the smaller one and the men dropped behind. Soon it was out of sight, but Bart pushed on. The Blue Ruin came out again and was passed from mouth to mouth. "Keep 'er goin'!" was sung to no particular tune.

Anna watched fearfully. Only she and Louisa were awake; the others had fallen asleep and were curled over and around the various bags of plunder. She stirred and stifled a moan as she sniffed in the wet, moldy smell of dampness. "Louisa!" Anna hissed. "The men! They're drinking!"

"I know! And Arthur... I haven't seen them for a long time!"

"The rapids, Liza! They're getting worse all the time!"

"I don't know what we can do, Anna."

"But the men! They're drunk!"

Louisa patted her knee. "Don't worry so... We've come through hard times before. Ma says the Lord is faithful. And I think He is."

"You *think*, Louisa?"

"See if you can't get some sleep. I'll watch."

"Keep 'er goin'!" the boatmen sang. Anna flattened a palm to her ears to shut away the sound. She leaned into a wet sack and watched Louisa until she could watch no more.

★　　★　　★

"ANNA! MARY!"

Anna jerked up. A loud hum buzzed and she saw that Louisa shook Mary Ann harshly. "*Wake up!*" Louisa screamed. "*Wake up! We are nearing the falls and the men are too drunk to know it!*"

A cold wave of horror swept through, making Anna reel. The hum was really a roar, and it trumpeted in her ears.

"Our Father, which art in heaven..." Ma rocked baby Loretta, her head bowed over the small bonnet.

"*The falls, Ma!*" Louisa screamed. "*Ma! Do something!*"

"Hallowed be Thy name..."

"MA!"

"There's nothing to be done but pray," whispered Mary Ann.

Anna didn't know that she screamed until Louisa slapped her. "*Shut up, Anna!*" Louisa hollered at her. "*For God's sake! Shut up!*" Louisa tumbled over the board seats and piles of sacks, catching herself as the boat lurched and flung her from side to side. "*You idiots!*" she screamed into Bart's ear at the bow of the boat. "*The falls! The falls! You're headed straight for the falls!*"

Bart shrugged and pushed his face into Louisa's. "Ain't no danger! Keep 'er going!" he yelled to his friends. Their paddles flashed.

"*You fool! You drunken fool! Turn this boat to shore!*"

"Yer a purdy lady when yer riled, Miss," Bart leered. He caught her about the arm and brought her face up to his. Bart's bloated face edged closer to Louisa's and she shrank back. He snapped her in, then dropped his oar to grab her face with both hands.

Bart kissed Louisa hard. "*You filthy fool!*" she screamed. "*Put this boat to shore or we shall all die!*" Bart pinned her tight, and Louisa twisted and kicked out.

The river boiled and churned on either side of the pitching boat; the roar of the falls was awesome. Suddenly Louisa broke loose, and with her hair tangled and undone she lunged at another of the men. "*LOOK!*" she screamed. "*The rapids! They are just beyond us! Please! Please turn this boat to shore!*" She shook him by the collar, then struck him across the face. "*The falls!*" she screamed. "*Can't you hear them?*" The man mockingly put a hand to his ear.

"Thar ain't no danger, Miss. Leastways not yet; wot's all this fuss about anyway? Jist ain't no danger..."

"*Oh, man! It will soon be too late! Think of your own life—*" But the man suddenly half-rose out of his slouch and knocked Louisa sideways with the abruptness of it. For an instant he froze, his eyes fixed ahead. "BART! THE LADY'S RIGHT!" he roared. His paddle struck the water.

The other paddles hit too. Bart leaned out of the bow of the boat and churned the water with long, quick strokes that went deep. The men swore in panic and confusion as they fought the swift current. Anna watched in mute horror. Ma prayed, Louisa buried her face in her lap and cupped her hands over her head. She had done all she could. Now it was in God's hands. The trees on shore swept past as the river hurtled them onward. A large rock loomed up out of nowhere and the bow of the boat slammed it hard. Bart pitched forward. Anna saw his paddle snap, his outstretched hand disappear in the boiling suds. The boat spun and tipped, the children screamed. Water gushed over the gunwhales, and for a moment the boat hung sideways, then righted itself.

Again it bounced into the rock. "ONE, TWO, THREE, FOUR!" screamed the boatmen, paddling in synchronization. "ONE, TWO, THREE, FOUR!" They paddled with desperation. Sweat and water spray mixed and ran from their faces. And then suddenly the boat broke free of the current. The men paddled into the shore, jumped from the boat, and pulled it up onto the rocky shore.

For a long time no one moved. No one said anything. Then slowly, almost carefully, they stirred, got a fire going, began again to spread out the wet things.

In the morning, when they were found, still nothing was said. Arthur, Dobbins, and John silently paddled the women and children back up the river to Mr. Chenowith's missed landing and tram road, being careful to stay along the peaceful river edge. The oarsmen returned to Mr. Tudor at The Dalles, without Bart.

Anna sat next to Louisa. Her hair still hung in tangles about her face. Dirt caked her exposed throat, and Anna reached out to touch her sister-in-law's hand. Louisa clutched Anna's fingers in her own. " 'Though the waters roar and be troubled we will not fear,' " Louisa whispered softly. Anna looked out to the river, to the foam that bubbled and spit along midstream. Sunlight made the water droplets sparkle. Somehow she had expected Louisa to say something like that.

The last few days of the journey were survived with only one thought in mind—*they were nearly there*. Pushed to the limit emotionally and physically, they took one day at a time, saying little to each other, reserving what little strength remained to do what had to be done.

Mr. Chenowith's tram road was just a simple cart and horse on a railing. The cart was for the provisions—the people walked behind, stepping over the piles of manure. Arthur carried Mary Ann in his arms the whole way down and around the falls, four miles of switchbacks and steep grades.

At the bottom of the falls, on the lower Columbia River, was Mr. Chenowith's brig, the *Henry*. It was dilapidated and no longer seaworthy, and was used solely for transporting salted salmon up and down the river—and for hauling passengers into the Willamette, now that the tram road was in operation.

The *Henry's* bulwarks had long since rotted away, so during the day the children were tied to the mast to keep them from slipping overboard. Nights were spent sleeping atop rows of fish barrels in the hold below and swatting at the swarms of mosquitoes. They buzzed and bit without mercy, and Mary Ann deteriorated rapidly.

Lack of wind and outgoing tides stranded them often on sandbars along the way. Arthur's ague started to bother him again,
and the others started to sweat and chill along with him. August
the 22nd they were moored once again on a sandbar, this time
outside Fort Vancouver in the mouth of the Willamette River,
where the Columbia and Willamette merged. Feeling somewhat
stronger, and greatly frustrated, Arthur picked up Mary Ann
and started to walk into Portland, three miles south along the
Willamette River

They found Pa, William Bell, Wiley, Samuel, James, and
David on the outskirts of town, with camp set up and supper
cooking. Too exhausted even to eat, Arthur sank to a bed and
scribbled the another entry in his diary: *"August 22nd. Footed it
up to Portland."*

"Welcome home, Son," said Pa.

"No, Pa. We're going on... Just as soon as the baby's born...
Just as soon as I can walk... soon as we can we're going to Puget
Sound."

Arthur slept, and John Denny covered his eldest son with a
worn comforter, then backed out of the tent. For a long time
he stood alone, watching his family, listening to the sounds.

David and Louisa were gone. James brooded sullenly by the
fire. And somewhere, as always, crickets sang plaintively.

Part Two

"In looking back over my pioneer life I can see many places where I would do differently if I had the chance to pass that way again, but knowing what I do now I would have come to Puget Sound, to Elliott Bay, and located just as I did before...that I would marry the same woman, join the same church, but endeavor to be a better Christian."

—David Thomas Denny,
April 30, 1896

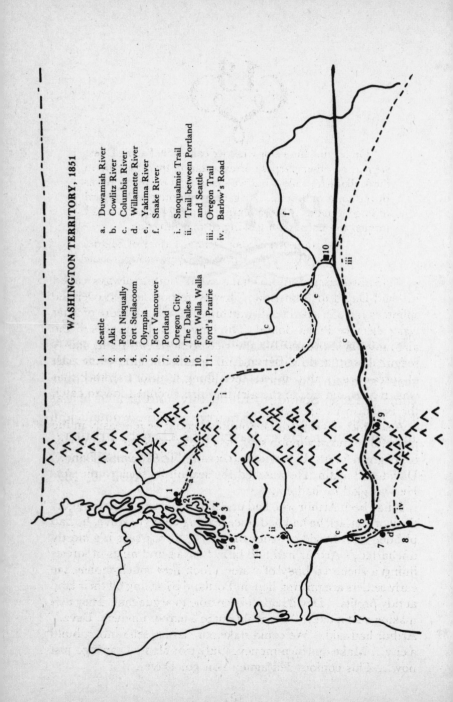

WASHINGTON TERRITORY, 1851

1. Seattle
2. Alki
3. Fort Nisqually
4. Fort Steilacoom
5. Olympia
6. Fort Vancouver
7. Portland
8. Oregon City
9. The Dalles
10. Fort Walla Walla
11. Ford's Prairie

a. Duwamish River
b. Cowlitz River
c. Columbia River
d. Willamette River
e. Yakima River
f. Snake River

i. Snoqualmie Trail
ii. Trail between Portland and Seattle
iii. Oregon Trail
iv. Barlow's Road

13

"On leaving home for what we called the Pacific Coast we had no other purpose or expectation than to settle in the Willamette valley, but we met a man on Burnt River by the name of Brock.... He gave us information in regard to Puget Sound.... My attention was thus turned...and I formed the purpose of looking in that direction."

—Arthur Armstrong Denny, Father of Seattle,
in *Pioneer Days on Puget Sound*

"The Promised Land. That's what Louisa always called it," said David to John Low. They were both leaned over the splintery rail of a small boat, watching the western shore of what was called the Puget Sound. The tang of early fall was in the air, and David breathed in the rich scent of earth and sea. A seagull cawed, and David tilted his head to the gray-white arch of spread wings and smiled, then flung a bit of hardtack that was in his hand out to the air; the bird swooped low to catch the bread in its open beak.

A serenity enveloped the Sound. It could be felt easily in the peaceful sound of wind in sails, fish breaking water, restful colors of green forests, blue skies and ocean. "The Promised Land," David said again. He watched the seagull fly back to the sky. He was glad he had come.

It had been Arthur who had urged him. Sweating out the ague, the worst attack he had had since leaving Cherry Grove, he had pleaded with David to scout the area. "Brock says it's mostly uncharted," Arthur had told him. "Miles and miles of forests lining a sheltered body of water. Look how much money the early settlers are making here in Portland by selling off their land at tidy profits." David hadn't been able to argue that. They *were* making a lot money. "We could put in a harbor up there, Dave," Arthur had said. "We could stake our claims, sell timber, build a city... Make our own money. Only trouble is, I can't go just now... This confounded ague. You go, Dave...."

On September 11 David and John left Portland—and their families. For two weeks they walked north along the Cowlitz River, pushing John's cattle ahead of them. In the Chehalis Valley, just north of where the Cowlitz veers east, they left the herd with a Mr. Ford to pasture for the winter. After 200 miles of twisted trail they came to Olympia, a small settlement on the southernmost end of Puget Sound.

Olympia was the clearinghouse, the furthest post of governmental bureaucracy. To the north lay land inhabited by Indians and a small remnant of the Hudson Bay British.

Olympia had about 12 buildings, including a post office, the clearinghouse, and a saloon or two. It was in one of the saloons that they met up with Captain Fay, sole proprietor of the fish business—salted, barreled, and sent to San Fransisco. When Fay offered them passage on his small sailing sloop for a nominal fee, they (along with another young man by the name of Leander Terry) jumped at the chance to be escorted further down the Sound with a more knowledgeable person. Fay had in mind to go as far as Elliott Bay, a few days' journey to the north, where he had heard the Indians like to fish and where the salmon were easy to find.

"Who is this Louisa Boren you keep talking about?" Captain Fay hollered suddenly. He was a jovial man, a man who liked to know what was happening—always curious, always thinking, always a smile on his rounded face.

David knew that John watched him closely. He could almost see the infuriating smile he had, sort of lopsided above the long beard that grew from just his chin. "She's my stepsister," he said quickly, letting it go at that.

"Sounds like this could be interesting!" the man hollered again.

"There's not much to tell you, Sir."

"I got all day!" Fay spit but missed the spittoon.

"Go on," grinned John. "Tell the man..."

David sighed. He wished he hadn't said anything to begin with. "My brother married her sister eight years ago. And my Pa married her Ma three years ago."

The captain raised a brow—a bushy, heavy covering atop his pale blue eyes. "Now that *is* interesting, lad!"

"No law against it," said David defensively.

"And I suppose you aim to marry her, this Louisa Boren?"

"I do." He would too, despite Pa. He couldn't help but wonder though, if Louisa would defy the folks if it came right down to it. He wondered if *he* would defy the folks if it came right down to it.

"And just how old of an upstart are you?" the captain drilled unmercifully.

"Nineteen, Sir."

"Nineteen, eh?" Fay said it slowly and rubbed the yellow stubble of his chin between his thumb and forefinger. "You got a long wait ahead 'a you, laddie?"

"How's that?" He knew what the captain was saying. He just didn't want to talk about it.

"You mean your folks'll let you marry 'fore you're of age? How old is she?"

John snickered, then laughed outright. "She's 24," said David quickly. He turned to stare back out to the water, to the shoreline, to the trees that grew thick and green, so green that they almost looked black.

"Twenty-four! Holy cats a-matin', boy!" Fay whistled and swore, then raised both eyebrows. He spat again. "So the young lad is going to marry himself a lady five years older than himself, is he? And his sister to boot!"

David tried to ignore the exchanged glances behind his back, but he found that his teeth were clenched and that his jaw ached. They all thought he was a kid yet. Pa had made that perfectly clear by denying him Louisa. James certainly viewed him as one.

He thought of James. He thought of James and Louisa together, and his guts twisted uncomfortably. The rail was hard and cold in his hand. The splinters dug into his palm. Why was Pa so bent on keeping him and Louisa apart? Was it just their ages? Unaware of his tension, he smote the railing. Prickles of pain buzzed in his hand.

"Elliott Bay!" Captain Fay swung into the southwest breeze. The boat nosed around what appeared to be a large tongue of land, passing by a long, wide, open beach. "What do you say we push into the bay and have a look-see?" Fay hollered.

David gazed behind him to catch sight of the western arm of the Sound, the Olympic Peninsula, which extended north-south as far as the eye could see. Its own mountains pierced the sky with jagged white peaks, resting against the blue like torn paper against a cover.

"This where the Duwamish River lets out?" John shouted. He motioned to Leander Terry to come to the bow of the ship. The younger man walked over, his head pulled down into his jacket, his collar turned up, his shoulders stooped over. He said that the wind made his ears cold. "What do you think?" asked John. "Think maybe this is the mouth of that river you've been hearing so much about in Olympia?"

"That's the Duwamish, all right!" Fay shouted, not letting Lee speak. "You can see the beginnings of it sprawled over the flats way south!" He pointed, then swung his neck around to look behind him. "I have a hankering that the beach we just passed by was Sqwudux!"

"You said what?" demanded John.

"Sqwudux! It's an Injun camping ground! Think I'll head back and nose in closer to have a look-see! Keep alert for any Injun signs! Them boats 'a theirs could be tucked up under the trees. If you spot anything, we'll pull in!"

"You *want* to go ashore if there's Indians?" Lee asked. He poked his head up out of his jacket to stare at Fay.

"And just how do you think I'm going to get my fish if I don't rub elbows with a few Injuns?" he demanded roughly.

"Fish 'em yourself?" Lee's nostrils flared, and he dropped his head back into his coat.

"The Injuns get the fish, Terry! *I* send them to San Fransisco!"

Lee's head shot out. "You don't *know* the beggars! What if they greet us all with a flying tomahawk or something?"

Fay laughed. "Of all the… These Injuns are about as peaceful as the preacher back home!"

"There they are." David pointed to the overhang of trees. "The boats, that is."

"Where, Lad?"

"Over there. Under the arbutus. Three of them. Canoes, I guess you call them."

"Injun boats, I call 'em! Come on!" All congeniality again, Fay bellowed orders to his crew, and the anchor was dropped. A small dinghy was lowered into the water, and the captain tossed over his bedroll and a few provisions, then motioned to David, Lee, and John to follow. "You three are coming with me. Who knows—this just may be the spot o' land you're looking for!"

John jumped with both feet into the tiny rowboat, taking the sway with his knees. David dropped in after him. Lee followed reluctantly.

"You row, Dave," commanded Fay. David set the paint-peeled oars into the rusted locks and took a deep breath of the salt air into his lungs. The blue seemed to have swallowed him, pleasantly so. It was everywhere—above, around, below. Cotton, bunched in endless formation, swirled overhead, and fish, arching neatly, broke the water beside him. He pulled back on the oars and dropped the blades neatly into the sea. He felt a contentment seep in, and he looked about, trying to visualize Arthur's city on the unbroken shores. He felt the power of his muscles as he pulled back on the oars over and over. The contentment settled in as sweat dripped from his armpits. The Promised Land. This was it. Louisa didn't know how right she had been.

The boat ground to a stop; the sand of the long, deep beach brought them to a rest. David climbed out and joined Fay and John as they surveyed the three Indian canoes. Lee hung back. It was obvious that the small boats had once been trees, but were now gutted out, shaped so that the bow and stern came to similar points.

A twig snapped and David jumped, startled to find how quickly the Indians had come upon them. His heart lurched and he felt the sweat come to his palms. For a moment no one moved, and he wondered if perhaps Lee had been right to be cautious, and Fay wrong.

"Klah-how-yah!" Fay said suddenly with an exaggerated cheerfulness. "Tillicum—skookum!"

14

"The little party spent their first night on the untrod shores of Sqwudux, the Indian name of the promontory now occupied by West Seattle."

—Emily Inez Denny in *Blazing the Way*

"Tillicum—skookum!" Fay said again. "Friend."

One of the Indians was at least a head taller than the others, and it was he who stepped forward. "Sealth," he said curtly, yet without animosity. He was striking to look at: his face was square and powerful, and his forehead was straight, in contrast to the slanted ones of his friends. David judged him to be about 60 or 65. Around his large naked frame hung a faded blue blanket which David recognized to be an old Hudson Bay item. It was held in place by a strong hand just beneath the neck. The most overwhelming impression, assaulting David's senses and making his skin crawl, was the stench that emanated from them all. It wasn't a smell that came from sweated bodies. It was worse—a rancid, sickening smell that killed all other odors.

The man who had called himself Sealth motioned to another man—smaller, maybe five feet, with badly bowed legs. He was sinewy and his body was devoid of any sort of clothing at all. He spoke with Fay, both of them almost painfully, using their arms to aid in the work, filling in where the words left off. Chinook was the language of the area, a compromise tongue of French, English, and the various Indian dialects. It had been devised by the Hudson Bay Company a century earlier, and its 300 or so words allowed no frills—only the basics of communication. David watched with fascination, his attention primarily focused on the apparent leader. It was clear that Sealth wasn't going to speak the demeaning language.

"Who's the man?" David asked as the natives moved up the beach.

"Sealth. Or Seattle. Whichever you prefer, I suppose. 'White man—Boston.' You learn your first Chinook there, Dave.

112

'White man—Boston.' Got it?''

David nodded. "You were saying?"

"White man, Boston, can't pronounce the fellow's name. Sort of have to swallow and die on the last of it to get it just right." He grinned slowly, showing his yellow teeth. "And since I ain't about to die, I just call him Sealth."

"Who is he?" Lee stepped forward suddenly. "And what are they doing here? What did they say? And why the squashed-in heads?"

"Why, Terry!" exclaimed Fay triumphantly. "Sealth's the great leader! Allied child of six tribes, head of two—the Duwamish and Suquamish!"

"And?" Lee urged.

"And their heads are squished in because their mamas thought it rather pretty. You really don't know anything, do you? What are you doing up here, anyway? Oregon's full of them flatheads, Terry! The mamas tie two boards to their wee little heads when they're first born, then squeeze 'em tighter and tighter until they get the look they want. Takes months." Fay paused and a wicked look of delight sprang into his face. "In Paris," he grinned, "it's the latest fashion. Only in Paris they got special hats instead of boards. And they use ostrich feathers to dress the whole thing up. Here they just let the rain drip onto the setup."

"You're a bore, Fay."

"And you're a coward, Lee Terry." Fay's smile vanished, then bounced back into place. "A lucky coward, though. The Injuns are stupid. If they were smart they'd 'a shot our heads off 'fore now. So far they don't know that Boston plans on coming in to stick up shipyards and dry good stores on their hunting grounds." He laughed and spit the phlegm from his throat. It hit one of the canoes. "This here Sealth just agreed to take his men fishing tomorrow—for me. We made a trade. His men's catch for one blanket. They like blankets," he added.

"You don't approve of our city idea?" John asked.

"Of course I approve! Just pointing out their stupidity is all!"

David glanced over to the Indians. They had a fire going and were fixing a duck onto a stick to roast over it. "You don't know that they're stupid, Fay," he said slowly, studying their movements and the way they spoke to each other as they accomplished what needed to be done.

"They're stupid, all right, Denny," Fay roared. "Why, you'd be a little on the dim side yourself, lad, if you had had your brains mashed flat!"

David squatted and absently turned over a small rock. A crab no bigger than the end of his thumb skittered sideways to the dark retreat of another rock. He liked Sealth. There was something about the man, a kind of knowing, yet sadness. His black eyes had shown fierce pride, yet a mournful resignation. The man definitely was not stupid. David flipped the second rock but took no pleasure in seeing the tiny crab scurry to a third stone. Gently he laid the rocks back into place, then rose up. "We going to take a hike around a bit before supper?" he asked casually. "The sun'll be dropping soon." He started off up the slope of land behind the beach, to the trees that crowded close and dark. John, Lee, and Fay fell in beside him.

David was impressed with the density of the woods. If they settled here, they wouldn't lack for timber. And the beach was a good place to build cabins. His thoughts and plans raced on. He only had to look at John to see that they thought and planned the same things. Even Lee, after a supper of hardtack, beans, and boiled coffee, relaxed and began to grow optimistic with them.

The sun dropped low and David looked out to the golden outline of the Olympic Mountains. He could see the wharves poking out into the Sound, seagulls perched on the pilings. The golden edge of the mountain peaks became brilliant as the sun lowered; it looked as if God Himself had touched the jagged edges with His own golden quill. The contentment that eased itself on David earlier returned, soaking into him like water to a sponge. Maybe it was a sign from God to him.

David's bedroll was cold and damp when he finally climbed into it. Overhead a large cedar tree bough covered him like a king's canopy. Moonlight spilled through and stars danced as the breeze swayed the branches. Waves rolled in at his feet. They had a pleasant sound—soft, continuous, persistent. He liked it. And suddenly he knew, without a doubt, that this was home.

A decision made, his thoughts turned to Louisa. He smiled with the realization that now, with a place picked out, he could go back to Portland. He would see her soon. A firmness came to his body and he stirred with the frustration it brought. A firmness came to his mind and he went over and over what he would say to Pa when he saw him. He would convince Pa. He and Louisa *would* marry. He knew that.

★　　★　　★

Salmon sizzled in Fay's large iron skillet and spit out tiny bits of hot saltpork fat. It was evening again, their third at Sqwudux. The golden sunset was hidden by gray clouds. Rain misted from a low fog—enough to dampen their clothing but not enough to put out the fire. David watched John's face through the warm steam of the frying fish and tried to discern his friend's thoughts.

"This it?" he asked suddenly, unable to stand the uncertainty any longer. "You agree this is the place? We leave with Fay in the morning to bring back the others?"

The dimple in John's cheek went deep. David let out a long sigh. Already he was figuring how many days it would be before he saw Louisa. Fay jabbed the fat side of one fish. It spit saltpork at him and he jumped back and sucked silently on his fist.

"I don't know about the both of you going back with me," he drawled after taking his lips from his hand. "Seems to me someone's got to stay behind and mind the store."

David frowned and pushed against the ridge over his nose with his thumb. Then he curled his fingers into his palms and shoved them into his jacket pockets. The air was chilly as well as wet, and his fingers ached. He stared at John. John stared back.

"HALLO THERE!"

David clambered to his feet, a reflex action. "HALLO THERE!" came the call again. David peered out to the fog and saw a large, flat-bottomed barge push into sight. A man waved. "Didn't know there were any white faces in these parts!" he called out. He used a long pole to glide in closer, and David saw that the man was about 45. There was a woman and a young girl beside him.

In the gathering dark and mist the girl could almost have been Louisa, and he stood trembling from the surprise of it. She was young, maybe 14 or 15 but her hair was the same dark color as Louisa's and curls framed her face.

"You got a claim around here?" David shouted, his eye rivoted to the girl.

"Got one up the Duwamish River! Best farmland around! Luther Collins is the name!"

"David Denny! This here is my partner, John Low! A friend, Leander Terry! And Captain Fay of Olympia!"

"My wife and daughter! Lucinda! Lucinda Collins!"

Lucinda? Louisa? Even their names were similar.

"You folks thinkin' of settlin' up here?" the man called Collins shouted.

"If no one beats us to it!"

"Well, the place is wide open, man! I got three friends who are out getting their winter provisions right now! We all filed alongside each other about two weeks ago! September 14, to be exact. Jacob Maple, his son, Samuel, and a bachelor."

Captain Fay bellowed out something in Chinook, and David wasn't surprised to hear the laughter. Suddenly he was tired of Fay's continual joviality.

"Well! We got a way to go yet!" the stranger waved. "I'll be by in about a month or so. I got an old claim up the Nisqually River near the Hudson Bay, and I got to be going after my team of oxen and other supplies still there."

David listened without hearing to the last-minute bantering of the Chinook and the clear laughter of the women. He headed numbly back to the fire and scooped one of the scorched salmon onto his tin plate. Settlers were coming in....

The scow moved into the dusty gray. Long after the mist had taken them he could hear their voices and more of the laughter leak from the fog and over the water.

Fay was right. David knew that. Someone *did* have to stay behind to mind the store. And it couldn't be Lee, since they didn't know him well enough. "I'll stay on if you want, John," he said suddenly, before he could change his mind.

"What's that?"

"I'll stay on while you go back to Portland." He felt an ache press into his stomach—sort of cold and hard at the same time. "I don't mind. I really don't," he rambled. "You have your family, your little ones to watch out for. And we'll be needing a cabin for them when they get here," he added quickly, before the ache moved up and pressed so tight he couldn't speak.

"You can do it alone?"

He swallowed. "If Lee's a mind, maybe he and I can do it together."

"Lee?" John asked.

"Never put one up before. But sure, I'll stay on. Got no use in Portland. What kind of a house do you want? One of those nice puncheon ones? Or a regular log house?"

"If I was you boys," interrupted Fay. "I'd build me a good stout log house." He couldn't hide his smile. He didn't want to. "It would keep off the stray bullets when them Injuns poo-mowitch!" The smile broke and laughter came.

"What's that?" David asked wearily.

"Why, laddie! That's when they shoot deer!" He winked at Lee. "What about Louisa?"

David caught John's eye through the light of the fire, and he looked down, away from the penetrating gaze of the older man. He was tired of Fay, of his jovial outlook. He was tired of John and Lee. He was tired of the smelly Indians, the hardtack, and the burnt fish. He was tired of a man's work that forced him into the wilderness in the first place and now forced him to stay behind. He was tired of being only 19. And he was tired of being without Louisa.

"I'll write a letter," he rose to his feet. "One to Arthur, telling him to come. Another to Pa. He'll listen. I'll word it just right." He looked up at John. "Then you bring me Louisa."

Their eyes met. "I'll do it," said John.

15

"We have examined the valley of the Duwamish River and find it a fine country. There is plenty of room for one thousand settlers. Come at once."
—Note from David Denny to his brother, Arthur
September 28, 1851

David limped painfully to the fallen logs, to the hole he had dug beside them. His foot was bandaged and his bare toes, poking out from the torn sheeting, dragged behind as he hobbled over the small stones, the clumps of dirt, and the broken twigs.

Sweat broke out, clammy and sticky. It ran from his back and his armpits, wetting his temples and catching in the thick beard that had grown since his isolation. Muscles shook under the sweated skin as David made his way back to the small shelter that he and Lee had made two months before. It had been patterned after the Indians' temporary dwellings: cedar boughs that leaned, propped together to make a small covering from the constant November rain that seemed to mark the winter in Puget Sound. It was a scanty shelter, but it kept him dry.

David sighed and panted heavily. Fog curled from his lips in sudden, quick puffs, and he watched the vapor as he leaned wearily into a stump that rose up out of a bed of moss. Pale green lichen scabbed the rotting bark, and he felt the roots give way under his weight, then rest. Too worn to go on, but too afraid to sit, he propped himself on the stump's edge and waited. Underbrush, thick and wet, clung to his pant legs.

Captain Fay, John, and even Lee were gone now. Captain Fay and John had gone in September, Lee left the end of October when Luther Collins had passed by on the way to his Nisqually claim. Lee had gone with him because Collins had offered the use of his froe if one of them helped him bring back his belongings from his old claim. They needed the froe to split cedar into shingles. The cabin was finished, except for the roof.

Of course Lee had gone. At first David hadn't minded being

alone. The Indians, more arriving each day, had seemed happy to have him there, and he had enough provisions to last him some time. But then he had chopped his foot and come down with neuralgia. He wished now that Lee hadn't gone. And he wished that he had some of Arthur's quinine.

David grimaced as he wiggled his toes. Despite the pain, they still moved, and he smiled with the encouragement. He was lucky to still have them. Only three days after Lee left he had been chopping wood when the ax handle slipped from his hands, neatly slicing through his boot and chopping into his foot. His scream had brought the Indians on the run. They found him doubled over and hanging from the waist, his hands clutching his foot where the blood oozed through his boot and dripped from his fingers.

Sealth had spoken softly, his words guttural and having no meaning other than compassion. And the others had gathered around to stare, open-eyed with curiosity, their half-naked bodies reeking with the awful stench. Only vaguely could he remember getting sick.

And now, each night, one of the squaws would come to wrap his foot with a new cloth. After the swish of their bark skirts had left him he would faithfully remove the dirty bandages and replace them with his own. A nasty infection had set in, but there was no way to deny the attention that Sealth insisted upon.

Moaning audibly, David rested his makeshift crutch against a bush and set his head carefully between his hands, gripping it tightly. His teeth clamped as the flash of pain darted through, shooting to his jaw. The wrapping he had made from a torn shirt to bind his head had done little to relieve the constant throb that had set in, and was useless now as the pain intensified.

Neuralgia. He didn't exactly know what it was, but it made a person's head hurt like blazes, and that was what his was doing. It came from exposure, and he had certainly been exposed.

More sweat came, soaking his shirt. He knew it was cold, although his fever kept him from feeling it. He could tell by the way his breath fogged up when he breathed. He had to get to a fire, but he didn't move.

Instead he sat alone, thinking, staring out to the water. The waves lapped tenderly, a sound he had grown accustomed to. But somewhere across the bay an Indian chanted, and he felt very much his aloneness. He thought of the two letters that John had carried with him to Portland—one to Arthur and the other to Pa.

The first letter had been a simple message. He had scrawled it quickly: *"We have examined the valley of the Duwamish River and find it a fine country. There is room for one thousand settlers. Come at once."*

The second letter had taken longer to draft. It had been carefully written, the pages long. David groaned again. Had Pa gotten the letter? Had Arthur? Were they on their way? Would Pa let Louisa come?

David finally stood and stumbled down the embankment to the beach, to his shelter and the roofless cabin. The evening sun played on the water, and David watched the myriad of colors. The last of the sun broke through the dismal gray, painting the world in pastels. He thought of Louisa and tried to picture her face, her eyes, the way she smiled. He tried to remember the feel of her in his arms, her kiss. But it had been too long.

A rustle, the whispers of scampering feet, brought his attention to where his shelter leaned, to where the incompleted cabin stood. He stared, horrified. The throb of his foot and his head, the frustration of his memories, were forgotten. A family of skunks, their saucy white stripes sharp against the black fur, had found his provisions.

David sank to the sand, unable to do anything but watch in dismal numbness as the last of his food disappeared. His foot began to bleed again. It oozed from the binding and stained the pebbles. The sun withdrew as the bottom fronds of a fern swayed then stilled. When David crawled to the shelter there was only one tea bag left, and it lay alone in the middle of the dirt floor.

★   ★   ★

The cup was hot in his hands and he felt the heat of the tea warm his belly. The lost sun had brought on darkness and it hung heavily about him, the light from his small fire staving it off from descending entirely.

The chant of the Indian across the bay grew louder, a chorus of sadness and sorrow. Gradually the rhythm increased, faster and more intense, and the wind sent hollow calls around the shelter, catching in the fragile boughs. Still the chanting pulsated on, beating harshly into David's ears and his fevered mind.

It began to haunt him, to mock him, to make him afraid.

He thought of the letters he had written, asking them all to come. What a fool! He plastered his hands to his ears in a vain effort to rid himself of the sound. The Indians—who knew them? Their ways were strange; they were different. And there were so many of them now. And what about the tribes to the north? The fierce Haidas? The ones that even Sealth feared?

Verses from the Book of James came to David's head—scattered verses, pieces that were disconnected and taunting.

"The trying of your faith worketh patience."
"When lust hath conceived, it bringeth forth sin, and sin, when it is finished, bringeth forth death."
"Do not err...."

His body jerked as the chill took over. He shut his eyes, thought of Louisa, agonized over which way to pray. He wanted her. He *needed* her. Would Pa read his letter and let her come? But her life? Could it be risked? More of James tormented him.

"What is your life? It is even a vapor."

He cried out and bit his lips to stop the noise, to stifle the selfish prayer. His body shook as painful spasms tore through his chest, pulling tight in his arms and legs.

Then gently, without noise, the rain began to fall.

November 5, 1851, the sun spread out golden feathers of light to awaken the dark valley of the Willamette. Indian summer was at its peak, and the yellows of the sky blended with the yellows of the earth to create a soft amber that reached out to the sagging trio of old and rotting tents that waited at the river's edge.

Louisa hadn't slept well and had arisen early. She stood with her feet lost in the golden stalks of grass as her fingers unknowingly pulled at the fat tufts of seeds, spilling them to the cold earth. Tears ran freely from her eyes, splintering the beauty the day offered.

The sunbonnets that Ma had washed the day before hung from a line—stiff profiles of starched calico and muslin. The beginnings of a breeze touched Louisa's cheek with cold strokes where her tears had run. The long ribbons of the bonnets danced.

Louisa pushed her sleeve over her face, then walked softly to the circle of rocks with its pile of graying ash. It took only a few moments to start the fire, and, after setting the heavy sadiron near the hot flames, she allowed herself to warm her fingers. The chill of the early morning drew small gusts of fog from her lips and she shivered, then winced as the heat of the flames burned her fingers. She pulled back a tiny bit, then pushed forward again—and thought of David. Her tears began again, dripping noiselessly from her chin. She had cried most of the night and had no energy to utter any sound with the release of her heartache.

Today was the day that Arthur and Mary Ann were leaving for Puget Sound, for the town that Mr. Low called 'New York.' Almost everyone was going: Arthur and Mary Ann, the children, Dobbins and Anna, and little Gertrude. Even the Bells were going, and the Lows too, of course. Everyone but her. Pa wouldn't let her go. She had prayed each night for him to change his mind. But he hadn't.

Louisa gathered the sunbonnets and pulled the iron away from the fire. She licked her finger and touched the tip quickly to the smooth surface. At the sound of sizzling spit she bent over the first of the bonnets. While she worked the family stretched and dressed quietly. Little was said this last morning together, although nods were exchanged. Louisa saw Pa comb out his beard, and she looked away. She sat back on her heels in the grass, not wishing to finish, too angry with Pa for denying her the chance to go to David. But the bonnets had to be pressed, and she dutifully bent over the task again. She ironed on the grass, on a quilt folded twice and laid out.

In the distance she could see the *Exact,* a sailing sloop that would take the others to New York, to Puget Sound. Her sails hung limply from her double masts, but the seamen had already begun to gather—at the *Exact* and other ships.

"Good morning, Louisa." Mary Ann sat down quietly beside Louisa. Her new baby fussed, then quieted beneath the heavy shawl. Louisa nodded and went on with her work. She tried not to think about the last two weeks, begun by Mr. Low's return without David. That had been disappointing enough, but then Pa had announced, after Arthur had shown him David's note to come at once, that he and Ma and baby Loretta would stay on in the Willamette. "And Louisa," he had said, looking at her with his blue eyes, "you're to stay on too. Wiley, Samuel, and James don't care to go on. I see no reason for you to go on."

"Why, Pa?" she had asked.

He didn't even blink. "Because I want to stay where the politics are. Oregon City is the territorial government seat, and I want to take a claim near there."

"No, Pa. Why must *I* stay?" she had asked.

"You're to marry James when you're ready."

"I want to marry David."

"David is too young."

Yes, she had prayed. And prayed and prayed. At night she had talked with God and seen the falling stars. Unanswered prayers falling from heaven?

Mary's baby cried and forced Louisa to stop the remembering, and almost gratefully she looked up at her sister and the two-month-old infant in her arms.

It had been a hard birth, both for the child and for Mary Ann. Still ill with the mountain fever and suffering from the ague, she had gone into labor 11 days after getting into Portland, bearing Rolland Herschel the next day in near-delirium. Her survival had been unexpected. So had Rollie's.

"I think he's going to die," Mary Ann whispered. She looked up at Louisa, resignation in her eyes.

"Die?" Louisa gasped. "Don't be silly! He's not going to die, and stop thinking such things! Stop *saying* such things!"

She took the baby from Mary, as if to protect him from a doom she could control. Rollie turned inward; his small pink mouth searched for her breast.

"See, Liza? He's always so hungry... I just don't have the milk..."

Louisa stroked the soft red curls and pushed a knuckle to his lips. The baby sucked greedily. His face pinked with the effort. But in a moment he let go and shrieked openly. His tiny fists punched at the blanket.

"Why don't you stay with us?" Louisa asked, brightening at the thought. "You could rest and regain your strength, and Ma could help you nurse Rolland when he's really miserable."

"You mean let Arthur go on?"

Louisa nodded. "He'll come back for you! Once they get this city of theirs going!"

"Ma can't nurse both Loretta and Rollie... I have to keep on trying myself. It's the only way the milk will come."

"But you haven't the strength!"

"There's just nothing else to be done." Mary Ann reached up and Louisa reluctantly put the baby in her arms. She watched Mary set the boy to her breast again, then picked up the iron. The baby fussed and Louisa concentrated on Kate's red bonnet. From the corner of her eye she saw Mary Ann shuffle back to one of the tents. After a time she set the red hat aside and picked up the last one to be done.

"Louisa?"

Louisa pushed the sharp point of the iron into a fold. "Hello, Ma," she said without looking up.

"I think we need to talk. You and I."

"There's nothing to say, Ma. You know how I feel. It seems to make no difference to you."

"It does, Liza. Please. Come to the river and we'll talk."

Small boats, tied to the wharves, bobbed on the water, and the *Exact* had her sails up. Men raced up and down the gangplank, full of energy and chatter. They bumped one another as they swore and laughed.

"David sent a letter to Pa," said Ma at last. She shielded her eyes from the sun's brightness, watching the activity instead of Louisa.

"When?"

"With John Low. Along with the one he sent to Arthur."

"You didn't tell me that!"

"It wasn't for you. There was no need."

Someone shouted, and Louisa looked up to see two men balanced precariously on the *Exact's* railing. They were playing a game and took jabs at each other, trying in vain not to go over. One with a bright yellow toque did.

"David's a mighty persuasive young man," said Ma. "Your Pa's been biding his time, waiting to see how things went between you and James." The men were forgotten.

"I don't love James. I love David."

"You *think* you love David."

"And how am I to know if I'm only around James, if I'm

never given the chance to be with David to find out? And how can James and I *ever* be happy with that between us?''

Ma smiled. ''Just the argument David used on his Pa.''

''And?'' Louisa's heart pounded fuzz into her head, and she had to swallow to clear her ears, to hear Ma speak.

''Pa's decided to let you go.''

Louisa stood stunned, hardly daring to believe the words, to even think on them.

''But on one condition.''

''Anything, Ma.''

''You're not to marry without our consent. Your Pa has agonized over this, tossing in bed every night, praying and not knowing what to do. His sense tells him to keep you here and let James marry you. It worries him about you going off to an uncharted land all alone, with no husband, living closely with a man...'' Her voice trailed off uncomfortably. ''Well, you understand, don't you?''

Louisa only stared at her mother, not hearing the words. She saw David—his face, his eyes, the way his hair waved in back.

''But your Pa isn't a man that feels restricted to doing what's usual or necessarily right, society-wise,'' Sarah went on. ''And he knows you to be a sensible woman with strong Christian principles, so he's decided to let you go. After all, you are a grown woman.'' The way she said the last sentence Louisa knew that it had been really Ma who had convinced Pa.

''Oh, Ma! I *do* love you!''

''You understand this is to be a trial period?''

''Oh, I do! Yes, I do!''

''Well, what are you standing about for? The ship's to leave in an hour's time!''

Louisa hugged her Ma—a quick, tight hug—then ran all the way back to the tents. Her fingers trembled with excitement as she went through her trunk, making sure it was all there—her mirror, her brass candlestick, the white dress she had made, the seed packets for Mary Ann, the children's Christmas gifts, Pamelia's sweetbriar. It was fall, but she could smell the sweet scent of roses, and she opened the pages of her Bible to where her sweetbriar seeds lay. God *was* good! A shadow darkened her Bible. ''Hello, James,'' she said without turning around. The smell of the rotting tent, of the decaying leaves that were caught between earth and canvas, of autumn swept in.

"Pa's just told me he's letting you go."

"Yes." She shut the lid slowly, turning the key. He took her in his arms, turning her face to his.

"He's five years younger than you, Louisa. Five years younger."

"Let's not argue, James."

"But I love you!"

"I'm sorry. I wish you hated me. It would make it easier, wouldn't it?"

He stood back as if stung. "Hate you?" She started for the door, but he came after her. "Don't walk away from me!" he said fiercely. "You can't leave me for David! You can't!" His mouth came down hard over hers.

"Please, James, don't…"

He let her go as suddenly as he had grabbed her. They stood motionless until her tears started to fall. He wiped them away with the back of his hand. "I'll wait for you. I'll wait forever. You know that, don't you?"

When she saw that his own eyes were full she knew that he was right. He *would* wait forever. "Perhaps you'll find someone else," she said, sorry for it as soon as she spoke.

James tried to smile, but it fell, and his hands came up to rub through his hair. "He's just a boy, Liza. Just a boy…"

"I love him, James."

"Don't do this to me! He can't even file a claim! He's only 19, Liza! He's just a kid!"

"Stop it! Just stop it! I have to go, James! I do!"

He walked away from her slowly, and when he stepped outside the tent, she followed him. He reached for her, kissed her, then broke into a run.

"Good-bye, James," she whispered. In her heart she knew that she would never see him again.

★　　★　　★

Everyone gathered to say good-bye—even Jonah, the old sheep dog. Everyone but James.

"Where *is* James?" Pa demanded. "I would think he'd want to say good-bye to you, Louisa."

"We've said our good-byes."

Sarah reached out to Louisa, and she fell into her mother's arms. She hugged tight, trying to catch the feel of it to hold in her memories. Then Pa took her and she let him wrap his arms around her. "I love you, Sugar Lump," he said hoarsely. "You be a good girl now?" She nodded, trying to hold back her tears. "I just pray that I'm doing the right thing by you," he whispered.

"Oh, Pa! You are!" she sobbed, unable to hold it any longer. "You are, Pa! You are!"

"Here, let me wipe your face." He pulled out his old red hand-kerchief and rubbed it over her cheeks, then patted the cloth under her eyes. Her tears kept coming. "You've got to stop your crying, Sugar. Someone'll be thinking I'm *making* you go off." He smiled.

She threw her arms about the man who had become her Pa. "I'm just too happy!" she cried. "Oh, Pa! I *do* love you!"

"And I love you too. Here." He thrust the handkerchief in-to her hand. "You keep this to remember your old Pa by. Remember that I love you..."

The gangplank up to the ship was long and narrow, and Louisa stepped carefully along the wooden slats until at last she stood on deck with everyone else—the Lows, the Bells, Arthur and Mary Ann and the children, Dobbins and Anna. Ma waved a white handkerchief, and for an instant Louisa saw Pamelia and Cherry Grove. "Good-bye, Ma!" she screamed.

The boat eased out into the river. Louisa clutched the red handkerchief in her hand, then waved it frantically above her head until everyone was gone. She wondered if James had seen her go.

"Hey! Look at the purdy lady!" someone shouted. Louisa whirled about just as the man who had earlier fallen from the ship's railing whistled. There was no mistaking the bright yellow toque. Her cheeks burned hot as he bowed and doffed his cap. "How do 'e do?" he winked. When he straightened he whistled again.

"Now, Ladies and Gentlemen!" Captain Folger said, nodding to the swarthy miners already engaged in a rowdy card game as they sat on the open deck. Wind filled the sails over them, making soft popping sounds. "There's bunks below and a small stove. It's take your pick, take your lot." The Captain winked at Louisa. He was a handsome man with thick, wind-blown black hair and a long nose that set off the depth of his piercing black eyes.

"The plan is to sail north, take the Juan de Fuca Strait, then head on down into the Sound, or up into the Sound, whichever you prefer. Olympia's the last stop. From there, of course," he looked again to the noisy men, "it'll be due north, north to the Queen Charlotte Islands, where I hear tell you boys aim to strike it rich."

"Aim to?" the man with the yellow toque spoke up. His cheeks were gray stubble, a dimple caught deep in his chin. "I'z cummin' 'ome with jingles in me coat, baby nuggetz the size of an 'alnut!" He roared and laid his hand out flat. "I take ye, Zir Zeke, it'z a royal flush."

The man called Sir Zeke groaned and gathered up the cards, then thumbed them quickly in a shuffle. He flipped them through his grimy fingers and dealt them swiftly. The tiny cards flew and slithered into tidy heaps around the "table."

"But then I z'poze them nuggetz 'won't be conzidered babiez, now 'ill they?" The man grinned and winked at the captain. "But then you wuz zayin'?"

128

"I was saying that I expect the trip to Olympia to last a week, week-and-a-half, maybe. Maybe more, depending on the wind. And any of you who want to get off before that better holler plenty loud so we can throw the anchor."

"Best see what's below," said Arthur. "We can divvy up the bunks and get some of that salmon of Mary Ann's cooking." He made a wry face and she pretended to scowl. Arthur didn't like salmon, but had allowed his wife to buy a large one just before sailing. An Indian woman had been selling them for a dime.

Sir Zeke stared openly at Louisa. In his hand he held all red hearts, four of them: an ace, a king, a queen and a jack. Louisa gave him a last look and followed Arthur into the hold. She backed down the ladder, forgetting the miners when she saw the cleanliness of the cabin. It was painted white, was cozy, and had a round porthole to let in some light.

"How do you do?" A happy woman came down after her, huffing loudly when she stepped onto the wooded flooring. She held out her hand to Arthur and smiled. "My name is Mrs. Alexander," she beamed. "These here are my two boys." She pointed up the ladder to the two pairs of feet that descended. "We're headed for Olympia. My husband's already there." She went to the window and peered out, taking a whiff of air—the scent of the salt and the rotting seaweed. "Mighty pretty country we're in, isn't it?" she said. "Like I've said to the old man, you sure know how to pick the land! Oh, say!" She turned to look at them congregate around her. "Where you folks headed? Will we be neighbors?"

"Puget Sound," answered Anna.

Mrs. Alexander laughed. Louisa liked the sound of it, open and free. It made her whole round body shake. "Land sakes, honey!" she chortled. "Up north it's all Puget Sound! I mean where on the Sound you going to settle?"

"Head of the Duwamish River—Elliott Bay. Place we call New York," said John Low, dropping into the hold.

Mrs. Alexander laughed heartily again. "New York? You say New York? You mean *alki!*"

"What's that?"

"Chinook for *by-and-by*. Dream on, Mr.——. What did you say your name was?"

"I didn't. It's Low, though. John Low."

"Well, pleased to meet you, Mr. Low." Introductions were made all around.

"Oops, who's this?" Mrs. Alexander made way for a tall man to squeeze past. He had a chest over his shoulder and he dropped it with a thud into a corner.

"The name's Charles Terry, Ma'am," the man said.

"Terry?" John Low stepped forward, eyeing the stranger.

"That's right. Charles Terry. I'm headed for Olympia to open up a mercantile."

"You got a brother named Leander Terry?" John asked. His fingers curled about his beard. "With blond hair, a bit curly, blue eyes?"

"Yeah... you know my brother?"

"I know a Leander Terry. Met up with him in Olympia. He and this man's brother," he nodded to Arthur, "are building me a cabin right now on Elliott Bay. We're starting a town— New York."

"Well, I'll be jiggered!" Charles ran a hand through his curly black hair. "That rascal! He and I left New York together to get gold in California. Only he petered out before me and the last I saw him he was walking north out of San Francisco! Where'd you say he is?"

"In New York."

Alki!" interrupted Mrs. Alexander.

"And you say you're starting a town?"

John nodded.

"You want a mercantile?" the newcomer inquired.

John thrust his hand forward and the two shook vigorously.

"Well, now that that's settled," said Dobbins, "we can see about that fish of Mary's. I'm hungry." He crossed the small space to the stove and ran a finger over the grease. It was a large stove and was pushed against the curved wall. It tilted, and a duct bent and stuck to a hole in the ceiling. "Where's that salmon of yours, Mary Ann?"

Mary Ann knew how to cook fish. She fried it slowly, letting it almost bake, and by the time it was ready even Arthur was hungry enough to eat it. Louisa pulled the children off the bunks and sat them on the floor.

"I don't feel so good, Auntie," whispered Kate. Her bonnet

hung limply from the back of her neck, and her hand pressed tightly on her stomach.

"Maybe you're just hungry. Here, have a bit of your Ma's fish."

"Three blind mice! Three blind mice! See how they—"

"WHAT IN TARNATION IS THAT?" Arthur took the rungs of the ladder two at a time. "What in the blazes is the noise about?" he hollered through the ceiling. Someone laughed.

"They all ran after the farmer's wife, who cut off their tails with a carving knife!" Someone made a loud whacking noise and more laughter followed. *"Ya ever seen such a sight in yer life as three blind mice!"*

"They're drunk! All of them drunk!" Arthur pulled his head down and dropped to the floor.

"The captain?" Memories of the Blue Ruin swept in, and Louisa felt the sway of the ship beneath her feet. Suddenly she didn't feel so well herself.

"No, the miners," said Arthur. "He sat disgustedly at the small table in the middle of the cabin.

"Three blind mice! Three blind mice!"

Louisa fixed a plate of fish for Laura Bell. The boat lurched and she had to push her leg to the stove to keep from falling.

"Here you go—eat up," she whispered.

"Our Father in heaven…" Arthur had his head bowed and the others quickly did the same.

"They all ran after the——"

Arthur said "amen" without finishing. The boat rocked and Louisa looked down at her plate. She felt her stomach turn…

"Land sakes alive! Whatever is the matter with the lot 'a you?" exclaimed Mrs. Alexander. Louisa staggered to the closest bunk. Dobbins was sick too, sitting with his head between his knees.

"It's that fool fish!" moaned Arthur. "I *knew* I shouldn't have let Mary buy it—dime or not!"

"Now, Mr. Denny, it ain't the fish. You all are just a bunch of landlubbers. Now me, I got a stomach made 'a iron."

"Okay, Mrs. Alexander," Arthur bantered, "you just fix a bit of that fish for *yourself!*"

"That, Mr. Denny, ain't a bad idea!"

In a few minutes, as Mrs. Alexander hung over the stove, a hand came to her stomach, another to her mouth. Arthur propped himself up on a pillow, his eyes sparkling. "I say, Mrs, Alexander!" he called out. "Why don't you go cook that fish?"

17

"I can't never forget when the folks landed at Alki Point. I was sorry for Mrs. Denny with her baby and the rest of the women.... I remember it rained awful hard that last day—and the starch got took out of our bonnets and the wind blew, and when the women got into the rowboat to go ashore they were crying every one of 'em, and their sun bonnets [sic] with the starch took out of them went flip flap, flip flap, as they rowed off for shore."

—Quote of "Grandma Fay" in *Four Wagons West*

The sky was gray the morning of November 13, 1851. The sea was gray. Everything was the color of dirty linens that hadn't been hung out in years. The gray hung over the *Exact,* making the ship gray. The billowing sails were gray.

Louisa shivered and pulled her cape tight under chin. Her eyes scanned eagerly the gray shoreline, seeing only the foggy outline of the trees, gray against gray. They had been sailing eight days now, all of them long.

But today was the ninth day and Captain Folger had hopes of coming close to New York any time. He *thought* they would, anyway.

"Keep your eyes open, fella!" the captain shouted. He stood near Louisa, and she could see the drizzle of the rain wet his cheeks and run from his face in long streams. But he didn't seem to mind. "If you spot the place, give me a holler!"

John Low bent over the bulwarks and peered into the heavy mist. "You sure you don't know, Folger?" he hollered back. "You haven't the slightest notion as to where Elliott Bay is?"

"Already told you! Don't know the Sound too well yet! 'Specially in this mud! But you say you've been there! You tell me where we're going!" The gathering miners laughed and Sir Zeke elbowed Louisa. She smiled hastily and stepped away.

"I haven't come at it from the north!" Mr. Low shouted. "I came up from 'Lympia! In the sun!"

"Well, if we miss, we miss. We can only wind up in 'Lympia anyway. And we can just turn right around and head back up! Doing that anyhow, remember? Going to deliver these boys to the Queen Charlottes and those Haidas!" Now it was the captain's turn to laugh, and the miners joined in weakly, as if it were something to laugh about.

"Yeah, and pay your fee for the extra passage," John muttered in the midst of the forced gaiety. Louisa moved closer to him and shivered. The air was wet and biting, with a penetrating chill that seemed to soak through clothes to skin and bone. She curled the ends of her fingers tight into her hand, then released them to set her open palms on the railing. Was it eight o'clock yet? Was David all right? Was he up?

Soon, soon, soon, the sails seemed to flap. Her fingers curled inward again.

"There it is! I see it! I see it!" shouted John exuberantly. There was a scramble of those on deck as they hurried to his side, and as the ones below clawed at the rungs of the ladder to push out of the hold.

Lydia set her arm over her husband's and stared with the others to the dark shape of land that loomed ahead. "Are you sure?" she asked hesitantly.

"Of course, I'm sure! Bell? Where are you? Arthur?"

"Doesn't look much like New York to me," drawled Dobbins dryly.

"It doesn't look like the Promised Land," said Lydia.

"Well, you haven't seen it when the sun comes out!" Mrs. Alexander exclaimed.

"You sure this is it?"

"Positive!"

The captain looked over his port side. "Don't know as I can let you in any further. Might get myself set high and dry on the mudflats!" He hollered for the anchor to be thrown.

"What do you expect us to do now?" John demanded. "Swim?"

"Naw... I got a dinghy or two. I'll let you load up your women and children, and you can take them as far as the first of those sandbars you see there. You can haul your plunder that way too. One of my mates can bring them back in when you're through. But you better work fast, before the tide turns!"

"This is a fine place for a harbor, Low," grunted Arthur as

the two boats were lowered and the children handed down. "Can't even put in a small sailing vessel."

"Sure you can. Folger's just scared to try." Arthur and John glowered a moment. Louisa pushed between them to break the tension.

The men worked quickly, depositing everyone and everything onto the sandbar. The fog thinned and the dark shapes that had gathered on the distant shore took form. The women gasped and looked away when they saw the nakedness of the Indians. Arthur stared with a lip between his teeth. The others quieted as his stare lengthened, as the muscles along his jawline worked against each other. The Indians congregated, and verbal bantering drifted over the shallow water. Louisa looked for David in the mass. She saw the cabin but missed the fact that there was no roof. She only knew that David *had* to be there.

★   ★   ★

David groaned and rolled over. Stiffness made it slow and he lay back, feeling the heat of his fever and the hunger in his stomach. His head felt odd, as if stuffed with wet goose feathers, and only vaguely could he remember that his supper had been only a cup of tea.

A loud clang made him snap up, but, wincing from the pain and dizziness it brought, he dropped back to his mat. What day was it? He tried to think, to put it together. He remembered that he had known what day it was yesterday, but that didn't help him today. "You're in bad shape, old boy," he said to himself, surprised to hear the hoarseness of his voice. He coughed painfully and cleared the phlegm to try again. "You're in bad—"

Another clang! This time he carefully pulled himself into a sitting position. Chains? The realization exploded the dullness of his mind, and everything came into focus. They had come! Arthur was here!

Pain forgotten, David scrambled to his knees and crawled from his shelter. The rain fell on his face as he stood.

The tide was out, way out. Sealth and his people swarmed the shoreline and David looked beyond them, out to the fog. It hung low, but it couldn't quite hide the ship. The heavy clouds sagged down to the tips of the double masts and rested there.

David felt his pants fall stiffly into place. His clothes were filthy and he thought of it now. Unconsciously he ran a hand over his beard and pushed his fingers at the knots of the torn shirt that still bound his head like a crown.

The rain, no longer a drizzle but a downpour, fell in sheets, wetting both his shirt and his skin. He shivered. Limping on, he made his way to the shore. Had Louisa been allowed to come? Had she wanted to?

Drips of rain fell from a knot over his forehead and dropped onto his nose. He pushed a hand over his face and stared out to see through the gray. He could see two boats, plus shapes of bonnets and skirts. Where was Louisa? Sealth said something. "My family," David said. "They've come." The Indian chief nodded, then smiled. He touched a hand to David's shoulder and gave it a slow squeeze.

"David!"

Louisa?

"David! David!"

"Louisa!" he screamed. He could see her now, with her blue cape and something in her arms. Hobbling over the barnacles, his toes getting scraped over the sharp edges in his haste, he splashed into the water. "Louisa! Louisa!" he shouted with energy he didn't know he had.

She handed her bundle to Mary Ann, then bent to gather her skirts and cape. But as she splashed into a tidal pool—the first of several that lay in narrow strips between long humps of sand—she let them go to run open-armed toward David.

The throbbing of his head forced him to shut his eyes a moment. Pain flashed down his cheek and through his jaw. "Louisa!" he shouted again, then went into the water deeper, feeling the cold go up over his ankles. "Louisa!" He crossed a sandbar and saw her smile. She was laughing!

Then he had her! They swayed as one, their arms locked. His breath came in gulps, painful and searing, and he could feel her warmth against him. The hood of her cape fell and he buried his nose into the coolness of her hair.

"Oh, David!" she cried, clinging to him, sobbing and laughing at the same time. Suddenly she let go and pushed him from her. Her eyes flashed. "Let me see you!" she cried. "Just let me see you!"

"I'm glad you're here," he said, remembering for some reason his last night's visitors. "The skunks. They've taken all my food."

"Skunks? Oh, David!" She laughed again, music after so long, and pulled him close. He held her, kissed her, touched his lips to her tears. She had come to him. They stared a moment, lost in their oneness, and then Louisa saw the bandages. And when she stepped back she saw his foot. Her eyes asked him what happened without having to speak.

"Chopped it three weeks ago," he said, trying to grin. She touched his head and ran a finger along the sheeting. "Neuralgia, I think," he said.

Arthur came up, his arms loaded down with sacks and bags. His face was wet. "It looks as though you could use some decent company!" He nodded grimly in the direction of the beach. Mary Ann walked slowly toward them and David stiffened at the shock of seeing her. She looked so weak, so fragile, her face so worn. Tears ran from her eyes, and he had never seen her cry before. She carried the baby in her arms.

"I wish you hadn't come," he blurted out without thinking, the full gravity of the situation hitting him like a blow between the eyes. The baby... It was too cold, too wet, for such a tiny infant. And Mary... She looked so weak. And there were the Indians, close to 300 now.

"*What?*" One of Arthur's sacks toppled. "*Are you out of your head?*" he demanded of David. "You say you *wish* we hadn't come? Thought it was you who *told* us to come! Thought it was you who said it was a fine country! Thought—"

"Be quiet!" Louisa picked up the fallen sack, let it drip, then plopped it back onto Arthur's load. "He's ill," she said coldly.

"I want to know what he meant by that little remark." Arthur glanced toward the Indians, and Louisa saw the muscles of his jaw tighten again.

"It's...the cabin," David mumbled. His head pounded fiercely and he blinked to try to clear his senses. "There's no roof...no way to keep everybody dry. Lee's gone...had to go get a froe for the shingles...." His words were too choppy, too slow.

"Where'd you say my brother went?" Charles Terry stepped up.

"I'm sorry...your brother?"

"I was told my brother would be here. Leander Terry."

Arthur interrupted. "I want to know what David meant about wishing we hadn't come!"

"Arthur!" Louisa turned on him. "Can't you stop long enough to see how ill David is? Look at his head." She saw him sway, then right himself. "Here," she commanded. "You've got to get out of the water, David. Lean into me." He felt her body support his. For a moment he hesitated, but then turned and let her lead him back up to the beach.

"I want to know what David meant! Are these Indians hostile?" Arthur thundered. "David!"

"He's about to collapse!" Louisa screamed over her shoulder.

"I'm not going to allow anyone to set foot on that beach until I know about these Indians!"

"I don't see any arrows, Arthur!"

A soft crying stopped them. It was more of a whimpering moan than a cry. "Mary Ann?" Arthur dropped everything and the bags lumped at his feet.

"Just stop it," Mary cried. She held the bundle of baby up close to her face. "We can't fight. We just can't!"

"Come on." Arthur asked Lydia to carry the baby, then hoisted Mary Ann up in his arms. "This is no way to begin pioneering," he said with a sudden cheerfulness. "You're right, Mary. As always. Louisa, you get that brother of mine into shore. I'll see to your sister." Charles Terry picked up the fallen bags.

★ ★ ★

Anna pulled at her skirts. They were wet, they dripped, and they clung uncomfortably to her legs. The salt itched. Gertrude, soaked through, fretted to be let down, but there was simply no place to set her.

So this was their Promised Land, Dobbins' dream—the Denny town. They had given up so much—good homes, a standing in the community. Anna had given up her family, her standing as the beautiful Anna Kays. Now here they were, here she was, just plain old Anna Boren, surrounded by stinking savages, standing helplessly wet, and subjected to the curious stares of the naked natives.

At her feet Lydia, Sally, and Mary Ann sat on a log, all of them crying. The children stood about in bewilderment, completely overwhelmed, but having enough sense to pull away whenever one of the Indian squaws reached out to touch their blond heads.

Anna had never seen Mary Ann cry before, and it frightened her. Mary was the inconquerable one, but now she sobbed over her baby. A lump came to Anna's throat, choking her in the rapid expansion. She tried to swallow away the knot. A warm trickle wet her own cheek and she wiped it dry. She wouldn't cry. But the tears fell anyway, noiselessly, dropping faster and faster, until they streamed down and mingled with the rain on her daughter's wet bonnet.

The men worked quickly. Charles Terry, once he was assured that Lee would be back, set to helping the others haul in the supplies that were to last them the winter in the wilderness. Barrels of flour, saltpork, cured bacon, sugar, and cornmeal were lifted and shared by two men. Bags of clothing and bedding were slung two at a time over shoulders. The ship sailed from sight unnoticed.

"I'm sorry," Mary Ann cried when Arthur finally came to sit with her, to see what he could do for her. She wiped her eyes and pushed the wet brim of her sunbonnet back off her face. "It's just that I'm so cold, so tired... And Rollie is so heavy. And he'll be wanting to eat again...*I just want a bed!*" she cried anew. "A real bed, warm covers, a bowl of Ma's hot soup! Oh, Arthur! Why am I crying?"

"Ah, tillicum..." Anna jumped at the sound of the old woman at her elbow. The squaw tried to touch her braids but Anna jerked back. "Oiahl," the Indian said. "Sealth—klootchman!" She grinned amiably and Anna recoiled at the ugly stained teeth, the gaping holes, and the wide, brown gums. The woman poked a finger under Gertrude's chin but Anna stepped away, moving from the nakedness, the stench, the familiarity.

The squaw spat at the sand and her black eyes flashed defiantly. She hobbled over to Arthur and tried to take the baby from his arms. But Arthur held fast and his eyebrows knit together over his nose in much the same way John Denny's did when he was disturbed.

"Ooh..." the woman cooed. But then she frowned and the deep wrinkles of her weathered face went deeper into her skin. She pushed her thumb through Rollie's reddish-gold curls.

"Acha-da, acha-da! Memaloose, memaloose!" she cried, and began to rock an imaginary infant tenderly in her arms.

"What does she say?" Mary screamed. She snatched Rolland from Arthur and sobbed hysterically.

"Acha-da! Acha-da! Memaloose!" the woman moaned.

"David?" Arthur looked about quickly. "David! Can you tell us what the woman says?"

"I don't know." David sat by a glowing fire. Louisa sat close. Wet sand caked their clothes.

"Yes, you do!" wailed Mary Ann. "I can see it in your face! You know what she said! David! Tell me! DAVID! *Please* tell me!"

"Her name is Oiahl," David whispered dejectedly. "She's Sealth's wife, the chief's squaw. She says, 'Too bad, too bad. He die.' "

"Oh! I knew he would! I knew he would!" Mary Ann screamed over and over. "I just haven't the milk! Oh, Arthur! Our baby! He *is* going to die!" Her wet bonnet flapped in the wind and covered over her face. Rolland awoke and wailed.

At the sound of her baby's cry, Mary quieted abruptly. She choked back her sobs and unbuttoned her dress. And the rain fell on her breast, on Rollie's cheek, and then mingled with the tears that still rolled from her chin unrestrained.

18

"About the time we had completed our winter quarters, the brig Leonesa, Capt. Daniel S. Howard, came to anchor in the bay."
—Arthur Armstrong Denny in *Pioneer Days on Puget Sound*

It was Louisa who first noticed the rainbow. It curved out of the sky in a break of clouds and dropped to the distant shore. The others, upon seeing it, drew in long breaths of air. Arthur stood and rubbed a hand over the back of his neck. "Well, Low," he said with an attempt of a smile on his face. "They say women are scarce in these parts so we best take care of what we got." He glanced up to the naked roofline of the cabin. "We'll get started on the roof."

"You need a froe," said David. "That's where Lee's gone."

"We brought one with us."

"You've got one?" David pushed again at the bandages on his head and grimaced with the fresh pain that zigzagged through. "Lee'll be a might perturbed when he gets back and finds that his trip was for naught."

Charles Terry chuckled. "I think you'll find, David Denny, that my brother likes to wander. Ants in his pants, our Ma used to say."

Lydia Low roused herself. Wiping her eyes dry, she leaned over to set a hand to David's forehead. "You, young man..." she scolded emphatically, "...you need to be taken care of 'fore you catch your death of cold. Come on, Louisa. Let's get this handsome man of yours fixed up."

She stood and surveyed the large trees that grew along the beach, set back and thick. The men wandered off and consulted together, while Lydia hollered for Alonzo, her oldest boy, to come and help. "We have a piece of tenting that can be strung over those boughs," she mused. "And that'll afford us a kind of shelter while the men build us a decent roof." She smiled at Louisa. "Good enough to keep the worst of the rain off, I expect.

Al-on-zo!'' she shrieked, allowing her voice to shrill with the last syllable.

"Now don't you fret about David, Liza Boren,'' she said, addressing Louisa directly. "He'll be all right. Now, I want you to rummage through the crate over there and get me some of my John's longjohns. They're good and warm—and dry, to say the least. That'll be a start. And while I'm getting him into them, you, Louisa, you start tearing up any sheeting you can find. Get the iron good and hot—set it right into the flames if you have to. I want those strips ironed brown—scorch 'em good. Then we can get this foot of his taken care of proper.''

It took time, but time was what they had. Eventually a fire blazed brightly and a temporary roof was hung. David was dried and warmed, and his foot was bandaged. Arthur's quinine was found and fed to him.

Rolland began to cry again and Mary Ann tried to nurse him, but it was no use. He screamed in frustration and hunger, thrashing wildly beneath his blanket. Oiahl appeared crying "Acha-da, memaloose,'' over and over until Mary started to cry again.

The stench hovered about wherever Oiahl went, and when at last she scooped up an old bucket and hurried out to a sand-bar Louisa turned to David. His face was flushed and he leaned against the trunk of a tree. He sensed her eyes upon him and smiled. "Why *do* they stink so?'' she asked him.

"Rancid dogfish oil. They smear themselves with it to keep warm. The rain just runs off them.''

"Why don't they wear clothes?''

"They used to. But the Hudson Bay gives them blankets for their furs. And they like blankets.'' He shut his eyes.

"Why do they prefer blankets to clothes?''

"Many blankets—more wealth.''

"You go to sleep.'' Louisa covered him with a blanket.

"Only if you don't ask me any more questions...''

"I won't.'' She turned her attention back to Oiahl. The woman had a sharp stick in her hand and she dug furiously into the sand. At times she reached down and scooped something up and plopped it into her pail. When she came back to the shelter she was smiling. Rain dripped from the bottom of the pail as she set it down at Mary's feet. Shells, round and about the size of the small trinket boxes that Louisa had hidden in her trunk for Kate and Nora's Christmas, filled the bucket.

Oiahl motioned for the caldron to be hung over the fire; then, taking a sharp stone in her hand, she began to pound on the shells, one by one, to break them open. Gray, pulpy flesh filled the interiors, and these she scooped into the pot. She added a bit of water from a bucket that had been set in the rain, and waited.

They all waited. Occasionally the men, straddled high on the walls of the cabin, would pause in their frantic pace to peer down, to see what it was that she was doing. But, like the women, they were unable to guess, so they resumed their work.

Dobbins and Arthur took turns wielding the froe, the small L-shaped tool whose scarcity had held up the completion of the cabin. The others pounded the newly made shingles into place on the supporting rafters that David and Lee had put up weeks before.

After a time, just as Sally Bell began to get impatient to start some sort of supper, Oiahl poured off the water, let it cool, then gently took Rolland from Mary Ann, who handed him over with little resistance this time. Louisa watched with held breath as the old woman carefully dropped some of the warm liquid into Rollie's mouth.

The baby sucked, then smacked his lips open and shut. "He likes it!" squealed Mary Ann. Kate and Nora peered above her shoulders and they all leaned in, laughing and exclaiming. Oiahl added more of the broth to Rollie's lips and then hugged the baby.

"What does she say, David?" Louisa whispered.

"That he's not going to die...that he will live."

Louisa smiled and watched Mary Ann watch her baby eat.

The sun went down but the rain kept on. By evening only half the roof was completed; the other half lay exposed to the constant drip of the darkened sky. Arthur, William, and Charles struggled to drape the canvas from the tree boughs and some borrowed Indian mats in an attempt to waterproof the cabin. When this was done Dobbins carried in the hot caldron, and they gathered in the small space to eat their supper. The cornmeal mush was filling, the stout log walls kept off the wind, and no one said anything about the muddy floors.

The last of the light vanished while they ate. And then, of one accord, they did their best to spread out bedrolls, everyone too exhausted to even clean up the dirty dishes. Sally Bell just set them outside the open door and the rain dripped into them. Louisa shook out her blanket and laid it next to David.

"I'm glad you came," David whispered in the dark. "Pa say it was all right to get married?" He spoke softly, just words of air, and Louisa had to lie close to hear them.

"Shh..." She touched his lips. "We'll talk of it in the morning." His hand was hot in her fingers. He was quiet, and his breath came in short and shallow swells. "Good night," she whispered, kissing his cheek. But he was already asleep.

Louisa lay awake for a long time, just enjoying being near David again and listening to the sounds outside—the waves, the wind, the lonely call of the Indians, the seagulls.

"The rain keeps dripping into my face," she heard Kate whisper. Mary Ann shifted her closer to the wall, and quiet settled in. Louisa kissed David again and he turned to her unconsciously. She leaned close, finally sleeping herself.

The next day the roof was completed, and by the first of December three more cabins were up. They were all in close proximity, edged up to the trees along the beach. They faced north and west. Elliott Bay was to their north and around the head of the land to the east. The Sound and the distant arm of the Olympic Peninsula were directly to the west.

Fireplaces were put into the cabins, made from numerous sticks and small stones, then daubed together with blue clay. Large stones served sufficiently as andirons, and flat stones for the hearths. A log, split lengthwise, was fastened to the wall as a mantel.

Lofts were added in some of the cabins so that the flooring stretched out over much of the cabin, making a place for the children to play during the long and rainy days. The girls cut paper dolls from a Godey's *Lady's Book,* and the boys were usually content to play with their army men, handmade from old clothespins, and to collect newer toys as David carved them.

Immediate survival concentrated everyone's energies during those first three weeks. Working from early morning, when the fog and rain blanketed their New York, the men sawed, hauled logs, and split shakes. The women made do with the scanty provisions and made home out of log walls. It wasn't until the last cabin was erected that concern for their future was given time for discussion. And, like sour milk, strained discussions took place.

"Tell me again which land you claimed, Low, and how much," said Arthur one day after lunch.

"My legal amount. 320 acres."

"Leave any for the rest of us?"

"What do you mean, leave any for the rest of us?"

"Just what I said."

"Denny! We're the only folks up here! Of course I left you some. Oh, excuse me... There's Luther Collins and his friends up the Duwamish."

"You've staked out the whole Point."

"Yes."

"And so where does that leave the rest of us when your harbor goes in, Low? I'll tell you. Sitting right here on *your* land!"

On December 10, eight months to the day after leaving Illinois, a ship sailed into Elliott Bay and dropped anchor. Captain Daniel S. Howard of the *Leonesa,* supplier of pilings to the city of San Francisco, introduced himself and presented a contract for timber. And so, like clabbered milk and butter, the friendships thickened; survival was dependent upon it, and they thrived. New York was begun. John Low had the site of the new city. And Arthur Denny threw in his muscle to make it work.

19

"Alki had not been a general camping place for the Indians, but soon after we landed and began clearing the ground for our buildings they commenced to congregate, and continued coming until we had over a thousand in our midst.... Although they seemed very friendly toward us we did not feel safe in objecting to their building thus near to us for fear of offending them...."

—Arthur Armstrong Denny in *Pioneer Days on Puget Sound*

"Mr. Denny said he'd carve me an Injun boat next!" shouted Alonzo down to Lydia. He had his head dangled over the edge of the loft. Lydia sighed and straightened, putting a hand to her spine, down low where it ached. Her face was warm from the fire and she gouged knuckles into her eyes, being careful not to drip any of the hot cornmeal mush from the long spoon. Not that it mattered. It was only a dirt floor.

"It's *Indian* boat, Alonzo," she said wearily, trying not to think of her lovely stove back home or of the new stove that Captain Howard had promised to bring her on his return voyage. "And how many times have I told you not to lean over that loft? You're going to fall one of these times and crack your skull." Alonzo slid back on his stomach and rested his chin on the flooring.

"Mama!" squealed little Mary. "He's got his feet on our dolls!"

"It's my loft too, ya know!"

"Well, we can play!"

"You don't live here, Laura Bell! Ding, dong, Laura Bell!"

"Mama! Alonzo is calling..."

The front door opened and Lydia jabbed the wooden spoon back into the caldron. For a while John's new door had worked well in keeping the Indians out. He had sawn it in two, bolting the bottom half shut and leaving the top free to swing open and to let light in—and to satisfy the curiosity of the natives. But before the month passed they had figured out how to take a long

145

stick and release the catch. As David had said, "They are not without intelligence."

"Hello, Curley," Lydia said to Suwalth, one of Sealth's men. They called him Curley because of his dark, curly hair. The man nodded and grinned, then began to snoop about as usual. He sniffed the mush, stirred the spoon and abandoned it, then crossed the floor to inspect a small sailboat that David had carved for one of the boys. Curley wore only a shirt with half the buttons missing.

"What do you want, Curley?" she asked him.

"Nothing."

"MAMA! Will you *please* tell Alonzo to quit it?"

Lydia hollered up to the loft and went back to the fire. She stirred the mush a few times, keeping an eye on Curley as he wandered and tried to ignore the fighting upstairs. Maybe John could take them for a walk when he got home, if he wasn't too tired.

The first three days after getting Captain Howard's order the men had managed to cut only 205 feet of timber. But they were getting better. The captain would return the first of the year, so that gave them just over two weeks to get the job done. He had said that San Francisco kept burning their wharves, creating a constant need for pilings, and if they could make his trip worthwhile they could have a steady livelihood. Lydia still didn't know if the man had been joking about the piers burning, but she certainly wasn't going to ask John. It was sufficient that San Francisco needed the lumber, and the men had the drive to make it work.

"Me and Johnny want the girls out 'a here!" shouted Alonzo, dangling from the loft again.

"Alonzo! I'm going to take this spoon to your bottom if I so much as hear another peep out of you! You hear? *Curley!*" she shouted. *"Where are you going?"*

The short Indian headed for the door with the last cured ham behind his back. Lydia whirled about and, without thinking, spoon in hand, she slapped the Indian across the bare buttocks. Hot cornmeal mush clung to his skin, and some dropped to the floor.

The ham fell and Curley grabbed his buttocks. His shriek brought the other women on the run. They gathered at the open door to stare in open-eyed astonishment. Curley bellowed in rage, hopping wildly about. He roared, waving a fist in Lydia's face. Five little faces, lined up and leaning over the loft, watched in horrified fascination.

"Stop right there!"

John barged through the door, gun low and ready to fire. Curley jerked to a halt, looking down the rifle pointed at him.

"You come near my wife again and I'll kill you!" John slammed the door shut and threw the bolt. Lydia sat down and cried.

★   ★   ★

From time to time the Indians, close to a thousand by the time the newcomers had been there three weeks, liked to show that they still had command. One day one of them had stepped out of the woods and had held a gun to Mary Ann's stomach while she hung clothes. She had merely returned the masked stare and turned away. The Indians generally seemed interested only in showing that they had power to frighten; they never inflicted real harm. But with John's threat they had all gathered. Sealth spoke, addressing the throng, and his deep and powerful voice carried down the beach. He spoke with authority, standing tall over them, one hand held out and the other, as always, holding his blanket in place.

Everyone crowded into the Lows' cabin for the night. The children were put to bed, although none of them slept. They listened intently to the converstion below, to the sounds that came from the Indian camp. Christmas next week was forgotten.

David stood by the door, his cap pulled tight around his ears. His fever had passed and much of his strength had returned, and although he favored the injured foot, that had healed too. He stood stiffly, hands in his pockets, concentrating on Sealth's voice and words. In just the short time he had been with the Indians, he had picked up a lot of their language.

"Can you understand anything, Dave? Anything at all?" Arthur asked.

"No. He's speaking too quickly. He's angry. I can tell that."

"Still trying to learn the fool Duwamish, Dave?" Lee asked. He had returned with the froe, and he now sat with a rifle across his knee. "You just don't give up, do you?"

All the men sat with rifles. The women paced the floor, praying silently, trying to smile. Lydia blamed herself for the whole incident but John refused to let her berate herself. "It was me," he told her. "I shouldn't have threatened him."

"They're not going to do anything," Arthur added. "Sealth's a decent sort, not hot under the collar."

"He's not got a collar," said John. Arthur glared and the silence came again.

Charles Terry got up to pace in front of the fireplace. "We need to be making plans," he said. He glanced nervously out the door. "I want to get my own cabin built, get my store operating proper. And I can see we're going to have to get a team of oxen somewhere if we want to continue this lumber business. We can't be hauling logs by hand out of the woods."

"Luther Collins was telling me of a team for sale in the Puyallup Valley," Lee put in. "I could go get them for you!"

"Collins tell you about a team?" Charles regarded his brother a moment. John went to a corner box, dug around a bit, then came over and handed Lee a roll of bills. "You want to leave first thing in the morning?" he asked.

"I'll help you buy them, Low," said Arthur.

"No, that's all right. I'll buy them."

"I'd like to share in the costs."

"No, really. It's my town."

Arthur's mouth went straight. "That's right, I do keep forgetting…"

"Hey! They're breaking up!" David stepped outside and everyone stood, hardly daring to look at one another, afraid to see each other's fear. Unconsciously the men gripped their guns. All watched David.

"Seems like they're just going to bed," he exclaimed. "They're just drifting apart, climbing into their separate shelters."

A stillness came to the beach—only the sound of the waves, an occasional snarl of a cougar, and the rustle of tree boughs rubbing in the wind.

"What do you make of it?" Charles asked.

The others just looked at each other. "Maybe we should all stay the night here," said William Bell. "We could post a watch."

Charles said, "All right. I'll take it. John, that all right?"

Louisa slipped up to the loft and lay down with the children. They watched her, their eyes following her movements. "Shh," she whispered. "I'll tell you a story."

Morning came as all other mornings came to New York— with the caw of a gull, the smell of Indian fires and smoking fish, and the laughing children. After a breakfast of cold biscuits and molasses, the men consulted, sent Lee off on his trip to Puyallup, left David behind to guard the camp, and then set out for the woods with saws over their shoulders. The women dispersed to their various cabins to do the daily chores that had to be done. Lydia set to clearing up the chaos of her house.

The ham still sat on the floor, pushed to the wall, and somehow she just couldn't bring herself to pick it up. The memory of her hasty actions and the danger she had put them all in was too poignant. Instead she started on the beds, pulling covers into place and fluffing out the pillows. The sun came out and she sent the children off to dig clams, the little round shells that Oiahl had shown them their first day on the Sound.

The door opened and Lydia stopped short. Curley stood in the sunlight, buttons undone on his shirt, hands behind his back. Behind him stood David, trying to hold back a smile. Lydia felt her breathing slow, her heart calm. "Hello, Curley," she said.

The Indian stepped in and thrust a burlap sack at her. "Sealth say stealing bad. Cultas," he added in the Chinook. He pushed the bag into her hand, and when she stood uncomprehending he dumped the contents out over the newly-made bed.

"Why, David!" Lydia exclaimed. "Come look! It's all the things we've been missing the last couple of weeks! Look! Here's my clothesline! And baby Rollie's nightgown! And look! Louisa's red handkerchief! Didn't she say your Pa gave that to her?"

David took it in his hand. "They love anything red," he said. "Sealth must have really been angry. Angry at them. They'd have never returned this without his insistence." He shoved it into a pocket. "I'll keep it. It'll make a good present."

Curley nodded and said hello. "You mean good-bye?" David asked him. Curley nodded again, then waved and was gone. David followed him to the door.

"Think you'll be all right now, Ma'am?" he asked. He looked around the room. "You got this place looking pretty good. All for this ham, Ma'am. You might want to rehang it before the raccoons swipe it.''

"Yes, Sir. I'll do that.''

And so when John came home for supper that night, they ate their meal in silence, the ham hanging off the wall behind them. And there it hung every supper the rest of the winter, for somehow Lydia couldn't bring herself to cook it. It was a comfort just to know it was there.

"Somewhere in the world, every year, there is a 'first' Christmas, in celebration of that first Christmas of all, in Bethlehem. So it had been since the birth of Jesus, and so it was on December 25, 1851, at Alki Point, where Seattle began...."

—Nard Jones, a Seattle historian, in an article written for the *Post-Intelligencer*, 108 years after that first Christmas at Alki Point.

" 'And it came to pass in those days that there went out a decree from Caesar Augustus that all the world should be taxed.' " A soft glow from the fire filled the small cabin with a cozy light. Louisa sat at the table—a puncheon one that David had made, with the rounded sides of the split logs facing downward and the top sanded smooth. She quietly wrote to Pamelia while Arthur read the Christmas story aloud from his Bible.

It had been a good Christmas. David had shot a wild goose and they had eaten the last of their potatoes. Visitors from the Collins settlement had come to share it with them, and they had all laughed and eaten, and gotten to know each other. Louisa paused in her writing to look over to the children. They were in bed, their small shell boxes and the trinkets she had given them tucked beneath their pillows. Their eyes were shut, the sound of Arthur's voice and the words of the familiar old story of Christ's birth having put them to sleep. Louisa smiled, remembering again their ecstatic cries upon awakening when they had discovered that Santa Claus had remembered to visit two small girls in so wild a country. Getting them to even hang their stockings the night before had been hard, for they had been convinced that Santa Claus only knew how to go to Illinois. But Louisa had insisted.

"Thank you again for the seeds, Liza," said Mary Ann, seeing that she watched the children. "And for their gifts." Rolland stirred in her arms, and she lifted her hand to rub his head, touching softly the tiny red curls that sprang up. "You've made the nicest Christmas I think I've ever had. Maybe because it was such a surprise." She smiled. "I still can't believe that you actually managed to keep such secrets all the way from Cherry Grove."

"Snuck them on board the night before we left," said David. He sat near the fire cleaning his gun.

"You knew too?"

"I didn't know about your seeds or the shell boxes. But I knew she was smuggling something." He looked over at her and grinned, then slowly raised his eyebrows. She felt color come to her face and looked down quickly at the pages on the table. Her mirror was still hidden, waiting.

"You mean Louisa had something else tucked away?" Mary asked. She got up to lay Rollie in his cradle—a crate, really, made over into a small crib. David blew into the empty muzzle of his rifle and Louisa picked up her quill. The new year would be in a week and it would bring Captain Howard. And he had promised to take any mail out with him. "Well, do you?" Mary asked, coming close to the table.

"Now what kind of a question is that to ask the lady?" David chided. "I expect if she does it'll come out of hiding sooner or later. Am I right, Liza?"

Louisa didn't look up and Mary went back to her rocking chair. Arthur had made it for her somehow, and she picked up her knitting. "Well, I can't wait until next Christmas," she laughed. "Will we know then, Liza?"

"Maybe."

"Well, thank you again for the seeds. Now I can start to plan in my head the fine garden I'll have come spring. You did bring some for yourself, didn't you?"

"You remember, Mary, that we're not settled yet," reminded Arthur. "We're on Low's land and will have to move on come spring. We need to get our own claim."

"I can still plan, can't I?"

Arthur shrugged and went back to his reading.

"You brought some for yourself, didn't you?" Mary asked again.

"I have enough." Louisa spoke absently, thinking now of Pamelia and their sweetbriar tryst. She missed Pam, the scent of Mr. Dunlap's garden, and spring. The wild roses that grew up on the Sound (finding root wherever the sun could come through) were nice, but not like the flowers back home.

"Louisa?"

Dark had settled in, and Louisa turned up the wick in the lantern. Shadows danced on the log walls, making large and lumpy shapes. "Yes, Mary?" she asked, forcing herself not to think of home, of sweetbriar in the spring.

"Is something wrong?"

"No."

"You're missing Pamelia, aren't you?"

"I am." She glanced up and saw Mary's gentle face, soft in the light of the fire and lantern. "But spring always comes, does it not?" Quill in hand, she began to write again:

> We all stood the hardships of the journey across the plains well and have reason to be thankful that neither sickness nor death overtook us. Soon after reaching the Willamette Valley, Father took a claim and settled on it. Arthur and Dobbins remained in Portland some two months, then boarded a vessel bound for the sound. After a short voyage we landed at New York. If I were to attempt to give a description of my feelings during that short voyage you perhaps would laugh. We all landed safely at the destined point, but when we reached land it was raining and we had nothing but a camp to live in; everything looked wild and gloomy. There was but one white family nearer than 30 miles except our own company, which consisted of four families. We are pleased with this country and I often wish that you were here, that you might take a view of the snow-capped mountains and evergreen valleys of our country.

"Would you like to go for a walk, Liza?" David stood behind her, his hands set over her shoulders. Louisa put the quill away and leaned into him, letting him rub her neck.

"I wish you wouldn't," Mary spoke up. "Arthur and I worry when you're gone, that you might let temptation overtake you!"

"Oh, Mary!" Louisa frowned. "There is simply no time for David and me to be alone without our walks!"

"You shouldn't be alone," interrupted Arthur. He set the Bible to his lap. "Not without a chaperone."

"Oh, for heaven's sakes! We are engaged! And everywhere

we turn in here there are eyes! Surely you can remember how it was when you and Mary courted!''

"The children..." hushed Mary Ann. She looked uncomfortable, her face strained.

"You are *not* engaged," said Arthur. "There's the difference. Pa's not granted you that yet."

"But, Arthur!"

"You are *not* engaged!"

"It's all right," whispered David. He bent low and gave her shoulders a squeeze. "Let's not spoil Christmas. Come, finish your letter and then we'll have a game of checkers and maybe sing some Christmas carols. Here, I'll set with you and wait." He pulled up a chair and sat across the table from her, watching her face in the lamplight. But Louisa, resolved that she would take a walk whether or not Arthur liked it, bent to her task. She wrote quickly:

> We are all well. Dobbins' wife is almost as flesh as your mother was when we left you. Little Gertrude can stand up at the table and call for salmon and clams.
>
> I would like to see any or all of our friends in this country—I do not think that it is a perfect paradise that is without fault. That country I never expect to find on this earth—but perhaps it has as few faults as any. The health, soil, climate and navigation is not surpassed on the western coast. All that it needs is enterprising permanent settlers to make it one of the most delightful countries in the world.
>
> P.S. Catherine and Lenora send their best love and want to tell Dully that they often talk about her, and that they do not go to school but they try to study their lessons. They send Dully some of Gertrude's and their little brother's hair. Nora says to tell her that his name is Rolland Herschel.

Louisa took the tiny curls of hair—Gertrude's black and Rollie's red—and laid them carefully in the middle of her pages, then took a deep breath. She let it out slowly to quell the rapid beating of her heart. "David and I are going for a walk," she said suddenly, not looking up. She pushed the cork into the ink bottle.

"I've told you my word on the matter," said Arthur. "And I had hoped that that would settle everything."

"It doesn't settle anything. I respect your opinion, Arthur, but I am, after all, 24 and not a child to be told what I can or cannot do." She rose, went to the pegs that stuck out of the wall by the door, and found her coat. "David, I'll be at the beach," she said as she passed him, then strode from the house.

Splintered light came from the other cabins. Laughter and loud guffaws at times penetrated the quiet. The tide was in, bringing the roll of the waves, and Louisa walked north along the water's edge, sidestepping tossed-up seaweed, bits of bark, and old stones that had never known rest. David didn't follow, and she blinked back the tears.

Words of peace on earth drifted from Anna and Dobbins' cabin and Louisa paused to listen. A log, round and wet, its bark long since battered from it, lay nearby, and she went to it. She sat and shivered, looking across the beach to the camp of the Indians, and to the moon—a beautiful Christmas moon, full and round.

David came and sat beside her. She felt his warmth, his quiet. He took her hand and slipped it into his jacket pocket. For a long time they sat silently, each thinking his own thoughts, wondering about the other's.

"We've gotten more than 13,000 feet of timber cut for Captain Howard," said David suddenly. He picked up a small pebble to toss out to the sea. It didn't call for a response, and Louisa knew none to give. The pebble hit the water with a plop.

"I suppose you're wondering why it took me so long to come out," David ventured. She nodded. "You'd never be happy married to me if you had to live with Ma and Pa's disapproval. And I can't do that to you, Liza. I love you too much for that. I want what is best."

"But I want you!" The tears came. "I'm an old maid, David! I'm 24!"

"I know. You told Arthur, remember?" He tried to smile for her.

"I'm not getting any younger!" she wailed.

"Hey, hey. I'm not either. Thank goodness," he added. She had to smile. "Our only hope is to wait, and bide our time," he told her. "You know Pa will eventually give in." He kissed her then, and she gave herself to him, to make her his own.

"Shh," he whispered, wiping the back of his fingers over her cheek. "You musn't cry. It's Christmas."

"Oh, David," she sobbed, clinging to him. "I just want to be with you, to be married to you! I don't want to wait."

He laughed and hugged her, walking her to the water. "I haven't had a chance to give you your present. You want it?"

"A present for me?"

He reached into his pocket and held out the handkerchief.

"Oh, David! Pa's red handkerchief. Wherever did you find it?"

"It was in the bag that Curley brought in last week. I just hung onto it—figured it would make a good Christmas present." His smile was soft in the moonlight. "There is no mercantile around here that carries anything pretty—no silver combs or anything like that. Charles has only boots and axes..."

"Oh, David..." She cried then. She cried hard. She cried for last Christmas, when David had told her that Arthur had picked out the silver combs when *he* really had. She cried for Pamelia, for Illinois. She cried for James and their broken relationship, for Pa, for Ma. She cried for herself, for David.

He held her, then began to walk with her around the Point. He said nothing, just letting her cry. She held Pa's handkerchief in her hand and on occasion lifted it to her eyes, only to cry some more.

When they came into full view of Elliott Bay David stopped and took the wet handkerchief from her. "This is my Christmas present to you." He tucked the red into her hand and closed her fingers over it. "It's my promise to you that we *will* marry. I, David Thomas Denny, *will* marry you, Louisa Boren. I promise." He closed his hand over hers so that the handkerchief was squeezed tight. "You hold onto that, Liza. You hold onto that and don't let go."

"Then we are engaged?"

"Yes, Liza. We are engaged."

That was all she needed. That was enough. She and David *would* marry! Someday. David had said they would.

The moon slipped behind a cloud. David's face was almost hidden by the darkness and his beard. "I love you," she whispered.

"Merry Christmas." David's lips were cold, wet, so alive, so tender. She felt his hands in her hair, pulling her silver combs loose.

Her curls fell, and the scent of spring, of sweetbriar, was strong.

21

"In February of '52, Bell, Boren, and the Dennys carried out their plan to explore the eastern side of Elliott Bay and take soundings offshore in their combined search for locations for claims and for a good harbor. At daylight on a cold gray morning these four men pushed their canoe off the beach at 'New York' and paddled across the Bay...."

—Roberta Frye Watt in *Four Wagons West*

January 1st came and went. The new year saw the return of Captain Howard, the arrival of Lydia's stove and of supplies for Charles' store, and an order of pilings filled. With the oxen that Lee had been able to get, they had filled the order easily enough, although they had had to go further back to get available timber.

Captain Howard was pleased and offered a larger contract, which the men accepted eagerly. He sailed away with orders for more flour, cotton batting, two bolts of calico, and a tin of pepper. And with his departure life slipped into a routine. The new year turned into one like any other. January passed. February began.

A cold, gray mist hung heavily on the morning of February the 11th. William Bell and Arthur worked together behind one of the cabins, sharpening the various saws (a task that had to be done every so often), blowing puffs of white fog to the gray from their lips.

"What do you say to taking the day off?" William Bell said suddenly. "We could go get some of those soundings we keep talking about." He waited for Arthur to think about it before expecting a reply.

Arthur set the saw in his hands to the wall of the cabin, then hung it on a nail up off the ground. He walked down to the beach to stare west out over the Sound. The distant mountains were misted over, and the sea absorbed the moisture that hung low.

Problems other than being on Low's land had come up, and Arthur looked to the gray sky. To him—and to David, Bell, and Dobbins—John's New York just wasn't going to work. They were having to go back too far to get their timber. Hauling it out to the beach wasted too much time. And the water was just too shallow. Large ships would never be able to put in. And while a wharf thrust out into the Sound would attract any traffic once it opened up, it would also be subjected to any winds that whipped up the Sound. If a city were to survive it had to be one that was born out of rich forests of unlimited trees, easily accessible. It had to have a deepwater harbor that was sheltered from wind. And Elliott Bay seemed to be the answer. They only had to get some soundings to find out how deep the water ran.

Perhaps that was why Arthur hesitated. He didn't want to find that Elliott Bay wouldn't work. He didn't want to leave the area, and it *was* unlikely that a bay could run as deep as was needed for large ships. John was no doubt right about *that*.

"You talk to David and Dobbins?" Arthur asked when he went back to where William waited.

"David's gone to see if he can't get a canoe from Jim or George."

"Jim? George?"

"Sealth's sons. You don't remember?"

Arthur shrugged. David was always talking of the Indians, giving them Christian names. "What'll we use for a plumbline?"

"Dobbins is working on it. He got some horseshoes from Charles and is trying to talk Mary Ann into lending us her clothesline."

Arthur laughed at that. Ever since the Indians had stolen Lydia's, the women guarded their clotheslines carefully. Dobbins would have to talk persuasively.

"Guess I'll go tell John we're taking the day off," he said.

"Was hoping you'd volunteer."

Arthur pushed his hands into his pockets and hurried over to the cabin they'd first built. "Hey, Low!" he hollered through the door. "I think we'll take the day off. See if we can't find a place for our claims!"

"Today?" John appeared, shaving cream lathered over his cheeks. He held a razor in his hand. "Wish you'd think on my offer. It still stands, you know. You can have your pick of land, and once we get this platted, it's yours for the taking."

"Thanks, John. But I want the acreage." They judiciously avoided talk of the harbor.

"Suit yourself, then." John motioned with his razor, crossing his neck under the long chin-beard. "It's your hanging."

"How's that?"

"Charles has that store of his set up now. We'll be getting newcomers come spring, not to mention the traffic between California and the gold mines up north."

"No one's going up there, Low. The *Georgiana*—the ship that sailed for the Queen Charlottes just two days before we left Portland—and those miners Folger took up haven't been heard of. No one's going to go up with that black cloud."

"Some think gold is worth it."

"Then you don't mind if we take off?"

John shrugged, then continued shaving his cheeks.

★   ★   ★

David watched Arthur coil the wet rope, twisting it around his elbow and catching it between his thumb and fingers. "Still can't find bottom?" He leaned over the canoe to help scoop up the horseshoes.

"Nope. Paddle south a bit. We'll try there."

Dobbins and William dipped the paddles into the sloppy water, and the borrowed boat shot forward over the small whitecaps. David grinned as the wind swept his cheeks. He pulled on his beard; he liked it now—now that Louisa had shown him how to trim it. It made him look older than his 19 years. Well, older than his 20; it would be his birthday next month, come Saint Patrick's Day.

All the men were grinning. Their pleasure over their findings escaped their usual restraints of self-control. So far, all of the eastern side of the bay was proving to run deep—deep within just feet of the shore. And they had taken soundings all the way from the very north point of the bay to about two-thirds of the way south.

"Let's not get too jovial," cautioned Arthur. "The most sheltered area is yet to come. Further south the winds will be at their least, and that's where we want the depth." He dropped the horseshoes into the water again, and Dobbins and William plunged their paddles in deep, the blades perpendicular to the canoe to hold them still. The horseshoes made a soft plop as they broke the surface, then sank, and Arthur let the line slip easily through his hand.

"Sun's high noon." William bent back his neck to look at the soft pastel blob of yellow beyond the gray. The fog had lifted a bit, and in spots blue peeked through. "Let's eat. I'm hungry."

"Good idea. My fingers are about frozen." Arthur pulled in the line, again unable to find the bottom, and set it to the floor of the canoe.

Dobbins set his paddle into the water, the tip of it angled ahead and to the left. The dugout followed the path that was pointed and they drew close to the rocky beach. All along the shore steep banks rose up, the thick forest capping them. In spots, massive roots protruded from the banks, bare twistings out of the clay.

"There's a small spring just ahead," said David. "Seems to have a bit of beach we can pull up on."

The canoe scraped the pebbles and the men climbed out, testing their legs carefully at first, moaning as the blood surged back into their feet. To ride an Indian canoe you had to kneel, your feet crossed under, to maintain the fragile balance of the dugout. Once they had learned the proper way to sit in one of the cedar boats it explained to them the terribly bowed legs of the Indians. Sealth didn't have the deformity: being of noble birth he had never had to paddle his own canoe and had been able to sit with legs stretched out straight along the boat's floor. It helped to explain his height too.

"Can't you just see it?" said Arthur. The lifting fog revealed the promontory of land that was New York directly across from them. "Any fool can see that New York is too exposed. Right here is where the harbor ought to be. Hey, David, can't you see the wharves, the ships by the dozens, the stores, the places of business lining busy streets right where we sit now?"

"It'll take a bit of clearing." David peered up the slope to the stream that trickled down past their feet to the water.

"There's a break in the tree line. Come on, want to explore a bit?" Arthur was already to his feet. Dobbins followed and they all scrambled up the slippery bank.

Fallen trees, their trunks burnt black, lay at every angle. Scorched, gnawed-off looking stumps stood in small clusters. But beyond the desolation the forest grew thick. The mountains, their snowtops seeming to hang from the sky like wash on a line, rested above the tips of the green. The ceiling of the fog hung like a veil over the beauty.

David ambled over to a fallen alder near the edge of the desecration. Its roots were torn up and were stretched out, tangled, as if still writhing with the throes of its death. One of the numerous wild rosebushes grew out of the twistings, tiny pink buds opening, waiting for the sun to warm the petals.

"It's a gentle reminder that life goes on, isn't it?" David jumped, unaware that Arthur had followed him, and his knee jarred the roots, making the pink tremble. Arthur watched the flowers, then looked out to the rest of the fireswept landscape.

"I like this, Dave," he said. "If we do decide to relocate over here, this is my claim. We'll put the port down below and see if a trail can't be opened up through the Cascades." He waved a hand behind him to the distant mountain range. "Give folks another option other than just heading on into the Willamette. They get sidetracked there. And, Dave." He paused. "We'll lose them if we can't grub a road through somehow."

"What about the others—me, our claims?"

"Patkanim told me there's a pass of sorts through there." Arthur spoke of Sealth's cousin, the chief of the Snoqualmie tribe. He was lost in his own plans, not listening to David at all. David sighed. The other two men talked excitedly between themselves. "What about our claims?" David tried again, this time louder and more direct.

"What?"

"Our claims. You can't just come in and say, 'This is mine. I like it.' "

"You can't file, Dave. You know that."

David rubbed his chin, feeling the bristles of his beard. It made him look older, but that wasn't good enough. The fact still remained that he wasn't 21. Wouldn't be for another whole year.

"Surely you knew that, didn't you?"

"Guess I didn't really want to think about it."

"What did you expect? The law to change just for you?" David walked away. He wanted to be alone, to think, to sort out the mess in his head. "Surely you knew that—that's the main reason Pa can't have you marrying Louisa," Arthur said, following him.

"What do you mean?" David spun.

"How can you give Louisa a home if you can't even hold property?"

Of course! It was so obvious! Why hadn't he thought of it before? He couldn't marry Louisa and still live under Arthur's roof. It wasn't so much the age difference that bothered Pa. It was the land that was the issue! "What am I going to do?" he asked, stunned, unable to think.

"Going to do? You're asking me?" Arthur sounded incredulous. "I'm afraid you're in this all by yourself. Things would have been better if you'd have just let Louisa marry James."

"Marry James!" David exploded. "Are you out of your mind?"

They made their way down the embankment and tossed the leftover lunches into the canoe. "You'll think of something," said Arthur, whistling up for Dobbins and William. "You're a Denny. Dennys always come out ahead. And they do that by thinking," he added.

They spent another hour or so taking more readings and found that the deep water did run all the way south. As they approached the tidal flats in the most southern piece of the bay, the water shallowed out and the steep banks along the shore leveled off, sloping gradually to sea level. The forest gave way to pasture, and another stream wound its way through the tall grasslands, running alongside an old Indian hut that was ready to fall. Wild rosebushes tangled all around the decaying structure.

A curious knoll pushed up out of the water just where the shoreline ran east-west instead of north-south. Its banks stood about 30 or 40 feet high and were steep. It was easy to see that at high tide the knoll would be an island. Dobbins stopped paddling to look at it. "Something about that makes you feel like you own the world," he said. "I like it."

"Sounds to me like you and Arthur have pretty much decided you like it over here," said William Bell.

"It'd make good farmland—this marshy area," said Dobbins. "We could bring up a couple of those milk cows that Pa's got waiting for us in Portland."

"Should we tell John we've found our place?" asked Arthur. "Should we put in our stakes?"

"I'm already working on a name!" Dobbins sat in the stern as he paddled toward home.

"How about Boston? Matches John's New York!" William suggested.

"I don't know, Bell. John and Charles have about given up trying to make the name stick. It'll be Alki, just plain old Alki, before too long. Especially once we get our town going. That's as certain as the tide turns."

David quit listening to his brother. He didn't care what they called the place or where they laid their claims. Pa wouldn't let him get married because he couldn't have land.

Land. It was everywhere around him, just for the taking—if you were over 21. And there was no telling what could happen in a year, with settlers coming out and grabbing it all up while he was forced to sit back and wait for time to pass on.

Why hadn't he thought of it sooner? He didn't know. He was too busy thinking about Louisa, scheming of ways to get Pa's permission to marry her, to minimize the age span. Day and night he had been trying to think of ways to convince Pa that he was mature enough, that he and Louisa really did love each other, that the age difference shouldn't matter. And all this time it had been the *land* that was the problem. He scowled. There was nothing he could do about that. Dear God, what could be done?

"Yup, once we get a road through Patkanim's hills, just watch this place boom!"

"Arthur is back to that," thought David. The man never gave up. He turned to look at the hills. In reality they were a formidable barrier between them and the East.

"You're thinking too big again," he said. "Can't you relax and wait for things to happen?"

"You mean drift?" Arthur's face went rigid, the muscles stiffening the line of his cheek. "That's one thing I won't do, Dave, and that's drift. Get an idea in your head and go after it. That's the only way to succeed in life. That and hard work."

Get an idea in your head and go after it. There was no use in arguing with Arthur, especially when there was a ring of truth to his words. His own idea was to marry Louisa, but that was getting him nowhere. Maybe he just hadn't gone after it hard enough.

William and Dobbins pushed hard and dipped their oars deep. Silent now, they worked rhythmically and powerfully, making the most of each sweep. The canoe skimmed over the choppy waves. The eastern shore grew distant and the head of New York drew close. They rounded the Point and came into view of the cabins and the Indian camp. David saw that Louisa stood on the shore, and he waved.

"Hey, Dobbins!" he yelled over his shoulder. "You say you'll be wanting to get some of that cattle Pa's got in the Willamette?"

"Yup."

"Want some company while you go after them?"

"Could always use company!"

David raised an arm to wave again, this time more vigorously. He would marry Louisa, and he would do it before he was 21. And he would have a claim too.

"On the 23rd of March...the *Exact* returned.... David
Denny and Carson [Dobbins] Boren took passage on the
ship for Olympia, and then went on to the Willamette
Valley for their stock, which they had left to winter there
after their trip across the plains."
—Roberta Frye Watt in *Four Wagons West*

February 15th was balmy. Seagulls screeched. Arthur, Dobbins, and William returned to the eastern shore of Elliott Bay
to pound in their claim stakes, marking the division between
their adjacent choices. They limited themselves to a half-mile
of waterfront, saving some to attract spring settlers. Their acreage
would spread straight back to make up the full 320 acres that
each was entitled to under the New Land Act of 1851.

William took the northern piece and Arthur the middle, including the spring and fire-gutted clearing, and Dobbins got the
marshland, forest, and knoll.

David didn't go with them. He and Louisa spent the day
together instead. After an early supper they walked around the
beach toward the Duwamish River. They sat together on a log,
one that had rolled in from the ocean and lay half-buried in the
sand. They were alone, facing east and the new town site.

The evening sun hung low, drawing soft colors of red and
pink over the treetops behind them. They held hands, fingers
entwined, talking of the new city. "Straight across, all along
where William and Arthur have claimed, the bank goes up about
40 feet," David told her. "All we have to do is chop down the
trees and roll them over the brink. And if you go south a piece
you come to Dobbins' land. It levels out to a marsh—tideflats,
really. It'll be perfect for the cattle."

"Cattle?" She looked up at him in surprise. "What cattle?"
David fidgeted and pushed his heel into the soft sand.

"David, what cattle?"

"We're wanting some of the stock that Pa's been keeping.

I volunteered to go." He hurried on. "Who else is there? Arthur can't. He's got Mary to think about. Besides, what if his ague comes on again while he's on the trail?"

"Thought this country was supposed to cure the ague. He hasn't had it since coming up, you know."

"One never knows...'"

"What about your foot?"

"It's mended good enough."

"What about William Bell? Or Dobbins?"

"Bell doesn't want cattle and Dobbins *is* going with me. Or rather, I'm going with him."

"I know!" Her eyes danced with enthusiasm and solution. "What about Lee? He likes to be off! And he hasn't been out since getting John's oxen in Puyallup!"

He hated to shatter what was an excellent suggestion. But the fact was that he had to go and see Pa. He had to go and see if there wasn't some way he could make Pa understand the urgency of getting land now, of seeing his way clear to allowing them to marry. He took her hand and turned it over, running his finger over her palm and tracing the lines.

"Do you remember the day of the buffalo stampede?" He waited for her to nod. "Well, we can get through this too."

"But we've been separated too much already!" She wiped her cheeks hastily, pulling her hand free of his in the process. The sun dropped low, the trees hiding what was left, and the sky muted as the color of it died away. Dusk hovered.

He kissed her. She started to speak. "Shh..." He found the hollow of her throat, warm under his lips. For a moment she stiffened, and he felt the brief hesitation. But then she gave herself to him more fully than ever before and he felt the surge of his passion, the tormenting swell, and he lowered her to the beach, his mouth closing over hers.

The sand was damp and cold beneath them, but neither were cognizant of it. Their eyes met, faces hidden by shadow. Mesmerized by her beauty, her vulnerability, desire controlled David's every movement. His hand, quivering, felt the creamy smoothness of her skin. "I love you," he breathed into her mouth. Her arms came around him and she pulled him closer.

Every man is tempted when he is drawn away of his own
lust, and enticed.

James! He groaned audibly and pulled back. Why had he ever
begun to memorize the book? He couldn't get away from it.

"David?"

"I can't, Liza. I just can't... not yet, not this way."

She was beautiful, more so in the moonlight, lying on the sand
watching him. He felt his hands rub over his head and found
that they shook—that his whole body trembled. Waves rolled
in by his feet and he forced himself to look down at them in order
to keep his eyes off Louisa.

He eventually sat numbly back onto the log. Louisa came to
him and slid in close. With a choked-back cry he pulled her
onto his lap. The moon, a round coin, slid in and out of clouds.

"Dobbins and I will go to Olympia just as soon as we can
get away," he whispered, still staring out to the waves, to the
moon.

"When?"

"Six weeks, maybe. There's lots to be done. Captain Howard
will be returning at the end of March and we've got to have
that order filled. Soon as that's done I expect we can take off."

"Will you kiss me, David?"

He did—harshly, angrily, caught up in the frustration of the
circumstances. Then, suddenly aware of what he was doing, he
let her go. Still she watched him, not letting *him* go. He pulled
her close again, her body small and warm in his arms. "I've
got to go and see Pa. We can't go on like this. Do you understand?" She nodded. The sounds of evening were still. Louisa
pulled Pa's handkerchief from a pocket. He took it from her and
tenderly wiped her face.

"Why can't we just get married?"

"You promised Pa. That's why. We've been all through this,
Liza." He spoke quickly, afraid that if he didn't he would give
in, that he would end up destroying her innocence and his own.
He took Pa's handkerchief and rolled it into a ball, then pushed
it back to her pocket. She grabbed his hand and held it tight,
and he knew the warmth of her thigh under his fingers.

"We have to marry, David," she whispered. "Please."

"We don't *have* to marry, Liza. And we're not going to *have* to."

She just cried. She sobbed into Pa's kerchief. "Come on," he said. "We best get home. It's a long walk." He took her by the elbow and gently walked her north and around the Point to the cabins of New York.

The puncheon flooring of Arthur's loft creaked under the weight of David's boots as he crossed the floor, stilling only when he lowered himself to his stomach and propped his chin on the edge of the loft. His eyes grew accustomed to the dark, and he could see that Louisa still sat on her bed below praying silently. She moved, then crawled beneath the covers to where she undressed. He sighed and reluctantly gave up his position to find his own bed, asking his own peace with God.

★　　★　　★

"It's a beautiful country up theer, Miss, jist beautiful." The *Exact* was back. It was March 22, and spring was just beginning to draw open various wildflowers. Purples, yellows, pinks, small bits of orange and reds sprinkled the dark floor of the forests, edging the woods with gaiety. Sir Zeke helped himself to another biscuit and drank clam chowder from his cup. "But them Injuns ain't too kindly." He shook his head and looked solemnly at Louisa.

She hadn't recognized him or the other miners when she had first seen them. Captain Folger had anchored his ship just after their noon meal, and, without having to be told, the women had hurried to fix something hot for the starving men. Their bodies were lean, their faces gaunt, from both starvation and trauma.

"Tell me about it," said Louisa. She handed him another cup of the chowder. He put it to his lips, buried now by a thick beard.

"You hear 'bout the *Georgiana?*" She shook her head. "It sailed out 'a Portland two days 'fore us, I think. The third."

"The third of November?"

"Yes, Miss, that's it. Well, theer was a storm, a purdy bad one, they tell, and the men, they done had to swim fer shore. And them Injuns, them Haidas, them dirty scum, they jist rounded thim all up and held 'em prisners. 'Course, when we done git theer, the captain, he knows nothings of the sorts, and he leaves us."

Impulsively Louisa reached out to the man. She didn't know

that she had until he took her hand and held it. "All theer was
to do, Miss, was to keep out 'a sight, wait fer Folger to come
git us. And thim prisners, they're still up theer..." Sir Zeke
pinched tight Louisa's hand and leaned in close. "Up theer,
Miss, a man kin git mighty lonely fer a woman."

"I beg your pardon, Sir!" Louisa yanked free and stood, but
her dress caught on a protruding stump and held fast.

"Here, lit me." The miner laughed softly and reached down
to loosen the material. "But don't yer be runnin' off now," he
chuckled, hanging to the hem. "I ain't never mint to be im-
proper, Miss. I's askin' fer yer hand the only ways I know ter
do it."

"Sir!"

"Now, now, I relize ye don't know me will, but I kin wait
till yer warm up. I'm a patient man whin I know I kin have
in the end."

Louisa tugged on her skirt and the material tore where it was
badly worn and frayed. "Would you mind letting go?" she said
tersely, looking about quickly. Dobbins and David weren't too
far away; they were speaking with Captain Folger—no doubt
making arrangements to take passage with him to Olympia.

"My, my, bit ain't you a purdy thing whin you're riled!"
Sir Zeke laughed loudly and pulled on her hand so that she was
forced to sit beside him. "Now, don't you go and scream on
me, Miss—I ain't about to attack yer in front 'a all my friends
here. What I do aim to do is ter marry yer. Make it legal,
religious, the blessings of the Pope hisself, if'n that'd make yer
happy."

"I'm not Roman Catholic."

Sir Zeke bent over her hand and kissed it softly, surprising
her with the tenderness. His eyes came up to meet hers, but she
looked away.

"I'll lit yer go fer now," he said. "But I'll be in touch, yer
kin bit on that." She rose and stumbled, and with her face burning she moved away from Sir Zeke and his open stare. She hastily
scrambled over the tossed-up logs, darting in and out of the
numerous naked Indian children who played everywhere, and
hurried past the other miners hunched over their meal.

"It'z the purdy Miss!" hollered one of them. She turned and
saw the man with the yellow hat, his dimple covered over by

thick whiskers now. Blindly she ran to the cabin, found David's bed in the loft, and crawled beneath the covers to cry alone.

★　　★　　★

When David and Dobbins had finalized the arrangements to go with Folger up to Olympia the following day, David went in search of Louisa. Not seeing her on the beach, he went to the cabin and was surprised to find her asleep in his bed. "Louisa?" he whispered, kissing her lightly on the cheek.

Her eyes flew open and she flung her arms about him. "Oh, David!" she cried. "Just hold me! Please."

"What's wrong? You're shaking!"

"Just hold me..." she sobbed, clinging to him. He felt her tears against his cheek.

"Liza... what is it?" The last time he had seen her she had been happy enough, helping Mary Ann and the others feed the miners.

"Oh, David... you're leaving tomorrow, aren't you?"

So that was it. "Yes, Folger's taking us to Olympia. We'll walk the rest of the way."

"Oh, David, take me with you! We can go to Olympia and get someone to marry us. And John'll give you a bit of land here! He's giving it out to anyone who'll stay in New York! You know that!"

Her hair caught about her face and he pulled it away, running his fingers lightly over her cheek. "We've been over this, Liza."

"But it's not fair!"

"Life is never fair. Do you realize that if we came out a year earlier, in 1850, that I could have had land? And that I could have even had double what the government is giving out now?"

"How's that?" She sniffed.

"The first donation act gave 320 acres to anyone over 18, double that if he was married. But in just months, I guess, the land was getting grabbed up and they had to lessen the amount and raise the age. And so you see," he gave her a kiss, "life is never fair. To expect it to be is childish, Louisa."

"It's not going to make any difference if you go," she said sullenly. "Pa's got his mind made up. As long as you can't file, there's no changing Pa's mind. *I* know that! *You* know that!"

"I have my ideas."

She said nothing, but turned away from him.

"Liza." He rolled her back and took her face between his hands. "I do have my ideas."

"It won't do any good."

" 'If any of you lack wisdom, let him ask of God.' It's in James."

"I thought you finished memorizing that."

"I did. But I still remember the words. That's the whole point of it, isn't it?"

"So what's your idea?"

"Ah! That is my secret!" He kissed the tears on her face. "But I do promise you, Miss Boren, that before I'm 21 you'll be Mrs. Denny."

"Like Mary Ann?"

He grinned. "No, Liza. You'll be Mrs. David Denny." He sat and pulled her up with him. "But for now, Miss Boren, I don't think it'd be such a good idea if the other Mrs. Denny were to find you in my bed."

Louisa nodded and started for the ladder.

"Your skirt. It's got a tear in it."

"Caught it on a log a while back."

"Oh."

He watched her descend the ladder carefully, lest she catch the tear and fall. They both jumped when Mary Ann entered the darkened cabin. But she pretended to see nothing and went straight to the fire to put the supper on.

23

"Another incident that was a combination of tragedy
and comedy occurred when Chief Sealth's wife died...."
—Roberta Frye Watt in *Four Wagons West*

A loud wailing awoke Louisa and she stiffened in a momentary spasm of terror. But it was only the Indians chanting over another death. She lay quietly, listening to the mournful sounds, strange and eerie, with a hopelessness that made her want to weep.

"Oiahl!" The spasm of terror returned and she sat in bed, her heart racing. "Oiahl!" Maybe it was for Oiahl that they wailed! The old woman had been ill—lung fever, Mary Ann had thought.

"Arthur?" she whispered. If David had been there she could have called him. But he wasn't; yesterday he'd gone. There was only Arthur. "Arthur?" she called again.

"Mm?"

"Could it be Oiahl?" She heard the rustle of bedcovers.

"Maybe I better go see." She saw that he groped for his pants and turned away.

"Your fever..." Mary Ann called after him. The quiet latch of the door seemed loud.

"Go back to sleep, Mary Ann," whispered Louisa.

"I can't. The noises... And Arthur, he's coming down with the ague again."

"I'll go get Anna. Maybe she'll be wanting company."

They all sat in the dark. Moonlight outlined the whiteness of their nightdresses and faces. "Did Oiahl's daughter come while she was ill?" Louisa asked Mary.

"You mean her stepdaughter? Yes, she did come. A good thing, too, it looks like." Mary Ann shivered. "Kickisomlo loved Oiahl. She was the only mother Kickisomlo knew. Her own died shortly after her birth."

Silence came. The moon created shadows. The children slept.

"She told me that she wasn't afraid to die," whispered Mary.

"Don't be silly. Everyone is afraid to die." Anna shivered and Louisa went to find her a shawl. She got one for Mary Ann too.

"No... Oiahl said that she and Jesus were good friends. 'Jesus, Oiahl, tillicum,' is what she told me."

"She said that?" Louisa asked in surprise. "Where do you suppose she learned that?"

"That Bishop Demur, I suppose."

"A bishop?" Anna stared at Mary Ann.

"There's one about these parts somewhere," Mary said.

Anna got up from the table slowly. Clutching the shawl about her shoulders, she went to the door to look out. "So even the savages know to fear God," she whispered. Louisa gently pulled her away from the cold and Anna started to sob. She lay her head on the table and wept with long, lonely wails, more agonizing to listen to than the Indians.

"Anna?" Louisa bent over her. "Whatever is the matter?"

"I want to go home. *I just want to go home!*"

The chanting went on all night. Anna stayed and slept with Mary Ann, and Louisa tossed about in her own bed. David had been gone only a day, but she missed him already. She worried about Anna. "I'll never sleep," she thought, but then sunlight woke her, falling in through the window that Arthur had put in. Mary Ann was singing. Anna had the table set.

"Sealth wants a Christian funeral," said Arthur. "Says the Bishop Demur had Oiahl baptized some time ago. Couldn't make sense of when or where. Sure wish David were around at a time like this," he muttered. "I did get that he wants her to be buried—not strung up on some platform or set in a canoe to rot, or whatever it is that they do around here. He says he wants her buried deep, in a coffin."

"Why, Arthur! That's wonderful!" exclaimed Mary Ann. "Does this mean he desires knowledge of God? That he is willing to be Christian?"

Arthur shrugged. "Who knows what the old man thinks? Beats me. Says he's going to Olympia. Knows a doctor. He's convinced that this Maynard fellow could have kept Oiahl alive. Wants to bring him back."

"To stay? Oh, Lydia will be so relieved!" Mary almost

shouted when Arthur nodded. He helped himself to more sugar and stirred it into his coffee.

"And why would Mrs. Low be so delighted to see a doctor in these parts?"

"Because she is with child again."

A baby? Louisa swallowed hard. No wonder Lydia had looked so pale of late. She had thought it was due to her distress in finding that the rest of them were definitely going to leave New York just as soon as Captain Howard and the *Leonesa* returned, leaving her the only white woman at Alki. But a baby? Louisa felt a twinge of jealousy and looked up at the empty loft.

"Well, I've got to go." Arthur stood. "William Bell and I promised the good chief that we'd build that coffin for him. Guess we better get started before he can change his mind."

"Are you sure you're up to it?" The happiness was gone from Mary's voice. "Your fever. You really ought to rest," she called after him. But she didn't stop him and he walked on out the door.

The service was a simple one. Arthur read from the Psalms, then turned in his Bible to the Book of Job. The Indians listened attentively, more curious than polite.

Louisa noticed the sweat on Arthur's brow, far worse than it had been at breakfast. It dripped down his temples and his beard, and when he bowed his head to read, the pages of his Bible were wetted. He licked his lips often, and his cheeks and mouth both had little color. His hands shook noticeably with fatigue, and Louisa was relieved when he finally prayed. The Indian nobles, the highest of the warriors, picked up the blanket-wrapped body to lower it into the coffin.

No one said anything as they struggled to push the body inside. The warriors, their faces set firmly, tried to wedge it in, but it was no use. Oiahl just wouldn't fit. Sealth looked distressed and spoke sternly to his men. But they shrugged.

"I think you've wrapped her in too many blankets," said Arthur dismally. Sealth spoke and the interpreter translated: The number of blankets dictated wealth—great wealth.

"That's what David said, Arthur!" whispered Louisa.

"He didn't tell me that! How was I supposed to know they wrap their corpses in them!"

Louisa struggled not to smile while the nobles tried again. Suddenly Jim, one of Sealth's sons, stepped up. He was a handsome Indian, although his nakedness forced Louisa to never really look at him. He strode over to his father, crossed his arms, then pointed back at Oiahl. He spoke quickly to the chief, the sounds coming from his throat in sharp and quick syllables. Sealth nodded and quickly the warriors took the body and rolled it over to peel away the several layers of blankets. This time she fit.

The chief wept. "Death? There is no death," Sealth said solemnly. Tears fell, marking his face like narrow scars. "There is only a change of worlds." Shamed, he turned away. Without looking back he climbed into a waiting canoe. At his signal 40 nobles paddled him away, taking him from view.

Jim was the one who dropped the first dirt onto the lowered casket. And just as it hit with a thud onto the wooden container a wild shriek came from the crowd. A woman, her face broad like Sealth's, burst through the people. Crying and sobbing, she threw herself to the coffin in the ground, her cheek pressed to the lid. George, Sealth's older son, hauled her up roughly and she retaliated with a kick. George swore and spun her around, pinning her arms cruelly behind her back.

The woman screamed. She jerked loose with surprising fury and strength. As she spun, her fingers curled, raking the man's cheek.

"Kickisomlo?" Louisa asked. Mary nodded. Louisa watched in paralyzed shock as the sister and brother fought. The nudity and utter depravity astounded her, and the brutality of it almost made her ill.

"It's just their way," David had said. He believed that the Indians were a law unto themselves, more honorable than some white men in their creed. But she wasn't so sure. The natives needed great enlightenment. She would have to remember to pray for Kickisomlo.

A small breeze touched Louisa's cheek and she saw the rosebush behind Arthur sway. It was like sweetbriar. With trembling fingers she plucked the prettiest of the roses, and, holding the promise of life, of spring, in her hand, she went over to Sealth's distraught daughter.

Kickisomlo stood raggedly, dirt smeared over her high cheeks. Her hair was long and black and tangled, and hung in wisps over her breasts. Mud caked her face, but her eyes were clear, large, and black—and strangely desolate. "Here," said Louisa.

She pushed the flower to the woman and noticed that the petals trembled in her hand.

"Here," she said again, this time her voice stronger. But the woman only stared at her, not comprehending her intent. "See?" she said, setting the rose on the lid of the coffin.

Kickisomlo shook her arms and her brother released her. She stepped quietly to the grave. Crying softly, she picked up the flower, touched it to her lips, and gently laid it back as Louisa had done. She made the sign of the cross and stood motionless while Jim and others proceeded to fill the hole, covering over the coffin—and the rose—with the dirt of the earth.

Louisa rested her hand in her apron pocket and toyed with Pa's handkerchief. She watched Kickisomlo nervously, afraid that the woman might erupt again. But she remained stoically rigid, and Louisa impulsively handed the red handkerchief to the Indian. "Would you like this?" she asked.

Kickisomlo smiled, then grabbed the red and hugged Louisa as a child his mother. Louisa gagged on the stench that assaulted her nostrils and staggered backward. "Tillicum—skookum!" the woman cried, over and over, hugging Louisa again. Then, just as suddenly as she had demonstrated herself, she pulled away and hurried down the beach. She ran with the red fluttering from her hand.

"Thank you."

The words were stuttered and thick with accent. Louisa looked up into Jim's dark face. He stood before her, his own black eyes, large and round, gazing down at her. "Thank you," he said again. Then he too turned from her and was gone. The muscles under his lean, oil-smeared skin rippled as he carried himself into the woods. He brushed past the rosebush but didn't wince as the thorns caught and tore his skin. It was as if they had not scratched him, as if he had not felt them or even known they were there.

★ ★ ★

Louisa turned the page, reading on. On balmy days she liked to read to the children, and today was one of those warm, balmy days. It was the last day of March, and the scent of the ocean was lifted by a gentle breeze as seagulls screeched and swooped out over the water. Louisa should have been relaxed and happy, but she wasn't. David had been gone a week, and she missed him sorely. Like a toothache, the pain of his absence wouldn't go away. The minutes of passing time were filled with worry for his safety and with wondering how he was doing with Pa—if Pa would say they could get married.

She was frustrated because the new town site was still just five markers pounded into the unbroken shoreline across the bay. Captain Howard hadn't returned, and the order was filled. They needed the supplies he would bring. And Arthur was sick again.

Louisa was worried about Anna too. Ever since Oiahl had died Anna had been restless, going for long walks but never telling anyone when she was off. She would be gone for hours, and Gertrude would cry and call out for her mother. The rest of them would worry and wonder. Mary Ann said that Anna missed Dobbins, but Louisa wasn't so sure. Anna was just unhappy.

When Captain Howard had returned at the first of the year he had brought (along with Lydia's new stove) a set of Dickens' works. It was out of these that Louisa read, with the little ones gathered close and the bigger ones seated not too far away. All listened intently. But today Louisa found that the pages would pass leaving her unaware of the words she had just read. Anna came to listen and Louisa wearily went on.

"What's that?" Anna interrupted the story and pointed to a large canoe and scow out in the water.

"Sealth?" Louisa guessed.

"Oh, keep on reading, Auntie!" some of the children called out.

"Wait a minute," Louisa hushed them. "Who would be on the scow?" She and Anna stood simultaneously. The large, flat-bottomed boat appeared to be piled high with provisions of some sort, and a man—a tall man with a raccoon-tailed hat—stood in the midst of the pile.

"Anna!" Louisa shrieked with realization. "It's the doctor that Sealth said he'd bring back! Mary! Laura! You two go see if you can't find your fathers somewhere. Mary Ann! Lydia!" she hollered, breaking into a run. "He's here! The doctor! He's come!"

Mary Ann and Lydia both ran to the beach to welcome the stranger. Louisa passed by the cabins and saw that Arthur stood at the door, propped against the logs, his face white and drenched with sweat. "You get back to bed," she scolded him. "You're ill—fever and ague, remember?"

"Where's Mary gone?"

"To meet the new doctor. Now you do as I say. Into bed. We'll bring the good man in to see you." She grinned. "If you behave yourself he might let us give you a bit of quinine." His had run out, most of it having gone to David. Mary Ann waltzed in, smiling, bringing the doctor by the hand.

"It's Doctor Maynard!" she exclaimed. "And Arthur! He says he's got something that'll perk you up in no time!" Anna followed, and she and Louisa exchanged glances.

The doctor had a kindly face. He wore spectacles, and somewhat of a twinkle caught in his eyes behind the lenses. He was a man who obviously enjoyed small pleasures and was given to life in much the same way that others fought it. He bent over Arthur studiously.

"Well, Sir," he said jovially, his presence filling the room as he spoke. "Prepare yourself to this being your last bout. I personally guarantee you no more spells."

Arthur lifted his head suspiciously off the pillow and stared the stranger down. "How's that?"

"This country cures the ague just as sure as it causes colds. Just mark my words. It's true."

"I'll believe it when I see it, Sir." Arthur lay back. "I'm going to hold you to it, though."

The doctor laughed. "I like you! What did you say your name was?" He pulled up a chair and sat on it backward so that his arms and chin rested over the back of it.

"I didn't."

"Well, then, man, tell me!"

"Denny. Arthur Denny."

"Well, now, Denny, seeing as how I like you, I'll tell you what I'm going to do for you. I got just the tonic you need."

"What's in it?"

"Oh, just a bit of opium dissolved in a bit of spirits."

"We don't drink. We don't believe it's good for you physically, spiritually, or financially."

"Teetotalers!" The doctor looked amused. "The more the pity, I say. A belt of something stiff'll make you so's you don't even care that you got the ague!

"But in the meantime," he went on, "I do have some of the quinine. Not near as good. But helpful. Got plenty soon as I can find it. Now," he said, setting both hands on his knees, "where's the rest of the folks around here? It can't be just you, Denny, or is this your harem?" He waved to all the women that had gathered, peering at them over his glasses. He smiled and nodded at them, as if inspecting merchandise.

Sealth came to the door and the women respectfully let him in. He spoke in his own tongue to the doctor, who answered him back in the same language. Sealth grunted, then signaled to several of the Indians who had gathered outside the cabin.

"Well," said the doctor, "now that this is taken care of, I need someone to show me around. Seattle and me, we have a partnership going. He catches fish and I salt them, barrel them, and ship 'em off to San Francisco."

"But—"

"But what, young lady?" jumped in the doctor.

"Nothing," Louisa said lamely, embarrassed now. Why she was embarrassed she didn't know.

"Come, come, speak your piece. I'm not easily insulted. You were going to object to something, weren't you?" He removed his spectacles to scrutinize her more closely.

"I was just going to say, what about Captain Fay, Sir?" she added. "He's in the fish business and has the Indians catching for him."

"Well, so he does, so he does. Now that Captain Fay of yours," the doctor said, walking about the room, looking at everything, "that captain of yours has an excellent ship line between here and Olympia. And that's a lot of territory."

The bottom half of the door swung open to match the top half, and John and William entered. The doctor shook their hands vigorously. "Now this is more like it," he said. "I'm glad to find some working men around here. Beginning to think I'd bumped into a hospital! Ha!"

"You've met Arthur then," said John.

"Yeah, he's met me." Arthur sat and pushed Mary away. "He's promised me some quinine, and if he doesn't get moving, I'm going to start doubting the man's word."

"Arthur!"

"Never mind, Ma'am," the stranger said. "He's got spunk.

I already told you I liked your husband, didn't I?" He raised his voice and hollered over to Arthur. "Keep yer britches on, man! You'll get it by and by. I've told Seattle what to look for!"

"Seattle?" William and the rest of them looked puzzled.

"What do you call the good chief?" demanded the doctor.

"Sealth."

The man shrugged. "Don't you like Seattle better? Now, how many of you are there?" asked the doctor.

"Well, there's Lee and Charles Terry," drawled John. "They're off somewhere. Don't know exactly. But Lee'll be leaving before too long. Says it's too wild and woolly out here for him. I think it's that there are no lady friends." He grinned and the doctor laughed. "And there's William and myself— and our families, of course." He nodded in the direction of the little ones at the door, peering in for a look.

"How many altogether?"

"Twenty-four—twelve adults and twelve children."

"Some of us aim to settle across the bay shortly," William put in. "We've been waiting for the *Leonesa* to return so we can help John here load up the timber we cut."

"You mean to say you actually got a regular means of support?"

"John does. We're moving on—something else will come up, I expect. Two of our men have gone back to the Willamette to get some cattle. Soon as we load the *Leonesa* we'll be settling our claims. We think there's a better chance for a harbor."

"But then who's to know?" butted in John. "Are you looking to settle? I'll be glad to let you have your pick of the land over here. Just say the word and I'll adjust my claim. The Terry boys and I could use the company. Besides, my wife is in the family way and we could use a doctor. And we do have a store already," he rambled on. "Charles and I call it the New York Markook House."

"New York?"

"The name of our city here."

Maynard laughed. "New York—Alki!"

John reddened and thrust a nervous finger down his collar. "Wait and see, Sir."

"I was sort of thinking about opening up a store too."

"Thought you said you were in the fish business!"

"Oh, I am!" The doctor clapped his large hands together.

"But now, Mr.—— what did you say your name was?"

"John Low."

"Well, there's nothing that says we can't have two stores now, is there, Mr. Low?"

The dimple in John's cheek went deep. "Come on! I'll show you around. Remember, whatever you want, I'll move over!"

"Generous of you, Low, is it? Well, then, show me your New York, your Alki!" He chuckled merrily.

"Apparently the man didn't mind competition," thought Louisa—at least not when it was him coming in as the competitor. But he appeared to be a remarkable man, she had to admit that. His command of the Duwamish tongue and the Indians showed that. And it was evident that Sealth, or Seattle, regarded him highly. And for that, no doubt, he and David would find common ground.

"You heard that Olympia is calling this place of yours Duwamps, Low?" the man was saying. "But I won't settle any place under that foul name, that I can assure you. You, Ma'am—I missed your name." He looked directly at Louisa.

"Louisa Boren, Sir."

"Married?"

"No, Sir. Not yet, Sir!"

He roared and she felt her cheeks grow hot. "Not yet, anyway! Oh, my, I like that!" He tipped his hat and the raccoon tail flopped. "I say, if I didn't have an eye on a missy already, I'd marry you! Yup, sure a good thing I got my own lady or I'd marry you tomorrow."

"It's a good thing you got your eye on your own lady, Sir," said Anna. Her eyes sparkled with life and fun, and Louisa stared in astonishment at the change. Anna stepped forward, hands in her pockets, her small chin pushed forward. "Because the only way you'll marry my sister-in-law is if you're the Justice of the Peace!" The doctor chucked Anna under the chin and grinned, merriment coming to his face. John reached for the man's elbow and steered him toward the door.

"I'll tell you what, young lady!" he hollered over his shoulder. "I'll marry that sister-in-law of yours! Just as soon as I'm Justice of the Peace for Duwamps, and just as soon as she brings me her young man!" John pulled him out the door.

"You tell that fancy doctor we'll move our claims any which

way too! Any which way!" Arthur shouted. He sat and hollered again to the empty door, then flopped back to the bed and moaned. "Low isn't the only one around here who's generous," he muttered, yanking the cover to his chin. "I can be just as generous if I put my mind to it."

The women, left alone, the flamboyancy whisked out from under their noses, stared at one another. Anna and Louisa started to laugh.

"What was his first name, anyway?" Anna asked.

"I don't know!"

"Maybe the fool doesn't have one." It was Charles. He had been standing outside the window the whole time, listening.

24

"As she was strikingly beautiful, young and unmarried, both white and Indian braves thought it would be a fine thing to win her hand, and intimations of this fact were not wanting. The young Indians brought long poles with them and leaned them up against the cabin at Alki, the significance of which was not at first understood...."

—Emily Inez Denny in *Blazing the Way*

With the coming of Dr. Maynard, life in New York accelerated. Just his very presence evoked a charge, an excitement, and Louisa found that the passage of time no longer dragged on minute by minute. Instead there were a lot of animated discussions and debates, and Anna, for the first time since leaving Illinois, seemed to be her old self—happy, full of laughter, her eyes bright.

By the close of the first day of April, Maynard had chosen his site: the bluff of land that rose up out of the tideflats on the eastern side of the bay. "The Point," as Dr. Maynard called the knoll, would be perfect for his fishing business. John was disappointed and Arthur ecstatic, but Louisa was worried.

"Isn't that the land that becomes an island at high tide?" she asked.

Maynard was all smiles and enthusiasm. "That's it!"

"But that's my brother's claim. Arthur, you can't go and trade off land that isn't yours!"

He spoke calmly to her, as one might a child. "Louisa, having the Doc around is advantageous to our town. Having a doctor and a fishing business, not to mention the possibility of a store, our city is well on its way to being established."

"It's my brother's claim, Arthur."

But the matter was dropped. And that afternoon the *Leonesa* returned, bringing in their new supplies and merchandise for Charles' store. The men loaded the pilings they had cut (even the doctor lent a hand), and John signed a new contract. "I'll get the Indians to help me," he said, signing his name boldly to the new order. "New York is not going to wither just because half its inhabitants leave to create competition." He said it with a pained smile.

On April the 3rd the sun edged the eastern horizon in bold, unobstructed yellow. By ten o'clock in the morning the day was warm and the sea blue. And Doc Maynard decided it was time for those who were moving to move. Arthur stayed at home in bed with his bottle of quinine, but the others—Louisa, Anna, all the Bells, and Doc Maynard—paddled themselves and their provisions across the bay. They used the largest of Seattle's war canoes (Seattle now instead of Sealth, as far as Doc Maynard was concerned) and Doc Maynard's huge scow.

Instead of heading straight east they followed the shoreline, unwilling to risk a spill out in the middle of the deepwater "harbor." It was hard work and they stopped frequently. Louisa's hands grew tender from where she gripped the large pole that the doctor had given her to push them along with.

But if her hands were sore then, they were even more sore by the end of a week's time. Within a week she and Anna had laid the foundation to Anna's new cabin. They felled the trees themselves, cut them to the right lengths, and laid them in a 16-by-20-foot rectangle just inside the tree line of Dobbins' claim, and uphill from the marshland and the Point.

On the Point itself Doc Maynard had his combination house-store entirely finished. It was a large structure put together by the Indians—a full 18 by 26 feet, with an attic overhead and planks to set to the walls below for shelves. He hung a sign over the front door proclaiming THE SEATTLE EXCHANGE. By April 10, 1852, a year to the day after the Dennys had started west, their town had begun—with neither David nor Dobbins nor Arthur present.

There was a dizzying sense of activity that hummed all day, every day. Wildflowers opened wide to spring sun, bees hovered over clover, spiders found their way into bedsheets at night. Louisa, Anna, and Sally Bell spent the days boiling sweat-soaked flannel shirts in pots over hot fires, cooking biscuits, and stirring cornmeal mush. Children laughed and explored, and on occasion got in the way. And Indians by the hundreds swarmed the Point, paddling in with canoes of pink salmon, helping the doctor fashion barrels, then salting the fish and sealing them inside. The sound of hammers hitting spikes and saws chewing into trees filled the air, bringing the welcome sound of civilization.

Before the cabins could even be completed, a ship sailed into the bay. It was the brig *John Davis*, manned by Captain George Plummer, looking for timber. A contract was signed and the cabins came to a standstill, just half-walls in freshly scarred clearings.

The beach in the new town was unlike the wide-open space of New York. It was narrow and rocky, and at high tide the sea came right up to the bank, blocking any sort of passage from one claim to another. The only way to get from the Bells' claim, in the far north, down to Dobbins' and Maynard's, in the south, was to walk along the sandbars at low tide. For this reason, until all the cabins were built (and Arthur was well and David and Dobbins had returned), they all camped at the Point under the doctor's invitation, coming together in the evening for lively debates and lengthy stories.

★   ★   ★

Louisa wrote to Pamelia. She sat at the Low's table, lost in the silence of thoughts and memories, writing quickly. She had been back to New York-Alki a week, tending Lydia's chores and children since learning of her near miscarriage.

"Louisa, I hear something," Lydia said suddenly.

"Just the Indians. They seem to be setting some poles against the house," Louisa answered. Even as she spoke Jim Sealth set one by the front door.

"No... It's more like a tinkling noise. Like a bell!"

Louisa laughed. "A bell? In these parts? You've got to be hearing things, Lydia Low!"

She sensed rather than saw him. Her papers flew and the ink spilled, but she noticed none of it—only David.

"Oh, David," she sobbed, running to him. She felt the warmth of his breath, the security of his arms. His lips found hers and she clung to him. Then his mouth was on her cheeks, kissing away the tears that wouldn't stop.

"Cows, Mama!" Two-year-old Minerva crashed through the door and knocked into David and Louisa. "Oh, Mama! We was coming home and we saw them! Real cows! Real ones, Mama! Can I have the first cup of milk?"

"It's *may* I have, and what do you say to Mr. Denny and Miss Boren?" Minerva looked demurely down at her feet. "Excuse me," she whispered.

"Where's Anna?"

Louisa whirled around at the sound of the deep voice; it was foggy and gruff. "Dobbins!" He hugged her, pulling her hair in a fist like he used to do as a boy. He laughed and pulled her head so that he could give her a kiss of his own. "Where's Anna?"

"Oh, there is just so much to tell you!" she said, laughing herself and tugging away from him. "We've moved over to the other side. There's a new man, a Dr. Maynard. Arthur's moved your claim, Dobbins, to accommodate him, and his name is David, just like yours!" She pushed into David's arms and folded them over at her waist so that he had no choice but to hold her.

"Where's Anna?" Dobbins asked again. "I'm going to get tired of asking the question if someone doesn't give me an answer."

David looked down at Louisa and kissed her again. "He has a surprise for Anna and can hardly wait to show it to her."

Louisa tossed her head and pulled David's face to hers. Their kiss was lingered. "She's across the bay," she mumbled.

"I'll take the cows on over, then. You stay and rest up, Dave."

"You can do it alone?" David pushed Louisa from him gently and held her an arm's length away. "I don't mind helping out."

"I'm a big boy." Dobbins pulled on his beard and grinned at Louisa. "Besides, I'd rather go alone. I'm weary of your company." The sound of a bell tinkling came as the cows stepped wearily forward at Dobbins' command.

"Hearing things, am I?" Lydia sat down at the table, but Louisa ignored her. She pulled David close. "What's the surprise for Anna?" she whispered as he bent to touch his forehead to hers.

"Glass windows for their new cabin."

"Real glass?"

"M-mm."

Suddenly Kickisomlo tore into the cabin, the red handkerchief that Louisa had given her draped over her head like a kerchief. "Mizz Liza! Mizz Liza!" she screamed.

Louisa looked over to David, feeling a sense of panic, but he grinned and shrugged his shoulders, and the tension passed.

"Come in," she said, taking Sealth's daughter by the arm. "I have a friend I want you to meet."

"No! No! Mizz Liza! You decide!"

"Kickisomlo, I can't understand you! You talk too fast!" But the woman went on, pantomiming and waving her arms, switching over entirely into the Duwamish in her excitement. David said something and she turned to him. "Yes! Yes!" she shouted, then was off again, explaining something to him that neither Louisa nor Lydia could understand.

"Do you suppose you and Louisa could find something to do inside for awhile?" David asked Lydia when Kickisomlo was quiet.

"Is there danger?" Lydia asked.

"Oh, heaven's no!" David laughed, the kind of laughter he used whenever he was enjoying himself. "I just want Louisa inside for awhile, all right?" He and Kickisomlo moved to the door.

"David? David...don't go. Not yet!"

"It's all right, Liza. Kickisomlo, is that her name? She and I will be back." Louisa reached up to touch his chin and he drew in close, lingering his lips over hers.

"Klat-a-wah!" Kickisomlo hollered. She pulled on David's sleeve.

He kissed Louisa quickly.

After they were gone Louisa went to the crate that held the flour as the children put their pails of clams up on the table. She smiled. "Go on out and get your clams scooped out and washed." None of them moved. "Go on with you. I'll use whoever's bucket gets cleaned up first."

She listened to the merry sound of their laughter and measured salt into her dough. The children congregated about the water keg, arguing and pushing as Alonzo examined the several poles that were propped together along the front wall of the cabin. Louisa went to the door, bowl in hand, and was surprised to see how many there were. "You children go down to the ocean to clean your clams. You know better than to use the drinking water.

"It's the strangest thing," Louisa said, going back in. "There are several poles gathered outside, and some of the Indian men have gathered not too far away. I get the feeling they're waiting for something. Just standing and waiting."

"I don't suppose it's anything to worry about."

"S'pose not. Jim and George are both out there. And others that I recognize." She laughed. "Curley is."

Just then Alonzo burst in. "Ma! Here comes Mr. Denny and that Injun squaw! And he's got one of those stupid poles of his own!"

"David does?" Louisa ran outside. David stood at the edge of the woods, among the Indians, shouldering another of the poles. "What are you doing?" she shrieked, motioning wildly for Lydia to come see.

"This is a courting pole, so Kickisomlo tells me! She says you're to choose the noble you wish to marry by touching his pole!"

Relief was her first reaction, then sudden, mirthful understanding.

"Have you gone mad?" The tips of her fingers touched her mouth to stop the bubble of laughter, and David dropped his heavy pole to the ground by the cabin. It fell against the wall with a thud. "Take your time," he hollered over his shoulder. He spoke to Jim and George and some of the others. They all pretended not to be watching Louisa.

It was so silly. "Have you ever heard of anything so insane?" she demanded of Lydia. "Just look at them!"

"Maybe you better hurry up and make up your mind."

David's pole was at the end of the long line, and Louisa stepped from the shadow of the door and started toward it. Hands behind her back, and stealing a peek at David and the Indians, she purposefully, and with deliberate casualness, sauntered toward it.

As soon as she touched it she didn't wait for David to come to her. They met halfway, at a run, and then she was in his arms. He whirled her about in mad circles until she had to cry out for mercy. Then, both of them dizzy, they fell to the ground, tumbling into the sand, laughing and kissing and laughing some more.

"Pa said yes?" she gasped, spitting the sand from her mouth.

"Of course he said yes! And..." He stopped.

"And what?"

"And he co-filed with me and we got land, Liza! Land!"

She sat astonished, unable to believe it. "Land, David? You mean land of our own? Our very own?"

"We got the northern claim across the bay. The half-mile north of Bell's, the section bordering a pretty lake."

He scooted up next to her, closing his arm over her waist, his face above hers. The Indians, acknowledging defeat, came to take away their courting poles.

"How'd you do it, Dave?"

"Do what?"

She ran a finger under his chin, beneath the thick beard. "Convince Pa."

"I appealed to James."

"*James?*"

"We had a long talk. He loves you, Liza. I hadn't realized quite how much. Almost felt sorry for him."

"I told you. I don't like being the booty between you two."

He kissed her quickly. "Don't be silly." He kissed her again, this time longer. "You know, it's funny," he sighed. "All my life I've been losing to James. But in what's counted the most, I've won." He pulled one of the silver combs from her hair and gathered the strands in his fist. "And you're not the booty, Liza... I love you."

She stopped him, holding a finger to his lips. "Tell me about him. About James."

"He wants you to know that he loves you. That he'll always wait. That if I turn out to be a cad you're to sail on the first ship to Portland."

Now *she* kissed *him,* but he stopped her. "He's given you up, Louisa. Said he'd co-file with me so we could marry."

"James said that? James?"

"Said it was to be a wedding present for you. I don't think he did it for me."

"But I thought you said Pa co-filed with you!"

"He did! As soon as James volunteered, Pa said no, he would. Had them fighting over who would get to help me out!"

"When, David?"

"When what?"

"You know... when can we get married?"

"Soon as I can get a bit of money together and our cabin built.

You don't mind having a cabin without fancy glass like Anna's has, do you?'' He pulled back and she looked into his eyes. They drew together. ''Not with you inside, I won't,'' Louisa whispered.

''I'll build it myself. I'll make it fancy, though. Been planning it all the way up here. It'll be as grand as King Solomon's palace. I'll make it as described in the first chapter of the Song of Solomon, the 17th verse. You're supposed to ask me what that is, Liza.''

''And what is that?''

'' 'The beams of our house will be of cedar, our rafters of fir.' ''

''Oh, David!''

''Wait!'' He pulled away, then sat and scrounged about in his pockets. ''I have something for you. A fellow by the name of Sir Zeke in Olympia said for me to give this to you.'' He pulled out a small box, the corners of it well-smashed. ''He says there's a note inside.''

''What is it?''

David shrugged.

''Did you peek?''

''M-mm.''

Louisa lifted the lid and gasped, ''It's a ring!''

''I know.''

She opened it again, slowly this time. The ring was a gold band with a gold nugget on top. The note was folded over beneath, and she carefully opened it out. The paper was small, folded four times, and the handwriting was tight. ''He wants to know if I'll marry him...''

''He also says he's sorry for ripping your dress.''

''It was nothing, David. Really, it wasn't.''

He pursed his lips, the bristles of his beard standing out toward her, and he watched her. ''Someday, Louisa Boren, you'll tell me about that afternoon.''

''What shall I tell Sir Zeke?'' she teased.

David dropped back to the sand and brought her with him. Her hair fell about her shoulders and he held it. ''I've been thinking of an answer for you all the way home.''

''Tell me.''

''You're going to tell the man...'' He paused and smiled, then reached up to kiss the tip of her nose. ''You're going to tell the old goat the ring doesn't fit!''

"There seems to be no record of the exact time that the name Seattle was chosen by the founders for the new town."

—Clarence B. Bagley in *History of Seattle*

Summer arrived gently, in much the same way that the new town, still without name, grew. The sun, growing warmer each day, lingered longer. The settlement, with the arrival of new settlers, another brig, and more oxen, expanded and rooted and gained strength.

The doctor kept up a hectic pace all through the spring months, barreling his fish, running his store, and trading with the Indians. And when spring gave way to summer, the new brig, the *Franklin Adams,* left with a hold full of the salted salmon, along with a contract for pilings, more cords of wood, and cedar shakes—as many as could be made. And with the two ships requiring timber, Arthur, David, William, Dobbins, and Maynard had little time to do anything but fell trees and roll them over the banks, where on the beach they were stripped and sawn into lumber.

The month of June saw long, warm days, cloudless blue skies, and mountain peaks that stayed out of hiding—as if intentionally, just to instill more deeply the settlers' conviction that Elliott Bay was indeed the most beautiful and productive country anyone could live in. The serrated summits sharply cut the arch of heaven, dividing the expanse of the firmament from the expanse of the earth and sea, making all the world layers, shades, and varying depths of blues and greens.

Two new settlers, John Chapman and George McConaha, arrived in Elliott Bay during those long and balmy days of June. Once arrived, they stayed, and added to the construction and survival of the town.

A postman, Bob Maxlie, started a mail run once a week out of Olympia, with the letters all addressed to Duwamps, Thurston

County—a name that rankled Doc Maynard and that made do for New York, the Collins' settlement up the Duwamish River and Doc Maynard's "Illahee," as the Indians had begun to call the new town.

Word was received that the Oregon Territorial Legislature had appointed Arthur as a commissioner for Thurston County, and in the evenings, after the hard work was put away, talk invariably turned to politics.

A movement was afoot for the area north of the Columbia River to split off as a separate territory from that of the area south. Oregon City in the Willamette Valley, the seat of the territorial government, was at least a two-week journey south. Any decision that had been enacted upon took at least two weeks to reach Puget Sound, and any dissension would take another two weeks to get back. "It is not a good situation for democratic people," Arthur would often point out.

Some of the more ambitious settlers were wanting to break the large Thurston County, of which they were a part, into four smaller counties, but Arthur, learning to curb his idealism with realism, began by calling attention to the issue of putting a road between Olympia and their "Illahee." "You put a road in from Olympia and you get settlers. And with settlers we become a city."

But others couldn't justify the time and expense, and so a compromise was worked out by putting in a road from Fort Steilacoom, a post about midway. Arthur appointed John Chapman, Luther Collins, and William Bell as viewers, and the work was begun. And Arthur, once chief surveyor of Knox County, Illinois, began to plat their new city streets in his mind that would one day come to pass.

Toward the end of June Arthur took his surveying equipment down to the beach and began to put on paper what he had pretty much in his head. A small canoe, which he at first ignored, figuring it to be just another of the Indians, paddled in close, but upon seeing that it was a white man, he hailed the stranger to come ashore.

The man was tall and lean, with a rugged look about his youthful face. The man smiled easily, and when he pushed his boat into the rocks so that a long scraping sound was heard, he laughed enthusiastically. "Ahoy there!" he hollered, offering a callused hand to Arthur. "Dr. Henry Smith's the name! Yours, Sir?"

"Denny. Arthur Denny."

There seemed to be a mutual and instant affinity between the two men, and they both laughed simultaneously. "What are you doing?" the new man asked. "Anything important?" He peered through the sights up to the woods along the high bank, a paddle slung casually over a shoulder.

"Just platting the streets of the most famous seaport this country'll ever see!" Arthur grinned broadly and ran a hand slowly down his beard. "*You* doing anything important, Sir? Or just out playing Indian?"

The young man set the blade of his paddle onto his boot and rested a hand and chin over the handle, then squinted purposefully at Arthur. "You say this spot will be a famous spot someday, Denny? Tell me something. You hear anything about a transcontinental railroad coming out here?"

"It's been rumored. But I don't take stock in rumors. Why? You know something I don't?"

"I've found out that Congress has appropriated funds for the location of just such a line, ending right here on the Sound. And I know it to be a fact."

"Where?"

"The guesses are out as to just where. That's what I'm doing. I'm out guessing."

"Oh?"

"I'm out to find the best place for the terminus. Can you imagine the money to be made? The way I figure it, all I need to do is find the best spot for a harbor and the railroad'll head straight for it. I want a hand in the windfall."

Arthur chuckled. "Well, this is the best place for a harbor. The water runs deep all along here," he waved a hand up and down the beach, "to within feet of the bank."

Now Henry Smith chuckled. He jerked his head to the east and the Cascade Mountains. "You hear any talk of a pass through those hills?"

"Patkanim, chief of the Indians out there, says that there is. Haven't had the time to look into it just yet myself, but I've no reason to doubt the man." Arthur paused and rubbed a hand over his mouth. "You hear of any talk, Dr. Smith?"

"There's a pass, all right. Runs right through the Snoqualmie tribe's territory." The two men stared at each other, then began to grin at the same time. "*If* a railroad can be brought through that pass, and *if* this seaport of yours is as good as you say it is, well, you tell me, Denny, where do you suppose the line should end?"

"Elliott Bay…"

"You, Sir, are no fool."

Arthur held out his hand again. "You are no fool either, Dr. Smith. I'm pleased to meet you." They shook cordially and Arthur pointed out the landmarks, showing the unavailable two-mile stretch of waterfront. "But beyond the Point is unclaimed," he said, "and up north it's wide open." Henry Smith smiled his thanks and stepped a foot into his canoe. "Say," Arthur asked. "Is it just you? Or do you have a wife?"

"No wife. But a mother." Henry Smith climbed into his canoe and shoved the handle of the paddle into the soft sand. It buried a few inches, then held, and the canoe slid backward. "By the way," he called as he backpaddled out to the deeper water, "What do you call this settlement of yours?"

"The Indians call it Illahee; the legislature calls it Duwamps!"

"What do you call it?"

Henry Smith was too far away to hear Arthur's answer. But it didn't matter anyway, for Arthur had mumbled, "Nothing, nothing yet."

★   ★   ★

Henry Smith, once convinced by Arthur and Doc Maynard that Elliott Bay was the best location for a harbor—and convincing himself that the northern tip of the bay was the best sight for the railroad terminus—pounded in his stakes along the shore, called the claim Smith's Cove, and made plans to return home for his mother and provisions. But he didn't go before the Fourth of July. He stayed for the celebration.

They celebrated without Arthur. As county commissioner he had gone to Olympia, paddled there by Jim and George Sealth, to attend a meeting that called for the separation of Northern Oregon. But the others gathered—from New York, the Collins settlement, and "Illahee"—to feast on smoked salmon, participate in more political debates, and set off fireworks.

Doc Maynard hosted the celebration. He had the Indians prepare the meal—filleted salmon stretched out on sticks over open fires, smoked for hours. Wapatoes (Chinook for potatoes) baked in the coals and boiled clams eaten right out of their shells completed the unique picnic, a sort of Thanksgiving that rivaled the original.

"We still haven't settled on a name for this town of ours," Doc Maynard said suddenly. "Seeing as how this is the Fourth of July, and seeing as how this will be the largest city on the Sound, and seeing as how the terminus of a transcontinental railroad will be up at Smith's Cove, I say it's about time we have a name!"

"I suppose you got one all lined up," Dobbins muttered.

"And I suppose I do." Maynard looked at them all, passing his gaze from one to another, resting at last on Sealth. "Who's the leading figure in these parts? At leastways 'fore we came on the scene?"

No one answered. Sealth started to say something but Maynard cut him short. "Who's the great leader? The allied chief of six tribes?"

"Sealth?"

"Not Sealth, you fool!" Maynard thundered at Dr. Smith. "Seattle!"

The Indian jumped to his feet protesting, speaking quickly in his Duwamish tongue.

"He doesn't seem to want a city named for him," said David.

"Get him to tell you why!"

David listened patiently, and when Sealth ceased to speak, he translated of the chief's objection for the others. "He says they believe that once they die the mere mention of their name will send their bodies rolling in their graves to see who calls. He fears that for eternity he will be spinning madly about in his coffin!"

"Have you ever heard of anything so ridiculous?" shouted the doctor. "Of all the harebrained ideas these Indians have thought up, this has got to be the craziest!" He laughed and winked at Seattle. "Talk some sense into the man, Dave! I can't."

"If he doesn't want..."

"Of course he wants! The man's a converted Catholic! It's

time he gave up his crazy notions. And Seattle *is* the name for our city; it sure beats *Duwamps!*" One by one he drew nods out of everyone, even David.

"But the man..." David still protested, even as he nodded. "...We have to respect the man's beliefs."

The doctor spoke to Sealth in Duwamish and then turned away. He walked the top of a wide, washed-up log, then stepped across a foot of sand to another. "Dave! You 'wah-wah' with the man! I'm going to get some gunpowder to celebrate!"

The low sun cut a rippled path of gold out over the water, outlining the distant jut of land that was New York—Alki. Ribbons of yellows and purples and pinks drew together over the graying blue. The youngest of the children were put to bed and some of the Indians wandered off. When Maynard got back they put the powder into a cache in a log.

The boom exploded all over the bay. Hats flew into the air; some fell to the sand. The reverberations scattered and then were lost to the sound of the wind in trees. The sun winked out, and all was summer-evening dusk.

And before long Seattle, really just a few log cabins and a trading house stretched along two miles of waterfront, lay hidden beneath the black woods.

26

"In one year they had survived their first winter among the Indians, established a lumber trade, expanded Elliott Bay, founded a city, surveyed and platted a portion of it into city blocks. They had increased their lumber output, made an attempt at packing salmon, and procured a sawmill. They had made plans for a wagon road, taken a most active part in forming a new and separate territory, and had acquired a very definite ambition to become the western terminus of a Pacific railroad. When, in later years, Arthur Denny was asked how they ever did it, he answered, 'By muscle and timber.' "

—Roberta Frye Watt in *Four Wagons West*

Summer passed with the sounds of axes striking wood and saws chewing into trees. The men who could use the broadax skillfully squared timber while the others got out pilings and corded wood and split cedar into shingles. Felled trees were rolled from the high banks and hauled by oxen along the beach to the Point, where most of the work was done. By fall the *Franklin Adams* alone had taken on 12,000 feet of squared timber, 8,000 feet of piles, 10,000 shingles, and 30 cords of wood. David was able to earn and save a substantial amount of money, and with the coming of fall he began to clear his land for a cabin.

Doc Maynard shipped out nearly a thousand barrels of his salted salmon, selling to both the *Franklin Adams* and the *John Davis*. Unfortunately, every barrel arrived into San Francisco spoiled, and the loss was great—to Maynard as well as to the two captains. But the doctor was not one to let it disturb him unduly, and he set to work immediately constructing and operating a much-needed blacksmith shop beside his store. It wasn't that he liked the job—it was that the job was needed.

New settlers arrived as leaves turned to amber, hung from dried stems, then fell. Other changes occurred as autumn ripened, and Louisa watched the men with a mount-

ing sense of excitement as well as impatience.
David still insisted on building the cabin by himself.
Lydia had her baby, a girl, and Charles Terry was given the
honor of naming her Amelia Antoinette. The territorial
legislature established a voting precinct out of New York, the
Collins settlement, and Seattle. "Duwamps" became the official
title, and everyone from all three towns cringed under the label.
The same legislature appointed Doc Maynard to be the Justice
of the Peace for the new precinct, and news of the appointment
came as a surprise. It gave them something to laugh about—at
least Anna, Louisa, and Maynard.

A welcome change was the *Columbian,* a newspaper begun out
of Olympia. It was born to support the cause of separation, and
it bore the proposed name change. Its first issue contained the
full speech that Mr. Bigelow delivered at the meeting Arthur
had attended on the Fourth of July, calling for the establishment
of Columbia. The first issue also carried a few lines that John
Low and Charles Terry had put in:

> Charles C. Terry, thankful for past favors, takes this op-
> portunity to inform their numerous friends and customers
> that they still continue at their well-known stand in the
> Town of New York on Puget Sound, where they keep con-
> stantly on hand and for sale at the lowest prices all kinds
> of merchandise usually required in a new country. N.B.
> vessels furnished with cargoes of piles, square timber,
> shingles, etc.

Doc Maynard, not to be outdone, advertised a few issues later
he was—

> Now receiving direct from London and New York, via San
> Francisco, a general assortment of dry goods, groceries,
> hardware, crockery, etc., suitable for the wants of im-
> migrants just arriving. First come, first served.

October brought in cold winds, gray clouds, and Mr. Henry
Yesler. A robust, middle-aged man, he paddled into shore one
day, a gray apparition in the gray blanket of fog. Even his hair
and whiskers were gray, not bringing age to the red and ruddy
face, but a look of distinction and maturity.

Henry Yesler had a sawmill, and he was looking for a place
to build it. Dobbins and Maynard offered to adjust their claims

to accommodate the much-needed asset. They ended up shortening the waterfront, and to make up for the lost acreage they took in land further to the east. Dobbins gave Yesler 300 feet of his beach and Maynard 100. The strip that lay between the two claims became Yesler's. It created a shovel-shaped claim, with the blade of it running along the water and the handle pushing back up the hill into the woods between Dobbins' and Maynard's land.

The *Columbian* ran its congratulations, and for the first time Seattle's name was acknowledged.

> Huzza for Seattle! It would be folly to suppose that the mill will not prove as good as a gold mine to Mr. Yesler besides tending greatly to improve the fine town site of Seattle and the fertile country around it by attracting thither the farmer, the laborer, and the capitalist. On with improvement. We hope to hear of scores of others ere long.

A cookhouse was built along the beach to accommodate the hired help that would be needed to run the mill. Everyone pitched in—even David, taking the time off from his cabin. The cookhouse was a large structure made of logs, and it boasted a puncheon floor. Just days after its completion, Doc Maynard, acting as Justice of the Peace, held Seattle's first trial.

One of the mates from the *Franklin Adams* was accused of misappropriating money and goods which belonged to the brig. He was found guilty, and Maynard, banging his fist on a bare table, admonished the man to never do the like again—and then let him go.

Christmas came to Seattle with blowing snow. It banked against the log walls in white heaps and caught along the fissures like white string. Some even sifted through the shingles, and powdered the lofts and beds. David's cabin, typical of the others, now stood completed. It was made with beams of cedar and rafters of fir and stood in a small, dark clearing a mile-and-a-half north of Arthur's.

In the cabin a mile-and-a-half south, Arthur read the Christmas story before the fire. The children slept with new tin cups under their pillows. David and Louisa whispered together in a corner. Once in awhile their eyes met and slow smiles came. Money was put away and the cabin was done.

27

"[Louisa] planted around the cabin door a few of the precious sweetbriar seeds that she had picked when she bade Pamelia Dunlap good-bye in the garden in Cherry Grove. The sweetbriar grew and scattered over the town, and old settlers called Louisa Denny 'the sweetbriar bride.' "
—Roberta Frye Watt in *Four Wagons West*

On January 23, 1853, cedar boughs hung from the rafters of Arthur's cabin. More of the greenery draped the mantle and looped over the door, and the scent of outdoors was poignant. Louisa, standing in the loft, gazed down at the busy preparations. Mary Ann had a new stove, and the wild duck David had shot was roasting in the oven, sending out its own tangible scent. Anna set homemade candles along the center of a long table.

"Can anyone help me?" Louisa called down. "I can't get the belt tied!" She wore her white mull dress, the one she had made a long time before but had never yet worn. David stepped into view, and she saw that he was dressed in a suit that *he* had never worn before either. Louisa had made it out of the skin of a buck that David had shot months earlier. All fall she had sewn it together, piece by piece, by the light of the old smelly dogfish-oil lantern. Jim and George had cured and tanned the hide for her and Kickisomlo had shown her how to dye it with the bark of maple and red fir. Now it was a soft brown, stitched together with deer sinew, looking just like a suit in a store window in Boston.

"You're dressed for a wedding!" David called up. His eyes were dark in the dim light of the cold winter day, and shadows crossed his cheek and smile. "Come on down and I'll tie up your belt!"

His touch brought warm shivers, and Louisa waited patiently for him to finish before turning her face up to his, before kissing him. He held her close, touching his cheek to hers. "I love you," he whispered in her hair, and she felt the muscles of his face move under his smile.

Then the guests began to arrive—Anna and Dobbins, William and Sally, the McConahas, Mr. Yesler, and all the children involved. Some of the Indians congregated about to see the "Bostonian" get his "klootchman," peering in over the half-open door of the small cabin.

"Where is the doctor?" Arthur demanded when all had assembled. "We can't start without him. Unfortunately," he muttered.

"He's probably still wrapped up in the arms of that new bride of his," Mr. Yesler said. "What's it been? A week?" Whispers broke out.

Arthur drew in a quick breath and bit down on his bottom lip. Louisa watched him carefully, aware of his disapproval and his efforts to keep it from showing. He had made it clear that he saw no good coming to a marriage performed by Doc Maynard. "There's no sanctity about it," he had told her. "Last month when he married that couple from Olympia he said she was over 18 just because she was standing on the pieces of paper that he had written '18' on! You don't want a man like that marrying you, do you?" He had leaned forward on the *do you,* fully expecting to hear her say, "Of course not." But she hadn't, and he had slumped back in his chair.

A loud knock interrupted the hushed whisperings, and Doc Maynard himself strode in. He blew the snow off his raccoon hat and pulled his spectacles off his nose. "My new wife!" he said grandly, shoving the glasses back onto his nose and ushering in the tall, slender, and very beautiful Catherine Simmons Broshears Maynard.

They had only been married a few days, and not all of Seattle had met Catherine. Louisa hadn't. Catherine was stunningly beautiful, with large, gentle eyes and a gracious smile. Louisa could see at once why the doctor had pursued her so ardently.

The woman held out a small, brown, wrapped package. "A gift," she whispered, setting the present into Louisa's hand.

"Why, thank you!" Louisa exclaimed, surprised and pleased and feeling like she had found a friend. "But really," she started to protest, "you shouldn't have. I wasn't expecting anything..."

"It's nothing, dear." Mrs. Maynard's voice was fluid, almost melodic. "It's just a few flower seeds. The doctor told me of your love of such things."

"Thank you…"

"You like that?" Maynard went to the door and hollered something in Duwamish at Curley. A sack was handed over the sill and the doctor dumped it into the middle of the floor. Odd noises came from inside.

"Chickens?" David moved toward the burlap bag.

"The very same!" Maynard set the sack up onto the hearth by the fire. "Here, make room! Can't have the poor beggars freezin' to death, now can we?" He howled and thumped David's back. "A rooster and a hen for you, Dave! May your nests be equally productive!"

Louisa reddened and looked away. Arthur said, "Shall we get on with it?" but didn't look happy.

Doc Maynard stepped up onto the short hearth beside the chickens. "Right," he said. He fidgeted a bit, then he began. "Dearly beloved, we are gathered together to witness…" His reading was short, and Louisa held fast to David's hand. His fingers were warm, steady, and comforting. She looked up, and he sensed her gaze, turning sideways to smile down at her.

"And now as Justice of the Peace for the newly-named King County, and for the soon-to-be Territory of Columbia," he added, "I now pronounce you man and wife!"

"You forgot the vows!" Arthur bellowed.

"So I did! Louisa, do you take this man to be your lawful wedded husband and all that?" She nodded. "And David, do you take Louisa to be your lawful wedded wife?" He nodded. "Well, then, I now pronounce—"

"You forgot 'For better or for worse, for richer or poorer, in sickness and in health—' "

Doc Maynard squeezed his eyebrows together and looked down at David and Louisa. "You want me to pronounce you man and wife or do you want me to get Arthur here to rattle off the formula?"

"Just pronounce us man and wife," said David calmly. "We've made our vows."

"Then as Justice of the Peace for King County, and for the soon-to-be-territory of Columbia, I now pronounce you man and wife. *And I dare anyone to contradict!*" Maynard glowered at Arthur.

"You forgot, 'What God has put together, let no man put asunder!' "

"What God has put together, let no man put asunder! You may kiss the bride!"

David's hands cupped Louisa's face, and she remembered the wetness of the thunderstorm on the plains and the boom of the thunder. The memory of the first time he had touched her became so real. Their lips touched, lightly, and she wondered if ever there was a time when happiness had been so complete.

"Here, here, that's enough!" Maynard stepped off the hearth and pushed in. "I get my turn. Oops...here come me own bride." Arthur took Louisa's arm. "Lunch is being served," he said quickly.

"Come with us, Catherine," Louisa invited. "Please... You and your new husband. After all, this can be a party for the four of us."

"It can?" Arthur looked at her, the blue of his eyes sharp. Arthur turned to David.

"It's her wedding, Arthur," he said, shrugging. "No denying that."

Arthur shrugged to match David's. "In that case, Dave," he said, handing Louisa over to him, "you show your beautiful wife to the table and I will gladly show the Maynards."

★ ★ ★

The cabin was dark and bitterly cold when David and Louisa finally got to it. David pushed open the door and dropped some of their supplies inside, then went back to the canoe (a gift from Sealth) to get the rest. The white stones that Louisa and the children had gathered all the previous summer were only small lumps beneath the layer of snow, dimly outlining the trail that he needed to follow back to the beach.

The snow had stopped and the sun hung heavy over the Sound, the Olympics, even the distant shoreline, lost in winter's dusk. David dropped the sack of chickens and fumbled with the knot in the sack, stopping to rub the numbness of his fingers against his thighs, then trying again.

Kicking the cabin door shut he said, "I'll get a fire going and you put us on some tea." They worked quickly, saying nothing, and soon the fireplace was blazing, flames crackling, licking out, casting off the needed heat, bringing light to the hazy cabin.

Louisa lit a candle in her brass candlestick and a circle of light haloed her face. She looked more desirable than he could ever remember her looking before. Knowing that she was his now caused him to tremble all over. He didn't trust himself to speak.

The flame gave off a soft glow and melted the roughness of the cabin's walls, dispelling the harshness of the dark. Louisa's hair, falling long about her face, with the silver combs holding back some of the curls, looked soft and beguiling, and he wanted to touch it. The teakettle whistled.

He enjoyed watching Louisa as she worked at the stove, then went over to her trunk to unpack a few things, then went back to the stove again. He felt himself relax. The tension, the weariness of his muscles started letting go.

Louisa hung a picture on the wall and stepped back to look at it. "What do you think?"

"I like it." It was a picture of a small child swinging on a gate, meadow grasses growing thick around her. It could almost be Louisa as a child. "Where'd you get it? " he asked.

"Ripped it out of my Godey's *Lady's Book*. Reminds me of Mary Ann when she was little." She hung a few more pictures, some steel engravings, and a "God Bless This House" sampler over the door.

The sun went down as they drank their tea, and the feeble light from the candle quivered, flickering, casting shadows. The fire in the fireplace settled, with only the glowing embers left, and Louisa's eyes looked dark and tired.

"Are you tired?"

"No."

"You look exhausted."

"Well, maybe I am. Didn't sleep last night." She smiled slowly. Their eyes locked. "Did you?"

"No."

"I have a surprise for you. Been saving it for a long time."

"Oh?"

She jumped up and went to her trunk. "Now close your eyes," she commanded him. The last thing he saw was the bed. He had made it from fir posts, crossing slats to hold the feather mattress. Over the top lay one of Louisa's comforters, one that she had used in Cherry Grove, a comforter she had pieced as a child at her mother's knee. It looked bright and cheerful, inviting.

"All right!" she cried excitedly. "You can open your eyes now!"

She had the mirror in her hands. She was beautiful and he could only stare at her. She laughed and the curls about her face fell back over her shoulders, shimmering black in the candlelight. Again he wanted to touch it, to feel the coolness, to hold it to his face. "You didn't know I had it, did you?" she teased, and he knew that he was supposed to say no.

"You were supposed to have taken it over to Pamelia's."

"But I didn't! I brought it all this way just for you! It's my wedding present to you!"

"Louisa, put the mirror down and come here."

She did as she was told. "I love you," he said, reaching for her. The candle flickered, almost went out, and he felt her tremble as she came to him.

"David?" she whispered. "Can you wait for one more thing?"

"What's that?"

"I have some seeds from Pamelia's garden in Cherry Grove. I want to plant them. It's like a tryst between us. They're sweet-briar seeds, David."

"You can't plant seeds now. It's January. May even be snowing again."

"I know. I just want to mark the spot. I want to be able to tell Pamelia they're home. That *I'm* home."

He sighed and pulled back, then let her go.

The door opened and a blast of cold air swept into the room. The chickens, nested beneath the door stoop, cackled in fright and jumped out, squawking, their wings flapping in panic.

He waited. The chickens settled back down. Finally he went to the door himself. She didn't see him. She stood looking out over the water, over the gray. The moonlight, an eerie glow through screening clouds, seemed to almost bathe her hair, and the snow, beginning to fall again, started to cover over. He saw that she shivered, the icy cold penetrating easily through her wedding dress.

"Louisa?"

He went to her and gathered her up in her arms. The door closed with his kick. Darkness fell as he blew out the candle.

"Louisa?"

"Yes, David?"

"Do you love me?"

"You know I do."

"If I ask a question, will you answer me honestly?"

"All right."

"Why did you marry a boy?"

He thought he heard her laugh. "There are no men about. I *had* to marry a boy...."

The blanket was warm on top of them, the colored squares and patches hidden in the night. And on the door, still swinging from the jolt of David's boot, hung two hats, a sunbonnet and a cap.

ACKNOWLEDGMENTS

I thank first and foremost Donna Jo Doepken, my friend, for calling to my attention books that eventually became the mainstay of my research, and for loaning me her slides and stories of her travels across the Oregon Trail.

I thank Rebeccah Chaffee, my neighbor and friend, who watched my three preschoolers many times while I buried myself in piles of books at the various libraries.

I thank Tresa Wiggins, my sister, who has always been my supporter and continual source of encouragement.

I thank Robert, John, and Richard Watt, sons of Roberta Frye Watt, author of *Four Wagons West*, for allowing me to quote extensively from their mother's book.

I thank Dr. Brewster Denny of the University of Washington for taking the time to talk with me and to supply me with pertinent information.

I thank the Museum of History and Industry in Seattle for their superb collection of information and their willingness to share this with the general public, and for their helpfulness in finding and digging out materials that I have found to be invaluable for the construction of this book.

I thank the University of Washington for allowing me access to their Northwest Collections Room, a room of old and rare scrapbooks, collections, and books.

I thank Larry Kent for his support of my endeavors.

And most of all I thank equally my two friends, Scott Wyatt and Celeste Neuffer, for giving me belief in myself.

BIBLIOGRAPHY

1. Bagley, C.B., *Scrapbook*, Vols. 1, 12, 15, 5. University of Washington, Northwest Collection Room.
2. *The Bible* (King James Version).
3. *Blazing the Way*. Seattle: Rainier Printing Company. © 1909. By Emily Inez Denny.
4. *The Buffalo Are Coming*. New York: Alfred A. Knopf. © 1960. By Gus Tavo.
5. *Chief Seattle*. Caldwell, Idaho: The Caxton Printers, Ltd. © 1943. By Eva Greenslit Anderson.
6. *Chief Seattle—Great Statesman*. Illinois: Garrard Publishing Company. © 1966. By Elizabeth Montgomery.
7. *Chronological History of Seattle*. By Thomas Prosch.
8. *David S. Maynard and Catherine T. Maynard*. Seattle: Lowman and Hanford Stationery and Printing Company. © by Thomas W. Prosch 1906.
9. *David's Diaries*. Seattle: Museum of History and Industry.
10. *Denny and Boren Family Files*. Seattle: Museum of History and Industry.
11. *Denny Family Pamphlet File*. University of Washington, Northwest Collection Room.
12. *Doc Maynard*. Seattle: Nettle Creek Publishing Company. © 1978. By Bill Speidel.
13. *Dubuar Scrapbook*, Vols. 77, 82, 86. University of Washington, Northwest Collection Room.
14. *Empire of the Columbia*. New York: Harper and Row. © 1967. By Dorothy O. Johansen and Charles M. Gates.
15. Fonda, W.C., *Scrapbook*, Vols. 5, 6. University of Washington, Northwest Collection Room.
16. *Four Wagons West*. Portland, Oregon: Binford and Mort, Publishers. © 1931. By Roberta Frye Watt. Used by permission.
17. *Frisbie Scrapbook*, Vol. 1. University of Washington, Northwest Collection Room.
18. *Genealogical Notes—Denny Family*. Seattle Public Library, Main Office. By Margaret Thompson.
19. *History of Seattle*, Vol. II. Chicago: The S.T. Clarke Publishing Company. © 1916. By C.B. Bagley.
20. *History of Washington*, Vol. III. New York: The Century History Company. © 1901. By Clinton A. Snowden.
21. *Oregon Trail*. Rand McNally and Co. © 1972. By Ingvard Henry Eide.
22. *The Oregon Trail Revisited*. St. Louis: Patrice Press, Inc. © 1972. By Gregory Franzwa.
23. *Pioneer Days on Puget Sound*. Seattle: C.B. Bagley. © 1888. By Arthur Armstrong Denny.
24. *Pioneer Seattle and Its Pioneers*. Seattle. © 1928. By Clarence B. Bagley.
25. *Post-Intelligencer*. Seattle, Washington.
26. *Sealth—The Story of an American Indian*. Minneapolis: Dillon Press, Inc. © 1978. By Mel Boring.
27. *Seattle*. New York: Alfred A. Knopf. © 1977. By Gerald B. Nelson.
28. *Seattle Daily Times*. Seattle, Washington.
29. *Seattle Memoirs*. Boston: Lothrop, Lee and Shepard Co. © 1930. By Edith Sanderson Redfield.
30. *Seattle's First Physician*. Clinics of the Virginia Mason Hospital. Dec. 1932, v. xii.
31. *Skid Road*. New York: Viking Press. © 1952. By Murray Morgan.
32. *Sons of the Profits*. Seattle: Nettle Creek Publishing Company. © 1967. By William C. Speidel.
33. *Souvenir of Chief Seattle and Princess Angeline*. © 1909. By Laura D. Buchanan.
34. *Washington's Yesterdays*. Portland, Oregon: Binford and Mort, Publishers. © 1953. By Lucille McDonald. Used by permission.
35. *Westward to Alki*. Seattle: Superior Publishing Company. © 1977. By Gordon Newell.